Night Kill

Books by Ann Littlewood

Night Kill
Did Not Survive

Night Kill

Ann Littlewood

Poisoned Pen Press

JAN 2011

*Poisoned
Pen
Press*

Poisoned Pen Press
6962 E. First Ave., Ste. 103
Scottsdale, AZ 85251
www.poisonedpenpress.com
info@poisonedpenpress.com

Printed in the United States of America

Night Kill *is dedicated to my mother,*
Pauline E. Parker, who set a good example.

Acknowledgments

This book benefited from the generous help of relatives, friends, writing buddies, and zoo professionals. Thanks, guys!

Especially: Nancy, Pam, Laurel, Lyla, J, the Steves, Jane, Brie, Susan, Mary Ann (Title Consultant), Jim, Cynthia, Christine, Michelle and Joe, Nancy, Marilyn, Dick, Dave, Joe, Liz, Mary, Jill, Sally, Mary Jo, Roland, Ralph, and my wonderful agent, Mollie Glick.

Chapter One

Hot breath from the lioness touched my cheek. Round dark irises in gold eyes, nostrils flaring and relaxing, a complex pattern faint on the black nose pad, the harsh breath of a meat eater. She stood as tall as I, reared up with her big front feet at my shoulder height. She was all about power: massive jaws, thick forelegs, heavy shoulder muscles. Power she'd never used, never run down and throttled her unwilling dinner, never torn it into fragments she could eat. The familiar fact that she was on one side of the wire and I was safe on the other seemed profoundly odd, a peculiar twist in the ancient relationship between our species.

She opened her mouth a hesitant crack. "Good!" I told her and pressed a miniature raw meatball through the heavy mesh. Her rough pink tongue, the size of a washcloth, worked carefully, scrubbing every trace off the wire.

Spice seemed to enjoy these training sessions as much as I did. She had the basics of the contract down—pay attention and she could induce me to produce something tasty. "Up" and "stay" were in place, and I could inspect her front feet and face up close. Soon I'd get a good look at her teeth, after we worked more on "open up." The near-contact oxygenated my blood with ancestral fear, diluted by familiarity and good steel down to a pleasant fizz. It was the booster shot I needed to face the evening.

I pulled the handle to open the guillotine door. She dropped down to the ground—class over—and padded outside to join the pride. When I got better at training, I'd see what I could do with Sugar and Simba. Spice was easy—smart and willing, fearless, the logical place to start my education.

Past time to leave work. Time to go home. A quick visit to Rajah, the old Bengal tiger, put off the duty. I strolled down the dimly lit cement hallway, passing empty night dens until I reached his at the end. Raj was an elegant slack rug, yellow and black ribs rising and falling. He opened one eye when I made tiger hello noises and didn't get up. Still mad.

Being late wouldn't help. Time to go.

I walked through the cool late afternoon of early October to the time clock at the Commissary, nursing Spice's success like my last bite of chocolate bar. Wet socks squelched in rubber boots, and my back was resentful of a day spent lifting and scrubbing. I swiped my time card and turned away from Finley Memorial Zoo, trudging toward the parking lot, where my good-looking, funny, hard-working husband waited for me. I reached deep to find a chipper smile.

Rick had punched out ahead of me and waited in his new pickup in the employee parking lot. Green paint glowed in the gray light, not yet dulled by road grime. I climbed in and we pulled away from the zoo as light autumn rain started. Windshield wipers gave rhythmic warning that summer was shutting down. We caught Interstate 5, vena cava of the Northwest, and headed south toward Vancouver, Washington. Finley Zoo is several miles north of town, in a once-wooded area yielding to row housing. My real sense of home still resided in Portland, across the Columbia River where I'd grown up, but I had picked up the Vancouver inferiority complex in my two years living here. No, not Vancouver, Canada. Yes, in the United States. Portland's little sister, just as Finley Zoo was an outdated miniature of Oregon Zoo in Portland. But Vancouver shared the Northwest rain and casual style of Portland, and Finley had lions and zebras as authentic as any other zoo. We flowed with three lanes of traffic past a mix of housing, strip malls, and industrial buildings.

When it became clear Rick wasn't going to break the silence, I asked, "How's the snake project with Dr. Dawson?"

"She laid ten eggs last night. They all look good."

Why wasn't he crowing to me? He and the zoo vet had worked hard for this, tinkering with diet and temperature. I shoved fatigue and worry aside. "That's really great. You did the research and made the changes and it paid off."

"Uh huh. Doesn't count until they hatch."

So that topic wasn't going anywhere. "Any news from lunch?" I'd eaten in the Feline kitchen with my friend Linda Carson instead of joining the group at the cafe.

Rick slid out of his preoccupation. "Denny says this big chicken processor is spreading hoof-and-mouth disease to cattle all over the world so that he can control the protein supply for everyone on the planet." He gave it to me deadpan, confident of my reaction. "He says there's a Web site with all kinds of evidence backing it up, but the Feds are going to shut it down any day."

Denny Stellar, fellow animal keeper, my ex-lover and Rick's current friend, did not confine himself to conventional reality. "Where does he get this stuff? He has got to be the most gullible and suspicious person ever born."

"Gullible *and* suspicious? Way to go, Iris." Rick fussed with one of many little knobs on the dashboard to get the airflow exactly right.

He didn't ask why I hadn't joined him for lunch. He didn't ask about the cats or my day. I told him anyway. "I'm doing a morning session and an afternoon session with Spice. She's picking it up fast. We're having a good time. I wish I'd started this a year ago."

"Good day, huh?" Rick said, slipping in a blues CD.

"Only the last part. The female clouded leopard isn't settling in. She's still awfully timid. Arnie screwed up the routine on my weekend and now she won't eat until I'm far, far away."

I supposed, briefly, that it was unfair to blame Arnie Bertram for my troubles since he rarely worked Felines. He was primarily the bear keeper and couldn't be expected to know everything. But I had left detailed instructions and he had ignored them.

"He didn't do the lions right either. Sugar's so confused she won't come in. Wallace said not to feed her until she does. So she's going to bed hungry tonight." Count on Wallace, foreman with heart of stone. "And Rajah is in a major tiger-snit because I locked him out of his den and put Simba in there for half the day to get a fecal sample. His den has lion cooties."

"Yeah. Sounds like a hassle." Rick tapped his fingers on the steering wheel to Billie Holiday.

> *The way you hold your knife*
> *The way we danced till three*
> *The way you changed my life*
> *No, no they can't take that away from me.*

After a mile or two of silence, I said, "You're good at training. Maybe you could come by late tomorrow and watch a session with Spice, give me some pointers."

"Sure."

Dial tone. File not found. Please call again during our regular business hours.

I decided my feet would rot if I left them wet another minute. I leaned forward against the seat belt to unlace them. "And my boots leak."

"We'll go out and have some fun tonight." He smiled at the prospect, already there.

We were off the freeway and heading through the outskirts of Vancouver, the north end of town.

I kept my voice light, no whining. "I was hoping maybe we could both stay home tonight. Talk, maybe plan for Christmas or something." Like we used to, I didn't add.

"I'd rather find some live music."

I gave up. "You mean, go out and drink a bunch of beer and feel like shit tomorrow?"

"You can always stay home and watch TV," he said as we pulled into the gravel driveway. "I've got energy for a little action."

Maybe there's a reason he's a reptile keeper, I thought. Maybe he lacks talent for warm-blooded species. No, not that many months ago, the world was rich with small joys and big possibilities when we were together. I remembered thinking he was the best listener ever. Then we married and he got tired of me.

Barefoot, I stepped gingerly across the gravel and up the cracked cement path, a dark green rubber boot and a damp sock in each hand.

Vancouver is a bedroom community for Portland and it's thick with lovely neighborhoods. This wasn't one of them. The little rental was a one-story wooden bungalow painted gray. The garage roof sagged and a huge Douglas fir tree waited for the next big windstorm to fall and kill us in our bed. Inside were two bedrooms, a kitchen, one unreliable bathroom, a living room, and two bored dogs. A six-foot wood fence around the backyard was what originally captured my attention, and "pets permitted" in the rental agreement corralled my signature, back before Rick. Then, the house had seemed snug and cute.

Winnie, my tan and gray shepherd mix, and Range, Rick's black mostly-Lab, were ecstatic to have their pack reunited, and thrilled that once again, we were going to shovel out the kibble. Rick got his beer out of the fridge and headed for the TV.

"Aren't you going to feed the dogs?" I asked.

He stopped to dispense kibble while I rummaged in the fridge. The dogs licked their bowls to a high gloss, then swapped places, each irrationally confident that, some day, the other dog would overlook a choice morsel. Recovering quickly from the inevitable disappointment, they nosed their way out the doggy door to the backyard.

I dug out leftover drumsticks, probably grown by Denny's protein conspirator. With mashed potatoes and frozen peas, they rode noisily on the microwave carousel. Rick took some of the peas and added grated carrots and lettuce. These he delivered to Bessie Smith, his green iguana.

We ate in front of the TV—Rick on the good sofa, me on the green recliner—watching the news with the dogs curled at our feet. Rick had his beer; I had leftover coffee.

I stared through the newscasters, unhearing. If we had a quiet evening at home together, maybe we could talk, maybe figure out why the affection and laughter were being swamped by irritation with each other. Maybe together we could find our courage, if courage was what was needed, to see what had turned a wonderful courtship into a stale marriage in a few short months.

I wondered if his drinking was the cause of our joyless relationship or the result. Despair had humbled me; I was ready to take whatever blame was my due. He just had to meet me part way. And soon, because hope was being run out of the territory.

"I'm going out to the Bird and find some people," Rick said. The Vultures' Roost was his favorite watering hole. "You coming?"

"No way. I'm beat. And it's your turn on dishes. Why not stay home?" I wasn't going to beg, damn it.

"Why not have some fun? They've been having live music. You suit yourself—I'm outta here when the news is over. I'll get the dishes in the morning." Meaning he'd be back after midnight, stinking of beer and cigarettes.

"You've been out every night this week. I'm tired of getting lit. Can't we hang out together for a change? I thought you'd want to hear that Muddy Waters CD you got in the mail."

"The CD will keep. You're tired, I'm not. So you watch TV or go to bed early or whatever. I won't be gone all that long. They have a new group tonight and I want to hear it." He flipped a piece of chicken skin to Range.

"Just Range?" Winnie was alert, expecting fair play.

"Give me a second, for Pete's sake." He tossed her a scrap.

"You're going for the beer," I muttered, getting to my feet.

"Hey, what's with you? I don't think I'm the one with the problem. I get up in the morning and do my job." It was a familiar riff between us, familiar and futile.

I gathered the dirty plates and hauled them into the kitchen, wondering how we always managed to get so sour so fast. If he would only tell me…Lousy sex? Not enough? My cooking?

Too much complaining? How did geese and wolves pull off this "mated for life" thing? More legend than fact, that's how.

After dumping chicken bones into the garbage, I put a plate in front of each dog for pre-washing.

"Hey, bring me a beer as long as you're in there," Rick called.

Whatever my failures as a partner, it was clear, beyond doubt or denial, that Rick was far more interested in drinking beer than in being my friend.

I went to the fridge and pulled out today's six-pack—down two bottles, neither into me. I took the whole thing into the living room and pulled out Number Three. The glass neck fit in my hand, a comfortable heft. I looked at Rick, oblivious in front of the television, and adulthood took a vacation. Winding up like a sixth-grade pitcher in Little League, I hurled the beer bottle across the living room and against the wood front door. The smash was delightful, definitely worth the smell and the flying glass. Both dogs were in the bedroom and under the bed in seconds. I could feel my face flush, frustration erupting into anger, rage drowning worry and loneliness. Bottle Number Four performed as well as Number Three. Number Five was a little wild, hitting the doorjamb, but I was still getting warmed up. Rick was on his feet yelling at me. I wasn't listening. My arm was loose; I was hot. Number Six was going right over the plate and through that door.

Rick moved fast and grabbed my arm. I like to think that I'm as strong as most men, but he had my wrist in a grip I couldn't begin to counter. "Are you out of your mind?" he shouted. "You knock that off or you are really going to regret it."

"Let go of me, you bastard. I've already got plenty of regrets." I jerked my arm free, but he grabbed the bottle away.

I walked into the bedroom, closed the door, and stood there waiting for my vision to clear. The rage drained out. I stood shaking. Through the thin walls, I could hear the hiss as Rick uncapped Number Six. I dumped a pillow out of its case and jammed some clothes in, grabbed my toothbrush from the bathroom. Carefully not looking at Rick, I got my jacket off a chair in the living room. Winnie and Range crowded next to me, worried but ready for a walk. I squeezed out the back door with Winnie only.

About a week after the Great Beer Debacle, my best friend, Marcie Altman, came over in the evening bringing cider and dark rum. I'd gone to stay at her place, across the river in Portland, the night I walked out on Rick, so she knew the whole story. Denny had found me at work the following day and told me Rick was staying with him, so I had the house back. I also had both dogs, since Range didn't get along with Denny's new dog. That was fine with me. I liked Range and he was good company for Winnie when I was gone. Denny relayed Rick's request that I feed Bessie, as if I would forget we had an iguana. And there we'd been for a week, me with the dogs at home, Rick camped with Denny.

Marcie heated up the cider, added a ladylike shot of rum to two mugs, and started working on me to go to a party that night, one we had both been invited to. We sat on the sofa: me in jeans and a gray sweatshirt suitable for vacuuming dog hair on my day off, her—as always—in something coordinated and clean. Today it was a blue pullover and charcoal linen pants. She's blond with big blue eyes, short and round and shy. Marcie's the alpaca; I'm the big eland. But she's as close to a sister as I'll ever have. We met as freshman roommates. Her tutoring and encouragement helped keep me in college for two years, and I stood by her through an ugly boyfriend crisis our freshman year. When I got a summer job at the zoo between sophomore and junior years, that was the end of my interest in college, but not my friendship with Marcie.

Turning down parties is not natural to me, but I wasn't up for this one. "It's a zoo party. Rick's going to be there. No way." I was curled up with my nice hot mug; leaping into confrontation had no appeal. Remembering my eruption still made me shudder.

"He won't be there," Marcie said, holding up her hand palm-out for emphasis. "He'll think you'll show up and start lobbing long-necks at him. Incidentally, it still smells a little funny in here."

Rick had cleaned up the broken beer bottles before he left and I'd wiped down the floor with ammonia, but a hint of stale beer lingered. The front door had a few new dents, a little chipped paint, nothing to worry about.

"I'll get a new rug soon," I told her, "and Rick will too show up. He never missed a party in his life. You have Saturday off for party recuperation, but I have to go to work tomorrow."

"Iris, you've avoided him for a week. You don't answer his calls, you dodge him at work, you take vacation days. You look like your dog died. You know," she went on, glancing at me sideways, "you have to talk to him someday. And you need to get out and have some fun." She emphasized "fun" with a little upward flourish of her hands.

"So which one is this party supposed to do—fun or spousal dramatics?" I asked, slouching on the couch the way my mother told me never to do. "Either one means standing around with all the people who can hardly wait for the next chapter of 'Iris and Rick: Pair Bonding Catastrophe.' Anyway, what's keeping you from going with that new guy, Jake?"

"Jack. Wrong type for a zoo party. Cars with animal names are his idea of zoology." She waved a hand dismissively. "Where better for you to run into Rick than with your friends? My guess is that everyone wants to see you guys work this out. Once upon a time, you two really made each other happy. Call me a hopeless romantic, but I think there's still a chance you could get that back."

"*I'm* the hopeless romantic, the one who ran off and got married on impulse. At this point, I have no idea where he's coming from, and I guess I'm afraid to find out." I squirmed on the sofa.

"You're scared, that's all."

"Well, that makes it simple."

And maybe it did. I set the condition that we take separate cars so I could leave early. I dug around in the closet until I found a clean white jersey and a lacy yellow sweater to go over it. The top was skimpy; a thin band of belly showed if I kept my shoulders back. Black jeans, a pair of stylish black boots, silver dolphin earrings Marcie gave me last year for my twenty-fourth birthday. The black boots were freighted with meaning, but I didn't have anything else in the way of party footwear. Rick had talked me into them a week after we were married while we were in Portland shopping for a Mother's Day gift for my mom. I'd stopped to admire the boots, gleaming in Nordstrom's window, and he'd urged me to buy them.

"No way!" I'd scoffed. "Too spendy. And those heels will make me look eight feet tall."

"I'll pay for them and I wish you *were* eight feet tall. I want you to put them on so I can rip them off your body." He had grinned as he reached for his credit card.

I did think I looked sharp in them and he did rip them off my body later, although, with boots, it's more tugging and yanking than ripping. Sex and laughter…My throat was suddenly sore, remembering. Living together hadn't been just irritation and argument, not at first. I checked the mirror. Dark hair was shoulder-length and needed a trim, a little untidy. I tried for a sexy tousle. Definitely tall with the boots. The jeans were new, clean, and tight in the right places. I sighed, wondering who or what I was getting dressed up for. A week without sex was addling my thinking.

We caravaned, me leading in my pickup, across the old Interstate 5 bridge to northeast Portland. People who live in Vancouver, USA, spend a lot of time switching states, hopping across the Columbia River to the big city.

Hap Ricketts, the Commissary manager in charge of supplies and animal food, held a rowdy, noisy party at least once a year. Marcie and I walked toward his stucco house, loud music inviting us in from the chilly evening. No one was likely to hear the bell, so we let ourselves in. The place was crowded with zoo people, both staff and volunteers; a few of Hap's half-feral bike club friends; and miscellaneous significant others. We added our jackets to a four-foot stack in the living room. I caught a glimpse of Denny's blond head. He was running the music system from a bedroom off the dining room: surf rock and lots of it. I gave that two minutes until Hap got the sound back to Motörhead.

Hap interrupted a story he was telling Arnie, the bear keeper, to wave and shout something incomprehensible at me that seemed to be a compliment. Maybe it hadn't been such a bad idea to come. Or to wear the boots. As long as Hap stayed away from the jello shots and didn't repeat the scene from last year's party—pinning me against the wall in the hallway to vow his eternal friendship and deathless loyalty. Rick had rescued me with high-spirited horsing around that left Hap laughing. If Hap's wife, Benita, had found us instead, she would have eviscerated me on the spot with a plastic spoon. I'd forgotten that little situation. Where *was* Benita?

Marcie fished a dripping soda out of a cooler and I found a bottle of wine and a plastic glass. I didn't want beer that close to my nose. The music hit a brief lull and I could hear Hap's parrots screeching in a back room.

I pushed through the crowd toward the dining room, where the food was likely to be. I love party snacks. I could hear howling—somebody was in a party mood. Next it would probably be gibbon hooting or competitive birdcalls. The crowd shifted and I stopped dead. In the middle of the room with a half dozen other people stood Rick, bright blue T-shirt with a black lizard design, worn jeans, and scarred motorcycle boots, waving a tall glass. He had his head back, eyes closed, and was howling like a particularly horny he-wolf. I stood stock-still, fight-or-flight reactions surging back and forth.

Flight won. I turned to go, but Marcie grabbed me by the elbow. "You big chicken. You can't run from him. You *work* together." She tried to whisper, but had to use a medium yell to be heard. Her fingers flicked "go in there." I hung back as pride and anxiety fought it out again. This time pride won. He wasn't going to run me out of a party with my people.

Sam Bates, the elephant and hoof stock keeper, was responding with a pretty good coyote serenade when I stepped into the
room. They were arguing about fox barks when Rick finally
saw me. He went still for a second, then nodded curtly. Sam
turned to see who it was. Somebody behind me said, "Let the
games begin."

Sam and others began drifting casually out of the room. Benita,
luscious in a tight red blouse and matching Capri pants, smiled
brilliantly at me and tiptoed out on her four-inch heels, leaving
Rick and me, plus a few innocents neither of us knew. I stepped
uneasily toward the food and grabbed a paper plate. Rick rocked
a little on the balls of his feet as I piled up chips, salted nuts, and
vegetables with dip, not looking at him. The tension was roughly
equivalent to Bonneville Dam's electricity output.

Done with foraging, I cleared my throat, something caught
in it. "Getting your daily quota?" I waved toward his glass.

"No. It's root beer. Sam makes it." He held it out to me. I
eyed the glass suspiciously.

The music volume dropped, changed to k.d. lang singing
about love. Denny setting a mood? Promoting eavesdropping?
You never knew with Denny. Rick said something softly; it might
have been "Don't quit me, babe," but I couldn't be sure.

"We should talk." Not that I had a clue what to say.

"Outside. My truck?"

I hesitated, then abandoned the plate. My stomach wasn't really
up for salsa-flavored chips anyway. We walked through the living
room and outside, ignoring people who were busy not noticing
us. I shivered as the night air hit me and kept on shivering in the
passenger seat. He started to reach out to pull me closer, but caught
himself as I growled. Cuddling was not on my agenda, cold or
not. He started the motor and turned on the heater. I shifted my
boots around a big envelope on the floor mat.

Rick twisted around to face me, leaning his back against the
door. "I been trying all week to figure out what to say to you,"
he said, slow and quiet. The streetlight left one side of his face
in shadow. "I was really hacked off at you for getting hysterical

and making a mess. It really bothered me that you spilled beer all over the house." He folded his arms across his chest. His voice stayed pensive. "Then I thought, why am I worrying about the beer and the house? We had something really good and it's all screwed up. I want to quit being annoyed at you and you being mad at me. It's too hard."

"Too hard?" I could feel anger rising to warm me and steady my knees. Too hard to find his own rental? Too hard to be my friend, like he used to be, before we got married?

"Yeah. Too hard going it alone. If it's going to be this tough, I want it to be from figuring out what we need to do. I want it back like it was before, not all the tension and bad feelings."

He looked through the windshield at the empty street. His face in profile was too much for my heart. I looked away.

"I miss you," he said.

I stared down at my black boots, invisible in the shadows under the dash, and tried to find a home for the anger. I couldn't. It eased on out. "What went wrong? I don't understand what went wrong."

He turned to face me again. "I figured out part of it, I think. You know how it is with your parents? You grew up knowing what being married is like when two people do it right, the way your folks do. It wasn't like that for me—I never saw being married work out."

It didn't seem the time to launch into a critique of my parents' marriage. For sure, it was better than ours. Rick's parents had died before I met him; he'd never wanted to talk about them. "So why did you want to get married?"

"I really didn't think about it. Maybe I figured it would keep you with me."

"What about your folks?"

"They really didn't like each other. Nonstop fighting and bitching. Fun for me was somewhere else, where they weren't. They were both heavy drinkers. It's probably why my mom got diabetes and Dad had a bad liver. They both died before they were fifty. My sister left when she was sixteen. I never really put it together until now. Pretty stupid, huh?" He was looking out the windshield again, not at me.

"So why did we end up doing them instead of my parents?"

"I don't know. It has to be me, but I just don't know. It's not what I want, that's for sure." He turned toward me. "It was so great at first. I feel like I wrecked it. Maybe we should have stayed together and not gotten married."

"Well, we *did* get married," I said. "So we either rerun your parents' marriage until we get divorced or we do something different." "Divorced" sent a shiver up my spine.

He flinched, too. After a moment, he said, "I'll try to quit the beer. I think you must be right about that, because the idea really bothers me, like I'll never feel good again. But I can do it. I've started."

He sounded like he meant it.

"I'm not sure what to do about the rest of it," he added. He ducked his chin and looked hard at me. "You still in the game, then?"

I shifted toward him, relief and a timid joy washing out the last of anger and sorrow. "Yeah, that's a start. Maybe get into a group or something for the alcohol. We can figure out the rest of it one step at a time."

He nodded thoughtfully.

We talked until the party emptied out, one or two at a time. We watched Denny walk Marcie to her car. One by one, vehicles coughed to life, headlights flared, and they retreated, leaving a quiet street dotted with pools of light from street lamps.

We talked until we ran dry and still we sat in Rick's truck, the motor muttering peacefully. When he pulled me into his arms, the last of the knots in my heart and stomach eased. We held each other like hurt children. Finally I raised my face and, gently, he kissed me.

That first kiss was sweet, filled with relief that we hadn't decided to part forever. The second kiss was a reminder that we'd kissed before and knew how to do this right. The third was between consenting adults. I slid my hand under his T-shirt, feeling warm skin over the muscles of his chest and back. He reached down and grabbed the big envelope next to my feet, dropping it behind his seat back. I twisted around and he shifted over to the passenger seat underneath me—a little difficulty getting the seat leaned back, my knees straddling his lap—then his mouth found mine again and it wasn't difficult at all. I noticed out of the corner of my eye that all the windows were steamed up. Then I forgot about the rest of the world.

Chapter Two

I hiked through the morning gray of early fall toward Felines the day after the party. I was almost on time. Well, twelve minutes late. I was short a few hours of sleep. Several hours of sleep. Still, I felt better than I had for a week. I hadn't let him come home with me, but Rick was my partner, at last, in figuring out how to be together. He was no longer just a husband on his way to becoming an ex. I was stumbling from sleepiness, but my heart gave a cheerful skip. I'd get through today, get some rest, and then we'd figure out what came next.

After four years at the zoo, even tired and preoccupied, I still felt a tingle walking toward the cats, past the old giraffe peering out of his barn, past zebras munching on the hay Sam had set out. Gibbons whooped and hoo-hooed their lilting morning song from over at Primates. A big peahen sailed over my head, gliding on set wings from her nighttime roost high in a Douglas fir. She landed heavily on the pathway ahead of me, caught her footing, and shook her gaudy feathers into place before starting a busy day of extorting hot dogs and popcorn from toddlers.

The air was moist with a fall tang of damp leaves that were still on the trees but starting to turn scarlet and yellow. Soon it would be time to shut the cats inside at night. The long, dank Northwest winter wasn't firmly in place yet; a sunny day was still a possibility, although probably not today. No noisy visitors, no soda cups or paper napkins littered the grounds. A quiet moment before the hard work of cleaning and feeding the animals began.

I heard muffled roaring as I turned the corner toward Felines. Two men were standing at the guardrail outside the lion exhibit, staring across the moat, their backs to me. One was too big and bald to be anyone but Hap. The other looked like Dr. Dawson, the zoo's veterinarian, in a dark green jacket. I got closer and was surprised to see people inside the yard, where the lions belonged. Wallace, the beefy foreman, was bending over something on the ground. The other, a keeper in the zoo's brown uniform, was removing his or her jacket. What were all these people doing? The lions were shut up inside and, judging by the noise, not happy about it.

I started to trot. As I got closer, I could see that the whole outdoor exhibit was wet, a lot wetter than the path or anything else around. A hose was draped over the guardrail. Someone had hosed the cats to drive them inside so they could be locked in the night den. The cats were trained to come in when I blew a whistle; surely Wallace and Dr. Dawson knew where to find the whistle in the kitchen?

A bad memory opened. Years ago, one of the maintenance staff had fallen in the moat with a pair of polar bears. Every new keeper got told the story a couple of times. The man had not survived the experience and neither had the bears. They'd both been shot to recover the body. Worldwide, big cats—lions and tigers—kill a careless keeper or visitor every few years. My heart started pounding. I could feel a sweat breaking out that had nothing to do with running.

The keeper inside the exhibit turned out to be Linda Carson, who gently draped her jacket over something large lying near the edge of the moat. The jacket left a bit of blue exposed— fabric?

Dr. Dawson had a dart pistol in hand. A shotgun rested on the guardrail next to him.

I loped toward the service entrance to get inside and do whatever a feline keeper was supposed to do in this situation.

Not a single thing from the crisis training a year ago came to mind. Out of the corner of my eye, I saw a long crimson smear on the cement slope from the moat up to the exhibit. Blood? Wallace looked up as I ran past the guardrail.

"Get in my office," he bellowed. "Now!"

I skidded to a stop, astonished. It was my area—I was supposed to be there. Hap took two quick steps and grabbed me by the arm. He swung behind me and put his other hand flat between my shoulder blades, propelling me away from Felines, toward the Administration building and Wallace's office.

"Let go of me! I'm supposed to deal with this."

"Not today you aren't." He kept shoving me away from the disaster area. With two hundred pounds to shove with, he was persuasive.

"Why not? What *happened?*" I tried to set my heels and lock my knees, but nearly fell over. I tried twisting sideways. Hap grabbed the back of my uniform into a bunch, lifted me to my tiptoes, and kept me moving forward.

"Stop it! Get your hands off me and tell me what is going on, damn it!"

He didn't answer and he didn't let go.

"Let go of me, you son of a bitch!"

"Shut up, Iris. Just shut up."

He hauled me across the zoo, into the Administration building past the astonished secretary, into Wallace's office. He kicked the door shut behind us and turned me loose. I whirled around. Hap raised his hands warily, ready to ward off a punch. I was ready to deliver one, except for the uselessness of it.

"Now you tell me what the hell is going on." Terror and anger left me spluttering. "Don't you *ever* grab me like that again. If you want me somewhere, *you ask.*"

Hap stood blocking the door, silent and immovable, beard and mustache half-hiding his expression. His eyes were grim. We were friends. Getting yelled at by Wallace was nothing new, but Hap shoving me around instead of joshing with me was scary. This was really, really bad.

I gave up on getting past him and struggled to get myself under control. Was that really a body I had glimpsed? "Who was that in the exhibit? You have to tell me what happened."

No response.

I tried to figure out how this disaster, whatever it was, could be my fault. Had I forgotten to lock a door? Did it happen somehow because I was late? Was I confined to the office because they were going to shoot the lions and didn't want me to watch? Would they do that, even if it was too late to save anyone? My heart was pounding and my hands were tight fists.

We both turned at wailing sirens. Through the window I glimpsed a police car and then an ambulance hopping the curb, headed toward Felines. I was getting the shakes.

"Hap, who was hurt? Was someone killed?"

Hap winced and stepped aside as Wallace banged the door open, slamming the knob into his kidneys. Wallace looked desperately at Hap, then at me. He took a deep breath, sweat darkening his shirt and beading on his forehead. "I'm sorry, Iris."

I stared at him, trying to decode meaning and coming up empty.

Wallace wiped a sleeve across his face. "It's Rick. The lions killed Rick. He fell in the moat last night and they killed him."

That was ridiculous. Rick was fine, staying at Denny's place since I wasn't ready to let him come home yet, probably still asleep since it was his day off. Some loony stranger, some mental case, had wandered into the zoo at night and climbed in with the lions. Rick wouldn't do any such thing. Rick was a professional keeper, not a reckless trespasser or a suicide. Then I remembered the scrap of blue cloth and Rick's blue T-shirt at the party last night.

Hap nudged me gently into one of the metal-framed office chairs. "I didn't want you to see him," he mumbled. "Sorry."

Wallace backed out uncertainly. "I got to be there with the police. Hap, you stay." He left, muttering that Mr. Crandall, the director, should be handling this, not him.

Hap stood and I sat in silence in the little room. I looked blankly at gray carpet, at an ordinary wood desk with an ordinary computer. I wasn't going to think about…anything. I studied the room carefully. Papers were piled on the desk. No photos of family. Instead, a framed drawing of clouded leopards. Color photo of Wallace with a young elephant when he was still a keeper, blue uniforms back then instead of brown. My previous visits were generally so that Wallace could yell at me about being late or letting the cougars chew up another hose. I hadn't ever really examined this room. I looked at every single thing with my complete attention. If I kept my eyes focused intently, my brain would lack the space to make up its own images. My heart was still hammering; my breath came in short gasps.

I wasn't nearly done looking when two police officers came in and shooed Hap out. The middle-aged woman sat down in Wallace's swivel chair, claiming the dominant seat behind the desk. Her brown hair was gray at the temples. She looked like she'd been up all night. Her uniform was a little tight and her gear—pistol and keys and unidentifiable things—clanked when she sat down. The lanky crewcut junior cop sat a little behind me in the other guest chair. He crossed his ankles and twitched one foot over and over.

The policewoman opened her notebook. "Mrs. Douglas, I'm sorry to bother you at such a bad moment, but we need to get a little information from you. Would you mind answering a few questions?"

I stared at the woman blankly. Mrs. Douglas? "Who?"

"You *are* Rick Douglas' wife, right?"

"I'm Iris Oakley. Yes, I'm his wife. Was his wife. Kept my own name." A dark wave started sweeping up from my gut. I looked hard at the clouded leopard drawing.

"How long have you been married?" she asked patiently.

"Five months? Since May." The bit of blue shirt wouldn't leave my mind.

"Has your husband acted unusual in any way recently?"

"Unusual how?" It came to me that the red smear on the concrete was made by the lions dragging Rick's body up from the bottom of the moat to the exhibit area.

"Anything different from normal."

"We had a fight," I told her, words emerging slowly through cortical smog, "and I left. Then he left, to stay with a friend, and I moved back in to the house." I paused, waiting for phrases to form. "Last night we made up, almost. I think we were getting back together. We were going to get back together. The two of us." My brain was stuck, stuck on never being with Rick again. Ever. My hands were tight knots in my lap.

"When did you have the fight?"

"About a week ago?" I guessed. A long time ago. Some other lifetime. The lions would have torn through the clothing and opened the abdominal cavity. I saw Linda pulling her jacket over Rick's face, over his chest.

"And then what happened?" Her voice was calm and steady, but her brown eyes showed a predator's intensity.

"Like I said—(had I said?)—I left. I stayed with my friend Marcie. Then Rick left to stay with Denny because it was my house, before we were married, I mean, and I moved back in." Would this have happened without the fight?

"But you reconciled?"

"Last night we ran into each other at a party. We sat and talked for hours." Warm in the truck, his quiet voice, his scent… "I thought we were going to be all right and work it out. He said he'd quit drinking. Did he fall in the moat because he was drunk?" Please, God, don't let him be drunk.

"We won't know until we get the lab reports back. Had he been drinking recently?"

"Huh?" I focused hard. "He drank a lot of beer. That's why I got mad and left. He told me he'd quit. I don't think he had any beer at the party." Who had dragged his body up? Simba? One of the females? Rick's one hundred seventy pounds wouldn't have been a problem for any of them.

"Was he depressed?"

Was he dead before they got to him? Maybe the fall had broken his neck instantly. I shuddered, staring blankly. The policewoman had said something. I ran the sounds through again and caught the meaning. "Depressed? No. I think, thought, he was glad we were making up. Happy."

"So you were together last night? Did anyone see you?"

"We sat in his truck and talked, until maybe midnight or so. I wouldn't let him come home with me. He was going to go back to Denny's for the night. We were going to talk again today." Which lion had gotten to him first? Spice, probably. The one who paid attention, the smart one.

"Why did he come up to the zoo late last night?" The younger cop behind me leaned forward. I'd forgotten he was there.

"I don't know." Why would he do that? Why didn't he go to Denny's, to bed? I pictured him falling over the rail, trying to catch himself, slipping…Spice watching with the same *interest* I saw in the policewoman's eyes.

"Were you alone at home, Ms. Oakley?" The policewoman was writing careful notes in a little pad.

"Huh? No."

"Who was with you?" she asked.

"My dog, Winnie, and Rick's dog, Range." I found I was rocking in my chair and stopped. "Can I see him?"

She looked past me, at her partner. "No. Later, if you want to."

The dogs. Winnie. I needed Winnie. "I want to go home."

"Do you have a roommate? Did anyone see you after the party?" Her voice was calm and patient, insistent.

"No. No roommate." I stood up. "I have to go." Could I leave? Did I need to go do my job before I could go home? What about Rajah? The old tiger hadn't been fed yet, or any of the other cats.

Just the lions.

I made it to the wastebasket—barely—before dumping my breakfast in gasping retches.

The policewoman closed her notebook and handed me a tissue. "Look, we'll have more questions later. You can go."

I wiped my mouth and stumbled out of Wallace's office into the lobby. Jackie Margulis, the administration secretary, stepped out of the bathroom, her eyes wide. The bathroom had a common wall with Wallace's office. It was a safe bet she was in there to listen in on my interview. Hap was gone. Wallace was sitting at Jackie's desk with his aggressive authority back in place, impatient to reclaim his office.

"Your mother said she's on her way," he told me. "The, uh, the body has to go to the police morgue."

I wanted to be alone, alone someplace where I could find the switch to shut off the pictures looping through my mind. My mother finally came, pale and shaking. She took my arm and walked me to the car, like I'd been sick at middle school and the nurse had sent me home. Wallace reluctantly followed us to the curb. I climbed into her car, a familiar place where sanity had a chance—and climbed out again.

"Wallace, are you going to shoot the lions?"

"No. I'm not going to shoot the lions." He turned away. Jackie lurked in the background, fascinated, a magpie gathering tidbits of gossip.

Mom started the car and pulled out.

Was that an honest answer or an evasion? Was he going to have someone else shoot the lions? Panic or anxiety or dread, or all three, filled me and flowed over, displacing anguish for a few short minutes.

Mom drove me home, her home. She and my father kept me there all day, then I made her take me to my house, to my dogs. She settled herself on the sofa with sheets and blankets. I called Winnie and Range into the bedroom and made them get on the bed with me. Curled in a ball in the middle, with Winnie pressed against my chest and Range snuffling at the back of my neck, I rocked us all until sleep stopped the pain.

Chapter Three

"What the hell are you doing here?" Hap stood gape-jawed in the middle of the Commissary, the combination kitchen and warehouse, with a cantaloupe in each big hand, ZZ Top thumping from a little speaker behind him.

"Going to work." I swiped my time card and turned to go.

"Does Wallace know you're coming in?"

"He'll figure it out."

"*Iris...*" faded behind me as I took the familiar path.

Felines smelled like it always did, like a lot of big cats that eat meat and then go potty. It was warm inside and ugly as only off-exhibit areas ever were—unadorned cement and metal. I caught the steel service door before it clanged shut behind me. Night dens stretched off to the sides—lions, tigers, leopards down the hall to the right, cougar, servals, bobcats, and clouded leopards to the left. In front of me, across the hall, a second door opened to the kitchen. Drop ceiling of stained acoustical tiles, double stainless sink, an ancient microwave, and an even older fridge. Metal table and two chipped metal chairs. Décor consisted of curling Gary Larson "Far Side" cartoons and a color poster of lions stalking zebras somewhere in Kenya or Tanzania.

Linda was there instead of Arnie, a relief. Arnie's cheerful incompetence was more than I could possibly tolerate and it was good to be spared the urge to kill him with a shovel.

She was standing at the kitchen counter in her brown uniform, by the little scale, weighing out ground meat for each cat and putting it in pans on the rolling cart. Lately she kept her thick red hair cropped short, no longer a ponytail between square shoulders. Wide mouth, strong nose, red-brown eyebrows raised in surprise. "Iris. I didn't expect to see you for a week. What's up?"

"I'm back, that's all."

"Wallace said you were on bereavement leave. Are you sure this is a good idea?"

"I'm done bereaving. I'll start feeding." I moved toward the food pans.

"Why don't you make us some coffee instead?" Her hazel eyes were worried.

It was disorienting. Come to work, do the routine. That was the plan. Coffee making wasn't for another two hours, at break time. And I directed the work, not Linda. Somehow I was at the sink, filling the kettle with water and setting it on the hot plate. I looked at it, puzzled, and then I was at the fridge, pulling out the French roast. Setting the filter in the pot and adding three scoops.

The water wouldn't boil for several minutes. What came next? This wasn't going the way I expected.

Linda washed her hands with the yellow gloves still on to get the meat goo off them, then pulled them off and washed her hands again. "Have a seat. I haven't seen you since the memorial service. What's been happening?" There was something funny about her voice, something carefully normal.

"I cried a lot. Then I got the toxicology report." I didn't recall pulling out a chair, but I was sitting at the battered metal table.

"And?"

"Drunk. Beyond DUI. Blitzed. Tanked. Empty bottle of scotch in the bushes by the lions, his fingerprints on it."

"Ah." Linda was sitting next to me. She was silent for a little bit. "What happened at the party earlier that night?"

"We talked. He promised to stop drinking. Reconciling. Like that." My voice sounded funny, too, clipped off.

"And he went on a binge a few hours later?"

"Yeah. Promised to quit drinking beer. Didn't say anything about scotch." Sweet-talked himself into my pants, then celebrated.

"Iris, that's a lot to cope with. You know, you can get grief counseling for free through the benefit plan. Jackie could get you the number. I'll help any way a friend can, but this is a big deal. You should get some help."

"I'm done with grief. He wasn't who we thought he was. You know that Billie Holiday song, the one Denny played at the memorial service? It's not true, not for me. They can take that away. The love away. Only it's not a 'they.' He did it all by himself. Marrying him was a bad decision. I can't change that, but I can move on and that's what I'm doing."

Linda seemed to pull into herself. She started to say something and stopped.

The water was boiling. I made coffee and we drank it, talking about the cats. The female clouded leopard was still nervous; the common leopards were spitting and snarling at each other. We didn't mention the lions.

I got up to start feeding. Linda stood and put her hand on my arm. I kept myself from shrugging it off.

"Iris, this is a dangerous job. You're upset. Your husband died in this building days ago. It's maybe not such a good idea for you to come back to work so soon."

"I'm fine. I *need* to get back to routine." She had a look on her face I didn't like. I didn't want her taking sides against me with Wallace. "Look, we'll work together, like always, and you'll see. I'm fine."

She nodded. We both pulled on rubber gloves and finished up weighing out the food.

I pushed the meat cart down to the lion den while Linda checked all the doors that should be closed and locked. Then I threw my weight on the cable that opens the door to the outside exhibit and she blew the dog whistle, two toots for Simba. The three lions shoved in through the narrow opening. They paced back and forth and in and out the cat door, a fast-moving tangle of tawny, powerful bodies and whipping tails. I waited; the lions and I had done this hundreds of times. This was the same as always, I told myself, but my hands didn't used to tremble.

Finally, only Simba, or most of Simba, was inside at the same time the females were outside. I lowered the door quickly, but not all the way because half of Simba's tail was still outside. The door was closed enough to block the lionesses. Simba stood there, whipping his black-tipped tail a little, and glaring at us. "Get your butt inside before I chop your tail off," I told him. He turned to exit. When his rear came around, I let the door slam down.

Simba and I looked at each other, his yellow eyes unblinking. Nausea rooted and flowered in my guts.

Senseless to blame Simba—he was exactly what he'd always been.

Linda dropped his raw meatloaf into the feeding chute. It hit the floor with a mushy plop and he dived onto it. He crouched with the meat cuddled between his forepaws. I shook myself and we moved on to feed the cougars and common leopards while Sugar and Spice moaned outside.

Simba had finished breakfast. Linda tooted three times, let the lionesses in, and shut him out. Sugar and Spice paced around, yowling throatily. Linda took one chute and I took the other. A lioness crouched below each. We dumped out both piles of meat simultaneously. Big teeth and rough tongues made short work of the meat. I caught myself thinking that after a lifetime of ground meat, they still knew what to do with a real carcass. Linda opened the door again and shut all three inside.

I was glad to be done with lions for the moment.

The phone rang while we were down the hall feeding the new VIPs, the two clouded leopards, in their separate night enclosures. They were named for their pelts, irregular open spots—"clouds"—shaded in black, gray, and tan. The male watched us warily; Losa, the female, quickly vanished into her den. The two were out of quarantine, but still settling in and hadn't been allowed time together yet. We had hopes for cubs, but male clouded leopards tend to have a character flaw—they kill their mates discouragingly often.

The phone kept ringing and I kept ignoring it. Linda walked down the hall to the kitchen. She came back and said it was Wallace, wanting me. Reluctantly, I walked back to the kitchen, Linda following.

"What the hell are you doing here?" Wallace asked, today's favorite conversational gambit.

"Working."

"Go home. You aren't scheduled until next Monday."

"I'm at Felines. I'm working."

"You won't get paid. You're not scheduled. Go home."

"Fix the schedule." I hung up. Linda stared at me wide-eyed. We went back to work.

We'd taken our break in the kitchen, so it was lunchtime before I had to deal with anyone else. Linda had a sandwich from home. I bought the tuna melt at the café and we sat down at a green plastic table inside. Two moms ordered for their indecisive preschoolers and took another table. The keepers started filtering in.

Denny had a variation on the theme: "You're supposed to be home until next week."

"You should get out more," I told him. "We've already done that conversation."

He stared at me—lean, blond, intense—before pulling up a plastic chair and taking out his latest form of nonconventional nutrition, a wooden bowl of brown rice and chopped kale covered with plastic wrap. Did he know about the toxicology report? I had a feeling they all did.

Hap came in and sat down cautiously with just "hello" and "welcome back."

"So what's up?" I asked generally. "I'm behind on the news."

"You missed a boatload of safety lectures from Wallace and Crandall. I've got Reptiles since Rick's gone," Denny said around a mouthful of fodder.

Hap gave him a steely look, as if this were inappropriate subject matter, and took control of the conversation. "We're short

on good news. Kids broke in about a week ago, the day after…"
He shied away from Rick's death again, like a deer smelling wolf
scat on the trail. "They, uh, fooled around with the water faucet
at the Children's Zoo." He settled into the story. "What a mess.
They got the wheel off, water everywhere. The drain got clogged
with straw, animals wandering around loose."

The faucet at the Children's Zoo was controlled by a metal
wheel set on the water pipe a couple feet above the ground. It
was almost a tradition for new keepers to turn the wheel the
wrong way when they were trying to shut it off. Turned far
enough open, the wheel fell off and a spectacular jet of water
shot about thirty feet up in the air. Wallace's scathing remarks
at my own initiation by geyser still stung.

"Diego was really pissed off," Denny said.

Diego, the night keeper, was hard to rile, but this would be
enough to seriously annoy anyone.

"They let the petting animals out?" I asked.

"Yup," Hap continued. "Opened the gate and propped the
faucet wheel against it to keep it open. Goats and ponies wandering all over, trampling shrubs and eating them. The gardeners
don't like herbivores anymore."

Linda nodded. "Diego hiked over to the Admin building to
the main shutoff valve so he could stop the water and get the
wheel back on. Then he had to wade in to clear straw out of the
drain. The goats didn't want to go back and one of them put her
head in that garbage can with the top that looks like an alligator,
trying to get at the trash, and got stuck and she freaked out. He
was still rounding them up when I got there."

Normal conversation. I could feel my shoulders relax. "Where
was the security guard?"

Linda rolled her eyes. "We got George that night. Diego was
also teed off at George. He didn't catch anybody and he didn't
help clean up the mess. Just sat there in his cart and watched.
He said wading wasn't in his job description."

George was known for his unfailing good cheer and for his
dedication to talk radio, which he listened to in the comfort of

a little office in the Administration building. He had an electric cart with which he was supposed to patrol the grounds. It was no surprise he hadn't seen the Children's Zoo invaders. I wondered if he'd seen Rick the night he died.

"The kids raised hell with the hoses at Elephants," Hap said. "They dragged one of them over to the zebras and got mud all over it."

That seemed to exhaust the topic. We chewed in silence for a bit.

"You're not going back to Felines, are you?" Denny asked.

"Of course I am," I said. "How's the new Asian exhibit coming along?"

The three did a collective glance that did not include me.

Linda picked up the thread. "No different from last week, scalped dirt with piles of trees and brush. The rain turned it into a sea of mud, and the bulldozer got stuck the day after the Children's Zoo break-in. It's mired halfway up the cab. They have to get another one to pull it out. Serves them right for starting a construction project this time of year."

"Crandall was peeing in his pants to spend the bond measure money," Denny said, getting up to go. "He hasn't gotten a new exhibit for ten years."

Denny was the only person I ever heard refer to the director by anything but "Mr. Crandall" and it always bothered me.

Denny stood shifting his weight restlessly from one foot to another, scowling at me, his gray eyes cloudy. "Wallace will put you in some other area if you ask him."

"Why would I do that?"

"Because one extreme accident is one too many." He frowned a little longer before he left.

I made it through the afternoon, although it felt like running through deep, soft sand with hidden snares. Linda never let me out of her sight.

In truth, working Felines alone was always dicey. Standard safety procedures, not to mention common sense, called for two people. But Finley Memorial Zoo ran on a scant budget, and

I wanted Felines to myself, to work at my own pace without straining to look unruffled. On the way home, I thought, no matter, Wallace doesn't have enough staff to double up at Felines every day. I'd be alone tomorrow, back to normal.

The red smear had been gone from the lion exhibit. Linda must have scrubbed it away before I got there.

I reeled in my wandering mind and focused on the freeway.

The dogs started yipping when I drove up. Once inside, I stopped to give Winnie the first installment on her evening ration of affection. Range was standing nearby, wagging his tail slowly, looking at the door.

"Hey, buddy. Come on over."

He complied and I fussed with his ears and scratched under his collar, with Winnie shoving her nose into my face. She needn't have worried. Range nosed my hand, then lay down facing the door, head on his paws. He liked me well enough, but I wasn't the one he was waiting for.

Winnie bolted her kibble, but Range ate only half of his and wandered back toward the front door. I rescued his leftovers from Winnie and took a good look at him.

He didn't look sick.

He looked discouraged.

After a TV dinner, I disciplined myself out of lethargy and took them for a walk. Range cheered up and was diligent about reading the pee-mail and contributing to the correspondence. Back at home, I sat on the rug with Winnie half on my lap and stared into space. It was good to be tired. I'd been right, going back to work was best.

Range came over after a bit and lay down next to me. My hand on his head found the blue nylon collar I'd bought as a gift for Rick. The matching leash was slung over the back of the sofa. Nylon for him, chain for Winnie, who would chew through nylon in seconds. Range inched over and put his head in my lap, next to Winnie's.

It seemed only right to tell him.

"Rick isn't coming back, Range. Not ever. It's me from now on." And just like that, I was doubled over on my side, crying like I'd never stop.

When that slowed down, I tried the deep breaths Marcie recommended for crises. A coffee mug full of red wine was more effective. Maybe I was on the same slippery slope as Rick.

Pain management—what was the trick of it?

Marcie interrupted my meltdown with a phone call. Articulating my miseries was too much for me, so I kept it short. We set a dinner date. I'd no sooner hung up than Linda called, asking for advice on whether to get a guinea pig or a ferret for an apartment pet. It was completely bogus, but I was calmed down enough to recognize contact calls, the noises monkeys make in thick vegetation that mean only "I'm here and thinking about you."

I sat back down with Range. "You poor dope. You picked the wrong guy to love, like I did." Range didn't seem to think so. "Why did we get our hearts broken?" Range had no idea. Winnie thought another walk might help.

Thinking of "whys," what was Rick doing at the zoo after the party? He'd been with me until midnight. I pictured him drinking hard in a bar to celebrate his conquest, then driving to the zoo. Maybe to check the snake eggs in the incubator, although that seemed unlikely. To meet someone? What did it matter? I stroked dog heads and tried to be done with tears.

Chapter Four

The schedule at the Commissary put me on Primates for the entire week, so my second day back started briskly with a shouting match in Wallace's office.

He was behind his cheap wood desk, his bulk filling the spavined swivel chair where the police officer had sat. He hadn't been surprised to see me. He interrupted my sputtering: "No one promised you Felines for the rest of your, uh, career." He'd started to say "life." "Keepers get scheduled where they're needed."

"It's not my fault the accident happened and it's not right to punish me for it," I said, failing to keep dismay and indignation out of my voice. "I've got the most experience in Felines." Standing with my feet apart and my hands in fists did not constitute good tactics. I straightened up and edged back a little from his desk.

Wallace's mouth moved the way it might if he needed to spit out a bug. "This zoo is too small for every keeper to own an area. I got to be free to move people around, especially since we're short-staffed."

"All the more reason to put me where I can do the job without training. What good would I be at Primates today? I haven't worked there since my orientation four years ago." That wasn't strictly true, but no need to pick nits. "And I researched the protocol to get the clouded leopards together without fighting. You can't turn that over to someone else in the middle of the process."

"Why in hell would you want to work Felines after what happened?" He seemed genuinely baffled.

"Because I'm still the cat keeper. That hasn't changed." Not if I could help it.

In the end, I stayed at Felines. Wallace said it was temporary and only because he hadn't replaced Rick yet and was having a tough time staffing all the areas. I figured that as long as I didn't screw up, he'd return to the old schedule and leave well enough alone. He moved Linda to Children's Zoo. As I'd guessed, I'd be there alone.

"Those lions may not act the way they used to," he said as I reached for the door to leave. "You watch yourself. I don't need any more trouble at Felines."

"You bet," I replied and got out of there.

Victory and relief eased the constriction that never quite left my chest. I circled the Feline building, checking on the cats from the visitor side, and spent a few chilly minutes watching Rajah watch a peacock perched on the guardrail on the opposite side of the exhibit from me. Peacocks had been known to blunder into reach now and then, a tiger's dream come true. Like almost all the zoo's inhabitants, he was captive-born and predation was a hobby, not a former career.

I could hear gibbons singing from Primates, a sweet tropical sound in the cold air. A weak sun fought through the overcast and a comforting barnyard smell drifted in from the zebra pad-dock behind me. Returning to my pre-Rick existence would soon dissipate the choking gray cloud wrapped around me since that terrible morning with the police. It was already working.

Dr. Dawson stopped next to me. He was tall, lean, and kept his shoulders back. Neat dark hair showed a little gray. I was not alone in respecting him for researching animal health problems thoroughly and for his creativity in preventing them. A white lab coat with syringes poking out of the pockets gave him the aura of a serious scientist. As usual, his air of disciplined professionalism rattled me. He gave Raj a quick once-over and turned to me.

"Good morning, Iris. Good to see you back. How are you getting along?"

This looked like one of those sympathetic episodes that I was incapable of managing gracefully. "Not too bad. You?"

The peacock hopped down from the guardrail to the walkway. Raj shifted his steady gaze to the vet. In his considerable experience, Dr. Dawson was nothing but trouble, most of it starting with a dart in the fanny.

"Where are you assigned now?"

"Felines, same as always."

An eyebrow twitch might have indicated surprise. "I hope you're being cautious. Rick's loss was a shock, a terrible tragedy."

Simba and Sugar paced to our right, impatient for me to get inside and start feeding. Spice stood still, golden eyes staring at us, then climbed down the sloping cement to the bottom of the moat.

I wondered if he knew about the blood alcohol level. He wasn't a close friend with anyone on the zoo staff except Wallace. "It's hard to know what to think. I never would have imagined this."

"Look, Iris, drop by my office if there's anything at all…"

His voice trailed off as Linda, heading out of Felines and toward Children's Zoo, changed course and joined us.

Relieved to have the conversation deflected, I took a deep breath and said, "I'm thinking it might be good to wait to put the clouded leopards together for a couple of weeks. Yuri is getting confident, but Losa still hides in her den whenever I come around."

The vet chose his words with care. "Yes. Well. Wallace wants to go ahead with the introduction as soon as possible. I saw your report from yesterday and I agree—she still looks timid. I'd rather not rush it. We'll wait until she's more settled."

I was pleased to hear him agree with my assessment, especially since I usually was as timid as Losa when he was around. We hadn't worked closely together until this clouded leopard project, and I was still uncomfortable with his formality.

"We may not succeed," he mused. "Clouded leopards should be introduced while they're still cubs, not two and three years old. They may be fine together for a while, then something will go wrong and he'll attack her. I don't think I told you—" his nod included Linda—"I finally contacted the veterinarian from the zoo that sent us the male. It sounds as if they did an amateurish job of introducing him to a female there. He tore her up badly. We may regret not going with artificial insemination."

"Did she live?" Linda asked.

"The person I talked to said they were still trying to pair her up, so she must have survived. That incident is the only reason Wallace was able to get the male. Nobody else wants him."

"Once a killer, always a killer?" I couldn't accept that. "We reviewed all the research, and I talked to keepers in other zoos that have tried this. We're using the best science available. I'm thinking that if we take it slow and careful and keep a close eye on them, the odds will be with us."

Dawson had the intensity of a falcon and a falcon's way of jerking his head up a little when something caught his attention. His chin twitched up now and his eyeglasses glinted in the pale sunlight. "Yes, of course. That's why I agreed to the plan. Caution is essential."

If only I were as confident as I'd tried to sound. After he and Linda left on their separate paths, I thought about how we would all feel if Yuri tore into Losa, which led to thinking about Simba tearing into…I pushed away from the rail and headed inside, trying to focus my mind on dinner with the folks or buying the new work boots I still needed or anything else at all.

I took a deep breath, then unlocked the service door and let myself inside.

I walked down the left hall, checking the cats that were inside, then toured the right hall. Everyone looked healthy and impatient for breakfast. In the kitchen, I weighed and laid out ground meat for the big cats, measured the rations for the small cats. It was wonderful to be alone, easing back to the familiar routine. Fog was fading, clarity returning.

After rolling the meat cart down the hall, I started with Rajah, pulling on the cable that opened the guillotine-style door so he could come inside. I blew my little whistle, announcing that the entrée was available. He padded in, chuffing tiger "hello" noises at me, and rubbed his handsome striped face against the mesh at the front of the den. I stuck my fingers through to scratch the coarse white and gold hair on his face, the closest we could come to rubbing cheeks the way tigers do with their friends. I made tiger "hello" noises back at him and he never corrected my accent.

After all the big cats were fed and shut inside, I fed the small cats on the other side of the building. Back at the lions, I checked the doors and locks and went outside to the exhibit area. Scooping feces and trash into a yellow plastic bucket with my little yellow-handled shovel, I focused on the mental trivia of everyday life, not looking for blood smears, not looking where Rick might have landed in the moat. I'd shop for rubber boots after work, go over to the mall on the Oregon side of the bridge and see what I could find. Get some new socks, too, synthetic ones that were supposed to stay warm when wet.

I was sweating when the lion yard was picked up and not from scooping poop.

It was time to let the lions back outside, but Sugar decided to let the neighbors know that this was Lion Country. She stood with her head thrust forward, chin close to the ground, her nose jammed into the back corner of the den. She closed her eyes, inhaled, and let go with a coughing roar. The sound bouncing around the concrete was deafening. Spice wandered around grunting the bass line. Simba watched awhile, then joined in half-heartedly.

When the featured artist paused for breath, I opened the guillotine door. The performers wandered outside.

I checked the doors and locks again, then filled a bucket with water and a splash of disinfectant and started cleaning their inside holding areas. I scrubbed the floor thoroughly, especially below the steel food chutes. Over the years, the cats' rough tongues had worn a depression in the concrete where the chutes dumped the meat. After rinsing with the hose and wiping away puddles with a squeegee, I filled the water pans, the thick fire hose turned down to a trickle. The hall smelled of cleaning solutions: strong chemical disinfectant, layered over with icky perfume.

I checked the holding area to see that Rajah was shut in, then opened the person door and went out into the tiger yard with my pail and shovel. A crow on a fir tree behind the exhibit rattled at me and a scrub jay yammered. The peacock was still loitering on the pathway. It was still early; the zoo wouldn't open for another hour.

Raj had taken his dump in the usual place, next to the pool.

The crow called again, then I heard a small, familiar squeak I couldn't place. It was vaguely troubling, but I couldn't think why.

I was about to turn and look where it had come from when something slammed me from behind and hurled me flat on my face. My cheek stung where it skidded on cement. I had no idea what had happened, but my body seemed to know. I rolled over fast and clutched the bucket, holding it over my belly. Raj had overshot and was a few yards away, coming at me in another smooth leap. Flat on my back, I teetered on the edge of the moat. If I went over, I'd tumble down the slope and land in a stunned heap at the bottom. I rolled away from the edge and scrabbled to hands and feet, desperate to stand tall. Predators equate height with size—low is vulnerable.

I had the bucket rim in one hand and grabbed the shovel in the other as I got to my feet, heart thundering in my chest, spots flickering before my eyes. Urine warmed my thighs. Rajah halted barely two feet away, crouched with his ears back and lips pulled up to show giant canines. He swatted at me hesitantly with a broad forepaw. I bashed him in the face with the bucket. He leaped away and turned right back, growling.

Threatening him with the shovel and bucket, I backed toward the open door. The tiger followed me step by step, tail lashing, head down and eyes intent on me. He looked enormous—the most dangerous thing on earth. His breath stank. His ribs vibrated with low growls.

He moved to my left, to circle behind me, a smooth ripple of yellow and black, tail thrashing. I rushed him in big steps, thrusting at his face with the shovel, jabbing his tender nose with the dirty point. He veered away and turned back toward me, closing in. I backed up, afraid to look behind to see where I was going, shovel and pail still in front of me, hopelessly inadequate. The tiger matched my steps, head low, eyes unblinking, vibrating. After an eternity, my shoulder bumped the heavy metal door. I stepped backwards through it and slammed it in his face.

Everything faded.

When I came to my senses, the door was locked—I couldn't remember doing it—and the tiger was out of sight, probably down in the moat.

I couldn't get up. I sat with my back against the cement wall, a spilled bucket of tiger shit next to me, the shovel across my legs. Nothing run by motor neurons worked. I could see and hear, that was it. Most of what I heard was thundering blood in my veins. Finally my hand obeyed and moved. The palm was skinned up and bleeding. I pushed the shovel away, bent a knee. It felt scraped also. I got up and leaned against the wall.

When I could walk, I looked in the den. It was empty, the guillotine door open. The tiger was out in the exhibit.

There was no doubt Raj could safely have ignored the shovel and bucket and taken me out. He chose not to. There was no real reason I was still alive, except maybe that he didn't want me dead, just back where he thought I belonged. I wanted to believe that he didn't want me dead.

What had happened—keeper error? Rajah had been in the den, but the door to the yard hadn't been closed? No, I had shut that door. Had I? Maybe I had checked, as always, but hadn't seen, looked but not noticed. I'd been so focused on thought control. Could I trust myself to know? I couldn't think straight.

It felt like hours since I first walked into the exhibit, but my watch claimed it was only minutes. I called Wallace and told him I was sick. He said he'd move Linda to cats to finish up, and I stumbled to the employee parking lot, thighs rubbing against cold wet uniform, and started home. Once on the freeway, I started shaking so badly I had to pull over and wait, teeth chattering, until I could drive again.

I tried a long shower to wash away the stink of terror and self-doubt, hot water stinging the hand and knee abrasions. The incident kept replaying with different camera angles and all the script variations: Rajah locked in like he should have been, no problems; the old tiger, far more agile than I would have thought, leaping up to slam me to the ground; teeth and claws sinking into my unprotected primate flesh; Raj shot to save my life. Or not, no one noticing until too late. The hot water tank finally ran out and I sloshed out of the bathtub, dimly aware that the water was ankle deep and staying that way. A clogged drain seemed trivial.

After a can of soup and walking the dogs, I paced around the living room and tried to figure out what had happened and what to do, the dogs watching in mild puzzlement. I considered talking it over with Marcie. This was too personal, too complicated. I felt too humiliated, frightened, and confused to tell anyone, even her.

Had I locked Raj in or not? Had I seen him safely in the night den before I went out into the yard? I circled the sofa and wandered in and back out of the kitchen, while I walked through the incident in my mind. The image was there—he was locked in. But was it true, or merely what I wanted to see?

If he *was* out in the yard when I first entered it, he must have been down in the moat. I'd been out there three or four minutes before he jumped me, a long time for him not to notice. More likely, he'd been in the den watching me through the open cat door. Had I been that oblivious? I had to admit it was possible.

I gave up on "what happened" for the moment and considered "what next." No one saw the accident; there would have been a big hullabaloo immediately if anyone had. Linda hadn't noticed anything amiss when she took over for the afternoon after I'd fled or she would have phoned to check up on me. I stared unseeing out the living room window into the gray day.

Range got up and started sniffing around. He found his tennis ball and nudged me hopefully. I stepped around him and paced on. Winnie snoozed.

If I reported the accident, Wallace would never let me stay at Felines. I wouldn't be a part of the clouded leopard introduction or train Spice or hand-feed the cougars. I'd lose the fragile clout I'd built over the last year as the feline keeper. At best, I'd be junior keeper in another area. Displaced, demoted.

If the incident had been an accident due to my carelessness, it was really a wake-up call that would make my job safer, not more dangerous, because I'd be paying close attention from now on. So I didn't need to report it.

Range laid his head in my lap, his lips bulging with the tennis ball. I took the soggy ball and tossed it for him. It rolled under the sofa and his claws scraped on bare wood as he tried to paw it out. Frustrated, he lay on his side and shoved his nose under the sofa. He moved it an inch or two. The sofa legs made a little squeal as they skidded on the hardwood floor.

The squeak. I remembered the noise, more of a high-pitched scraping sound, and I remembered what it was. It was the sound of the guillotine door being raised, the door that let the tiger out into the exhibit. Someone had pulled the cable and opened it for Raj.

Chapter Five

I sat on my bed, sipping my first coffee as I finished putting on my uniform. Why had I thought I hadn't closed and locked Raj's door to the exhibit? With the fear and adrenaline gone, I was positive I *had* locked that door, like always, with Raj on the inside where he belonged. Maybe Linda or Wallace had come into Felines, not seen me in the yard, and opened the cat door to let him out. Maybe the schedule changes had confused someone into making a major error.

I wiggled one foot into a rubber boot and pulled it on. My hands and knees hurt from yesterday's scrapes, and I was sore all over. My cheek was a little bruised, not too noticeably.

What about the main service door into Felines? When anyone came into the building, it slammed itself shut. Unless you were careful with it. I didn't hear the door slam while I was out in the yard. Linda would close it quietly. Wallace might not have bothered. Dead end.

I pulled the second boot on and tried to picture the foreman letting the tiger out into the yard. Or a keeper. Why would they? Even if they thought it was their responsibility to let Raj out, they would check the yard first—that's what the little windows were for. Arnie came to mind. He tended to be casual about standard procedure. Or was it wishful thinking to believe someone else opened that cat door?

I could keep quiet or I could tell Wallace. I knew perfectly well what I *should* do—tell Wallace and let him deal with it. And he would assume it was my fault because I was feeble-minded from grief. He would move me to another area forever, a new routine to learn under another keeper, another chunk whacked out of my life.

Losing Felines…my heart turned cold in my chest. Only a year ago, hard work and random luck had made me the right person to get the assignment when the old feline keeper retired. It was everything I wanted in a job and I'd given it all I had. Now restless luck was blowing the other way.

I brushed my hair, filled the dogs' water bowls, and climbed into my truck, parked side by side with Rick's on the driveway. Getting to the zoo took about twenty minutes. Nothing became any clearer. I should have called Marcie last night and talked it through with her. Too late now.

I'd pulled into the zoo parking lot when questions about Rick's death clinked against the accident with Raj. I sat behind the wheel, the motor off, trying to figure out whether any real connection could exist. If I brought that up, mentioning two peculiar accidents in one breath, I'd be labeled "deranged" for sure. Besides, I couldn't get it to make any sense. What could the incident with Raj possibly have to do with the puzzle of why Rick fell in the moat a few hours after midnight? Did he get drunk here or on the way? Did I care? I wasn't sure.

Regardless, I had two options for today's dilemma: stay silent about the episode or find out who let Raj out and then tell Wallace. I tried to pull myself together. This wasn't necessarily a career disaster, just a problem to solve.

I caught Linda at the time clock and walked with her to Felines. The path was wet from rain in the night, littered with a few yellow leaves and yesterday's visitor trash.

"You must have had a mild case," she said. "Hap had the flu for a week. My number's probably up next."

"Linda, did you go back to Felines after we talked to Dr. Dawson yesterday morning?" So I wasn't going with the silent strategy. According to Marcie, I never knew what I was planning until I said it or did it.

"I went to Children's Zoo. That's where Wallace put me. Why? What happened?" She stopped beside the zebra exhibit, facing me with her freckles wrinkled in concern.

"I think somebody let Raj out on me. I wasn't hurt, just scared."

"You went out into the yard and he jumped you?"

"Right. Did you let him out?"

She was slow to answer. "I didn't do that. I never went back to Felines. You could have been killed." She stared at me, pale. "Why didn't I know about this? Didn't you tell anyone?"

"Just you. I need to find out how Raj got out."

"Iris, are you sure you didn't leave the cat door open? You've been—a little distracted."

"I know the routine. I'd never make that mistake." It sounded totally unconvincing.

"People are already worried about you, worried about an accident. If Wallace hears about this…"

"Yeah. I know."

Hazel eyes stared me resolutely in the face. "I'm not sure how to say this, Iris, but it doesn't seem likely that someone else opened that door. Why would anyone? You don't seem to be quite yourself yet, and no wonder, considering all you've been through…"

"I had to ask. It must have been someone else."

"Iris, we're friends, but you'd better give this some thought before you question anyone else. It sounds pretty…unrealistic. People will worry even more about your state of mind. And they might take it as an accusation."

"Yeah, you're right. Just forget it." I started toward Felines.

"Iris…" her voice trailed after me.

I found Arnie at Bears, hosing the grizzly moat, a small, faintly ridiculous figure in his brown zoo uniform and a Western hat. He always wore cowboy boots, no doubt for the extra couple of inches, and didn't seem to care that constant wetness wrecked them fast. Bushy mustache, beady eyes, and buck teeth qualified him for Rodentia, not Bears.

He switched off the water, never reluctant to stop working. "Why, no. I was busy as all git out yesterday. Never went near the cat house. I heard you got the flu. Was it the trots kind or the upchuck kind? Did you get the shot this year?"

I told him it was the stomach kind, which was close to the truth, and left before he could ask anything more.

I leaned my forearms on the guardrail and stared at the cougars, lying high on wood platforms, indifferent to the cold, on their sides with pale bellies turned toward me. The night keeper had left the big cats with access to the outside yards, probably for the last time until spring. The wind bit through the thin brown jacket with my name stitched on the left breast. "Just a problem to solve" wasn't showing much promise. Any of a dozen people might have a legitimate reason to go into Felines. If I asked them all, they would probably put me on desk duty forever and hide the scissors. A culprit could lie about doing it, out of fear for the consequences. And it was still possible, barely, that I hadn't locked Raj in properly.

The female cougar stood up, stretched, and jumped down, hitting with a solid thud. The male rolled off his platform as limber as mercury and landed beside her, biffing her shoulder with a paw. She floated up eight feet to a log and he followed, then down again, two graceful bodies at play.

Given that I couldn't save my bacon by determining how Raj got out, could I resurrect silence as an option? Linda knew and Arnie might guess. If I asked her to keep quiet, Linda might not talk, and Arnie was not good at guessing. But silence had its own dangers—the risk of getting fired, not just losing Felines, if Wallace found out I hadn't reported the accident.

Hap and Dr. Dawson walked by the lion exhibit, apparently on their way to the Commissary. Hap waved and I waved back. Dr. Dawson nodded toward me. The three lions had been inside the night dens, out of sight. Spice emerged, eyed them, and padded down the cement slope to the moat at the bottom. Simba stuck his head out, then retreated back to the warmth. Next door, Raj was shut inside, a wise decision considering his age.

When the cold got to be too much and a happy ending still declined to materialize, I pushed myself upright and went inside. My stomach hurt and my head hurt. I wished it *was* the flu.

I found a tennis ball in a kitchen drawer, walked down the hall to the left, and climbed into the serval exhibit. The servals were always good medicine for troubles.

This exhibit was completely interior—no yard—and blessedly warm. The inside was done up with rocks and logs. I sat quietly on the ground. Spot, the female, came up to me right away. She had been bottle-raised and retained a skittish tolerance for people. She was calm for a serval—which was to say, jumpy. All the small wild cats are high-strung, at least all the ones I'd met. They are predators, but also prey and have a prey animal's wariness. I scratched lightly along Spot's spine and rubbed under her chin. Her fur, yellow with black spots, was a little stiffer and coarser than a house cat's. She didn't seem troubled that I hadn't brought a food pan.

Pele, the male, was zoo-born, but mother-raised. While he wouldn't tolerate actual contact, he wasn't afraid of me. He kept his distance and did a little odoriferous squirting to make it clear that he was Top Cat in this corner of the world and I was only a visitor.

How could I find out who had come into Felines yesterday morning? A security camera would be just the ticket, a video clip to review, but there wasn't any. And no cover story I could think of would keep people from guessing the truth if I kept asking questions.

I rolled the tennis ball across the exhibit, along the fake dry streambed. The ball skittered around the embedded rocks. Pele pounced on it, leaping high in the air and coming down with his feet bunched. He batted the ball around, Spot making ineffectual passes but staying out of his way. He was bigger than she and much more committed to killing tennis balls.

Linda thought I was genuinely at risk. Would she sacrifice our friendship, go to Wallace, if she thought it would save my life? She would.

The ball got stuck in a crevice. I scooted my butt over to it and tossed it high up in the air. Pele leaped three feet up, the way servals snag flushed birds in African grasslands. He smacked it a good one with a forepaw, knocking the ball hard into the glass. It rebounded and hit him in the face, scaring the daylights out of him. I held still until he got his nerves under control and his dignity back.

Rick had died dumb, a stupid, clumsy, *unprofessional* accident. Professionals didn't hide behind lies and silence.

I gathered up the ball and climbed out of the exhibit. Spot and Pele watched me, side by side, probably wondering where breakfast was.

"Thanks, guys," I told them sadly and shut the exhibit door. I put the ball away in the kitchen and walked to the service door and out.

One chance left.

He was sitting sideways to me at his desk, belly up against the keyboard tray, blue denim shirt straining at the snaps, poking at the keyboard with two index fingers. His face turned wary. "Oakley? What do you need?"

"Mr. Wallace, did you open the cat door and let Rajah out into the exhibit yesterday morning?" I looked for alarm or evasion.

"Of course not. I got better things to do than your work." His eyes narrowed. "So what happened yesterday?"

"That's what I'm trying to find out. I think somebody let Raj out."

"And where were you?"

On break? Visiting Primates? In the bathroom? "In the yard."

"What happened?" His full attention focused on me, boring holes in my heart and stomach.

"Raj chased me back out. I wasn't hurt, just skinned my knee. He didn't get out."

"And that's why you went home sick." He drummed his fingers on the desk. "You didn't report the accident immediately. That's grounds for disciplinary action."

"I'm reporting it now. I think someone might have opened the cat door. I think I heard it while I was in the yard." Wrong, wrong. I shouldn't have said "might have."

"Or else you forgot to check and went out there with the door still open."

Honesty was a lousy policy.

The thick pads of his fingers tapped on the desk. "Look, you got special circumstances, with Rick and all. I never should of let you go back to cats, so maybe this was my fault too. I'll forget about the warning in your file—this time. You let me know anything at all happens, any kind of accident at all, hear?"

I heard.

He picked a piece of paper off his desk and studied it. "You work Primates today and tomorrow. Linda does cats. You get Saturday and Sunday off, then you move to Birds under Calvin Lorenz mostly and Primates under Kip Harrison when they need extra help."

I opened my mouth to argue. Or beg.

"Get to work," he ordered. "And be damn glad you're still alive."

Defeated, I walked out and slunk toward Primates.

Chapter Six

A day scrubbing walls inside monkey exhibits added aching muscles to my sore spirit. Kip Harrison, the senior primate keeper, was delighted not to have to do it herself. It was mindless, wearying toil, about all I was good for.

Somehow word was out about my encounter with Rajah, judging by the glances and silences. No one came forward, embarrassed and apologetic, to confess they had let Raj out. Instead people treated me with uneasy thoughtfulness, as though a harsh word might send me into a psychotic episode where I'd hang myself with a hose. I could hardly wait for the weekend.

That evening, Marcie called as I sat huddled on the sofa in my robe and soon extracted the whole story about Raj evicting me and the consequences. She eventually collected herself enough to say, "Iris, I appreciate that you add spice to my dull little life, but this is excessive. I'd really prefer you stay alive." I pictured her hand flying up in alarm, the other white-knuckled on the phone.

She decided that dragging me to a big dog show at the Portland Expo Center on Saturday was essential to my mental health. That morning, she picked me up at the house in her Saturn and was determinedly chipper on the drive. I heard all about her job at the furniture store, which she hated, and the malnourished kitten she had recently adopted and was introducing to her other two cats. She talked with one hand on the steering wheel, the other illustrating important points.

I wasn't much help keeping the conversation going. During a pause, a huge red semi swept past us. A snarling tiger was painted on the side ten feet high, part of an ad for Olde English 800 malt liquor. "Beer can with tiger attacking. My personal eighteen-wheeler from hell," I sighed.

"Yes. We need to talk about that. You don't look so good."

"Just tired."

She gave me a look.

"Watch the road. I've lost Felines—how would you expect me to look? Telling Wallace what happened with Raj was the most adult thing I've ever done. I'll never do anything that mature again as long as I live. Way too painful."

Marcie put both hands on the wheel and stared straight ahead. "Your way of dealing with grief is not exactly the mature one."

"What's that supposed to mean?"

"Pretending Rick didn't happen isn't working."

"I'm not pretending. I'm rebuilding my life. What do you want me to do—wail and snarl and feel sorry for myself?"

"Take it easy. Keep in mind that I'm actually on your side."

If Marcie's goal was a relaxed outing, this was not going according to plan. We rode in silence for a few minutes, with me regretting angry words.

Marcie found her positive energy before I did. "You might actually like Birds, if you give it a chance. More rounded experience, good career move, all that."

"No cats. Calvin. Second banana."

She gave up on cheerful. "What's wrong with Calvin? I thought you liked him."

"Calvin's fine, as long as we're eating lunch together. My gut feeling is that he's an old-fashioned guy who remembers when being a keeper was a male thing. Arnie was his relief keeper for years and I don't think he got to vote on swapping Arnie for me." I stared morosely at the green struts of the Interstate 5 Bridge. "Now Calvin's my boss. I liked not having a boss at Felines."

"You had Wallace."

"True, but I mostly ran Felines the way I wanted. I wasn't a senior keeper, but I got to make decisions like one. Calvin *is* a senior keeper for Birds, and I'll try to do as I'm told. It's that or leave the zoo."

"You learned Felines from one of the old guys. You got along fine with him."

"I was brand new. I didn't know any better than to do whatever Herman told me. He was a 'clean it, feed it, go play cards 'til 4:00 PM' keeper. I don't know if Calvin is just putting in his time until retirement or not. And another thing. We're finally starting to use training instead of drugs and physical restraint. I'm working with the cats so that we can do exams and medical procedures without getting them stirred up or knocking them out. Calvin isn't doing anything like that with birds, and he's not likely to let me start a bunch of new procedures."

"Maybe a whole lot of dogs will help."

We pulled off the freeway and began the circuitous route that winds to the Portland Metropolitan Exposition Center.

Inside the Expo Center, a maze of show rings and exhibits was strung out over three big buildings connected by enclosed corridors. People of all ages wandered around, many of them attached to dogs. Crowd noises were spiced with barks and yelps; the huge space smelled of popcorn and canine grooming products. We were swept into the slow stream of dog-loving citizenry.

I had issues with some practices in the pure-bred dog industry, such as mutilating the ears of Doberman pinschers and developing breeds that can't give birth without caesareans, but I had to admit that the dogs looked to be having a great time. They got treats to keep their heads up, to let the handler set their feet right, to trot without frisking. They found wonderful opportunities to make new friends or new enemies, depending on personalities, and were socializing nonstop. My sorrows were supplanted for the moment by busy canines and their obsessed humans.

We meandered around dogs being brushed and fluffed on benches. I cheered up enough to flirt with a Bernese mountain dog on a grooming bench, who slobbered sweetly on my fingers, while Marcie cooed at a bright-eyed Lhasa Apso. This was fun after all.

"Marcie," I said, "we are both already in relationships with companion animals. Don't be promiscuous."

"You should talk. You got as much drool on that dog as he got on you."

"You still hanging with that Jake guy?" I'd met him once—quiet, low-key, some sort of doctor's assistant.

"Jack. Not for a while."

Smart, cute Marcie hadn't had a relationship last for more than a month since college. "Deeply flawed?"

"More like stale-dated. A high school basketball game is still the high point of his life."

"And I thought fear of commitment was a male trait," I said.

"Look, sometimes I wish I could toss my heart over a cliff and dive after it, but I do things differently."

"Scared to crash-land at the bottom like I did. You should be braver—there can't be that many guys as bogus as Rick."

"Let's get tea," Marcie said. "I want to sit at the ring with bleachers and watch the Finnish spitzes."

"We need doughnuts with sprinkles on top. That should go well with spitzes."

We got our treats and found space on a narrow bleacher bench. I'd never seen a Finnish spitz in my life. They looked like foxes, small and red-gold, with tails curled over their backs. One particularly lively female yipped firmly at her handler when the tidbits came too slow. As long as the action kept up, the ache in my chest lay dormant.

"Thanks for rooting me out of my cave," I told Marcie. "I'm almost enjoying myself." I had colorful sugar sprinkles all over me. They left a little stain on my jeans when I brushed them off.

"That was the idea," she said, eating her doughnut with not a sprinkle out of place or the slightest mar on her khakis or pink sweater.

"Obedience trial," I said, waving at the ring.

German shepherds, golden retrievers, and several other breeds heeled perfectly, heads up, close to their handlers. Their rears dropped promptly when the handlers stopped, except for a young Rhodesian Ridgeback, who wandered off to greet a poodle. Her handler caught her up and clipped on the leash.

"I'm the Ridgeback, but I have to act like a golden retriever."

"Which means...?"

"Do what Calvin tells me to do instead of thinking for myself. That's what's required to survive in the rubble Rick left of my life. If only I'd never started going out with him..."

Marcie wiped her fingers on a napkin and wadded it into a tight little ball. "You're acting more like an abused Doberman."

"What?" I wasn't sure I'd heard her right.

"This bitterness is corrosive. You aren't eating, you aren't sleeping, and you blame Rick for all your problems. Maybe you need to quit being so angry at him and try a little forgiving." She unwadded the napkin and started tearing it to shreds.

"Get real. He lied to me and manipulated me and died drunk." Acid roiled in my stomach, bitter in the back of my throat. I dug around for patience, wishing I'd found a gentler voice. Romantic Marcie, too wary of men for a serious relationship herself, trying to salvage the Rick ♥ Iris story.

"Denial has its uses, but this is not going to work. You're trying to pretend you never loved him and he never loved you." Marcie's face was flushed, her jaw set stubbornly.

"I'm trying to move on with my life, but he's cost me my job."

"It's his fault you have to move to Birds?" Marcie's hands flew apart in amazement.

"Oh, yes. I'm supposedly demented by grief, so everyone thinks I left Rajah's door open. People were quick to assume I screwed up. Nobody took me seriously about hearing someone open the cat door. They think I'm as incompetent as Rick."

"Give them a break. They lost one friend and they're worried about you. Besides, you always told me how competent Rick was." Her face turned fierce. "You've erased everything good about him. You might try to remember he was more than a liar and a loser, a lot more."

I bit back a sharp answer and waited for softer words to come. "Yeah, I still believe he was a decent animal keeper." I stared at the ring, barely registering the chocolate poodle jumping over a little fence, considering the depth of Marcie's loyalty to Rick. "Look, I know you liked Rick, everybody did, but he wasn't who we thought he was. You have some accepting to do yourself."

Marcie looked away, her face unreadable. "Let's go look for dog toys."

This was not going well.

We wandered around the commercial displays for another hour. People told us that we could pet the dogs after the show ring, but not before, to preserve extreme fluffiness; that the skin of whippets tears easily; that salukis are much less maintenance than Afghans. The air smelled of dog shampoo. The only mess I saw was a kicked-over can of cola.

When we'd seen it all, we stepped out of the noisy, warm exhibit hall to hunt for Marcie's car in the huge lot. On our right, outside the grounds and beyond a cyclone fence, a lake gleamed dully in twilight. The gray sky above it was crowded with dark waterfowl, circling and settling on the water. Their cries sounded like puppies yelping.

Driving home, Marcie broke our silence. "You loved Rick. I saw it. And he loved you."

I sagged back against the seat, weary to my bones. "I was drugged by pheromones and hormones and didn't see what was really happening until too late. That's all there was to it."

"That's not just stupid, it's mean and unfair." Marcie's round face, pale in the headlights of oncoming cars, was constricted with anger. "You're stupid to keep denying who Rick was, what you guys had. I know it went sour, but I saw the whole thing, remember? It was real. You two had big problems, but that wasn't the whole story. You'll never get over this if you keep pretending."

"Baby and bathwater?"

"Yes, damn it."

"What the hell good does it do me to remember what's gone forever?"

"I don't know. But lying to yourself isn't working. I feel like I'm talking to a stranger every time Rick comes up."

The Columbia River was slow-moving pewter in the gray light. Mt. Hood and Mt. Saint Helens were both invisible. Ahead lay a long, cold winter, an empty bed each night, endless regrets and questions, ugly dreams. Sorrows circled like ducks at the lake. Words to salve a bruised friendship failed to touch down.

We took the Vancouver exit for my house and rode through the outskirts of town in silence. I sought a scrap of common ground. "Marcie, you said one thing right. Rick *was* competent. He didn't make bonehead mistakes, especially on the job."

She nodded, unappeased.

"Even drunk, he didn't stagger around," I mused. "He got flushed and loud, that's all. He *said* things that were a little dumb, but he never *did* anything reckless or stupid." Unless disconnecting from me in favor of drinking could be called stupid.

She turned into my driveway and the dogs started barking from inside the house.

I sat in the warm car in the dark, gathering the will to get out. "Falling into the lion moat doesn't make sense. I need to know why Rick died at the zoo."

Marcie looked as exhausted as I felt. "Anything but staying like this. It's not what I had in mind, but start facing reality any way you can."

Chapter Seven

I swiped my time card a full half-hour early in the deserted Commissary and walked through the cold, quiet dawn to Felines without seeing another person. Peacocks and peahens were still abed; gibbons hadn't tuned up yet. The air smelled of fall and frost and rain to come.

The cats were locked inside for the night. My key turned in the lock, as familiar as brushing my teeth. Inside was sharp-smelling warmth. Water dripped somewhere and a half-hearted sawing roar came from the direction of the common leopards. I walked down the hall, rubber boots soft on the concrete, paying my regards. The cats were calm, accustomed to me, confident breakfast would be served soon. Even the twitchy clouded leopards were relaxed. My steps echoed softly as I walked back past the kitchen to the lions. All three lurched to their feet and started pacing. I watched them and they watched me. Across the aisle, the leopards ignored me, black Bagheera and yellow Kali, too cool to notice me. I went on to Rajah. Damned if he didn't say hello, a rough, short purr, like he always did.

"Good morning, Raj, good-by, Raj," I told him. "No hard feelings, not toward you."

I left by the service door and walked toward the Penguinarium. With every step, my identity as a cat keeper faded. Did I have the fortitude and energy to adapt, to become a first-rate bird keeper? No choice but to try.

Calvin was already busy in the Penguinarium kitchen, inject-
ing liquid vitamins into small dead fish with a big syringe.
Square-built with thinning gray hair and blunt fingers, he looked
like an old farmer despite the brown uniform. He'd started wearing glasses not long ago and been kidded about it. I'd never spent
much time in his company aside from lunch breaks.

The kitchen had a doorway open to the African penguin exhibit,
a wooden baby gate jammed across it to keep the birds where they
belonged. The room smelled to high heaven of penguin poop. The
little waddlers were braying and squalling at the gate. There seemed
to be a lot of them for the size of the exhibit. Calvin grunted at me
in a neutral way and showed me the diet charts. He demonstrated
how to vitamin-enrich their breakfast and soon I was coated in fish
gunk up to my yellow-gloved elbows. I finished shooting up the
fish—smelt and capelin and mackerel—while he pretended to tidy
up and not watch to be sure I was doing it right. He climbed over the
gate to the exhibit side and hand-fed the penguins clustered around.
Each bird got a little conversation. "Dotty, pay attention. Bandit,
knock it off; you'll get your share. Neal, there's a good boy."

That done, Calvin stepped back over the baby gate and
started washing up at the sink. "Can you carry a bag of duck
feed?" he asked over his shoulder, out of the blue. "Or should
I get a hand truck?"

I considered the question. I could be a weenie who couldn't
handle an ordinary bag of feed or I could eventually pull a
muscle in my back and make a chiropractor rich. I stalled for
time. "How big are the bags?"

"Fifty pounds."

I could handle fifty pounds if necessary, but it wasn't my
idea of fun. "Can you stack two on a hand truck?" Right, we
should use a hand truck for efficiency, not because I didn't want
to struggle on slippery footing with heavy bags.

"Yes, but we don't feed two bags. Just the one."

Rats. "I can lift fifty pounds, but I guess I'd have to know
the routine better to decide whether we need a hand truck. I
could let you know."

"I'll go ahead and get one. Don't need no worker's comp reports to fill out."

He smiled to make it a joke. It wasn't funny.

The rest of the morning I followed him around, trying to remember everything and not hurt myself or let anything escape. Under close supervision, I picked up mealworms, captured crickets in a Styrofoam cup, and created evil-looking glop in a blender, all for outdoor aviary birds.

I lugged a bag of duck food to the outdoor pond and poured it into a trough without hurting or embarrassing myself. The open-air pond was a winter resort for half-wild uninvited guests. A huge crowd of freeloading mallards swarmed over the trough and my boots and each other to get at the mash, a seething mass of avian avarice. Each duck grabbed a bill-full and fought its way back to the water to dabble and swallow.

Calvin identified the zoo ducks for me: wood ducks, redheads, Australian shelducks. The last were handsome birds in black, white, and chestnut. The zoo waterfowl swam around impatiently, waiting for the mallard bullies to clear out. I hadn't realized birds could get so aggressive. Only the big swans, "mute swans" according to Calvin, waded through the duck riot. I made a mental note to look up "mute swans" to see if it was a species or a defect.

Calvin warned that a parrot bite could require stitches, that owls attack with their talons, and that cranes would peck my eyes out. I hit my head on branches, slipped on mud, cut myself on wire mesh, and got whacked in the shins by a nene, an assertive Hawaiian goose. I walked miles carrying food pans, climbed ladders, and crawled through underbrush on hands and knees to retrieve food bowls.

Calvin left at lunchtime to eat with Kip; I ate my peanut butter and banana sandwiches alone in the Penguinarium kitchen, tired in body and mind from the strain of learning a new routine.

The hasty lunch restored me a little and left time to pursue yesterday's resolution, starting with a look in Rick's locker. Perhaps he'd left something there that would shed light on his last night.

I detoured past the new exhibit area on my way to Reptiles. The price for "Asian Experience" was passage of a big bond measure and destruction of the last patch of natural forest in the zoo. A scraggly ridge of topsoil and mashed understory plants fringed a wide area of mud now sculpted into hills and depressions, replacing the hills and depressions there originally. Mangled second-growth firs, maples, and alders lay in a heap to the side. The bulldozer was still mired in mud. Revenge of the landscape? I paused for a moment's memorial to summer lunches in the woods, the occasional woodpecker jackhammering on a snag, white trilliums in the spring. The new exhibit would be great, but the woods had been fine the way they were. I mourned things that would never be the same again.

In front of the Reptile area service door, I gathered myself, preparing to enter Rick's old territory. Denny emerged before I was quite ready, with his little canvas lunch sack in hand.

"Hey, Ire. What's up?" he asked.

"Don't call me that," I said, instantly irked. "You know I hate that." I stepped inside, keeping a wary eye on the floor and elsewhere. "I'm going to clean out Rick's locker."

Denny followed me inside, put his lunch down, and turned toward the two padlocked cabinets at the back of the service area that served as personal lockers for keepers assigned to Reptiles.

I stood inside the door. "Denny, I don't need help. You go on to lunch."

He stopped. "What's the problem?"

"I'd rather do this alone."

Denny looked unsettled. "Why? What do you think is in there?"

"Spare socks." Denny deserved better, but I couldn't find what it took to be nice. He'd done his erratic best to help at the memorial service and, at times, I felt a lingering loyalty toward him. He was a disaster as a boyfriend, feral and unreliable, but he'd never been devious or dishonest. I simply wanted to do this alone.

He didn't leave, but he stayed near the door, watching as I edged past him and through the narrow corridor between two curving rows of wood and glass boxes, their clear faces turned toward the public area. Each contained something reptilian—I hoped. Once when I was there with Rick, I'd nearly stepped on a small boa. By some miracle, my heart had restarted itself and Rick never noticed how close I was to screaming or bolting, the archaic primate response to an unexpected snake. He had scooped the snake up with his hands and plunked it back where it belonged, adjusting the lid so it couldn't go roaming again, no big deal.

I got to Rick's cabinet, the one left of the sink, without any unplanned encounters, but was stymied by the padlock. It was the kind that requires turning a dial first one way, then the other to hit each of three numbers. I had no idea what the combination was. Denny might know, but I didn't feel like asking him and giving him an excuse to watch over my shoulder. Frustrated, I gave the padlock a yank, and it opened. Rick had used the zookeepers' trick of leaving a padlock so it looked locked but wasn't, saving time. His hand had been the last to touch that lock, I realized as the ache reawoke in my chest.

Inside were an old fleece jacket, wadded up on the top shelf, and an empty yogurt container with fuzz from an ancient lunch brought from home. Rubber clogs to the rear of the bottom shelf. A tiny snake skin in a little plastic jar, frail translucent scales the reptile had left behind. Also in the jar were two small leathery eggshells, each split open and empty. No socks, but Rick was present, vivid and whole for an instant. I stood paralyzed.

I pulled myself together, hauled everything out, and set it on the counter, standing on tiptoe to be sure the top shelf was emptied. Denny couldn't tolerate not seeing and came up behind me. I handed him the yogurt container to throw in the trash.

"Why do you think the padlock was open?" he asked. "Did Rick leave it that way or did someone else go through the locker already?"

"Why would anybody care? The lock was open because Rick couldn't be bothered to protect some crummy clothing. You want this jacket and the clogs?"

"Yeah, sure."

I went through the jacket pockets—empty—and gave it to him with the clogs. Denny peered over my shoulder into Rick's cabinet, then opened the one to the right of the sink and stuffed the items inside.

I closed the door, wanting to be gone, then opened it again. "There's a lot of dirt inside. Where's some paper towels or a rag?" Clean, it would be ready for someone else to use, resolving one of the many messes Rick had left behind.

Denny handed over a wad of paper towels. I swept mud cookies and grit over the bottom edge of the cabinet and caught them in my hand. I was about to release it all into a wastebasket when a small bit of light-colored rock caught my eye. I picked it out and threw away the dirt. The "rock" turned out to be a small, stained tooth. I dropped it in the jar.

Denny plucked the jar from my hand and held it face-height to examine.

"Give that back," I snapped.

"Box turtle eggshells," he said. "Rick hatched them out a year or so ago and one survived. I don't know what the snake skin is."

"It's mine, is what it is." I grabbed his wrist. "Give me that."

Denny recoiled. "Hey, chill! Oh—do you think this is why Rick was at the zoo? Maybe he was investigating poaching or smuggled animal parts for Asian medicine. Or maybe—"

"Give me a break. It's stuff he found." I took it from his fingers. "You've got a nerve." I put the lid on the jar and stuck it in my pocket.

"Man, you are harshing everyone these days." He rubbed his wrist and looked at me, speculative. "You expected to find something else?"

"No, not really. I gotta go." I started to edge past him toward the door.

He didn't move out of my way. "You eat already? I'm headed to the café."

"I ate."

"Catch a look at the baby garter snakes before you go. Cute."

Cute snakes weren't quite enough of a concept to hook me, but Denny blocked my path and waved me down the aisle. I gave in, wondering what was really on his mind, and walked to an off-exhibit box with a suspended lightbulb and newspaper on the floor. Little stripy snakes each the size of a pencil oozed around a jar lid confining red earthworms. Perfect little scales covered their shiny, big-eyed snakey heads; tiny pink and black tongues flicked in and out, except for the ones that had their mouths full as they slowly ingested their worms. "Cute" was stretching it, but I could see the appeal, like slithery jewelry.

"Shit!" Denny yelped in my ear, and galloped back to the cabinets. He flung first one drawer open, then another, emerging with a pair of scissors. "They can't let go," he said, hustling back to the baby snakes and leaning over two wee reptiles that each had an end of the same earthworm. They'd swallowed toward each other until they were close to touching. He snipped the worm in two between their noses and straightened up, relieved. "If they meet head to head, one of them has to try to swallow the other, like corporate takeovers. Mutual assured destruction." He checked that everyone had a worm without any sharing and pulled the jar lid out.

Denny was positively parental, a side of him I'd never suspected. Reptiles did that to some people. No wonder he and Rick had been friends.

Staring down at the little snakelets, he said, "I wish Rick were here to teach me how to run this section. He knew so damn much and I have to figure everything out a piece at a time."

"Denny, do you know what Rick was doing here at Finley that last night?"

"No."

Just "no." I waited, but he was focused on putting the earthworms away in the refrigerator. "Would he come to check on the snake eggs that were incubating?"

"The blood pythons? If he did, he would have written some-thing in the log. I was going to ask *you* why he was here."

This was like pulling teeth. "I have no idea or I wouldn't be asking. So was there anything in the incubator log?"

"Nothing."

"I'd like to see it." I was careful to keep my voice neutral.

But Denny heard some hint of doubt. "I checked it. You think I wouldn't bother? He was my friend." He closed the fridge door and walked back to stand too close to me. "I'd like to know what came down that night."

You could get skin damage from Denny's full intensity. "I want to see it myself."

"It's got zip, Ire."

"Let me see the goddamned thing."

Denny recoiled, then led me to a tattered spiral notebook next to a large box of clear plastic with fancy equipment on top. The box contained a tray of kitty litter, or perhaps vermiculite, with a dozen or so white eggs nestled in it. The eggs were shaped like kiwi fruit, lacking the taper to one end that a hen's egg has. I'd seen the incuba-tor before with Rick, when we first started dating. He'd explained that the faintly penciled X on top of each egg was to help keep the orientation consistent. I was a novice bird keeper, but I knew bird eggs need regular turning and that reptile eggs won't tolerate it.

The notebook was a record of temperature and humidity for incu-bations dating back years. The blood python section was the most recent, with notes every few hours back three weeks. The last entry with Rick's initials was 3:00 PM the day before he died. I studied the page carefully. It had nothing to tell me. I set it down.

"See?" Denny said.

I took a deep breath. Why did he always get to me? "Don't knock yourself out, but if you think of anything useful, you might mention it to me."

"Sure. Does that go both ways?"

I looked at him and shrugged, uncertain what he was get-ting at but prepared to be annoyed. That was how it went with Denny and me.

I pulled the plastic jar out of my pocket as I walked back to the Penguinarium and took another look at the contents. The little snake shed was appealing, a perfect translucent sketch of a snake, and I'd never seen turtle eggs before. The tooth was probably unidentifiable and it wasn't even interesting. Maybe Rick had found it in the woods before the construction started. We all had our collections of zoo bits. My tokens of the wild world included a bird's nest made of lion and tiger whiskers, a red-shafted flicker feather, and a nice squirrel skull from a roadside rest.

But I was kidding myself. The little objects in the jar weren't just tokens. They had power, power to bring Rick out of the vague gray shadows, to make him real and let him bushwhack my heart once again. I put the jar back in my pocket, wondering if I should toss it into the nearest trashcan, and willed him gone.

Calvin was waiting with a big stack of food pans he wanted me to scrub while he filled out reports. Then he wanted help hauling gravel in a wheelbarrow and shoveling it onto the path at the pond.

"Time to head for the barn," was all he had to say at day's end.

I drove home exhausted. Calvin's concern about every detail wore on my nerves, but it was what I would do in his place. Nitpicking suited me far better than Arnie's blithe indifference. Calvin had made it clear I needed to prove myself and that he expected eight hours of hard work. It was looking to be a long week.

That night, bed seemed like the best place on earth. But soon I was lost on a cloudy trail, following tiger tracks in blood-streaked mud, frightened and alone. I must have cried out, because Winnie jumped on the bed and woke me. The rest of the night was lost to regrets, recriminations, and riddles.

Chapter Eight

Tuesday, Calvin remained taciturn and cool. He showed me once again how to fix vitamin-enhanced fish. After sharing herring and pleasantries with each penguin, he told me to start on the aviary diets and went off to check other bird areas and collect the food pans. I chugged an extra cup of coffee to beat back sleepiness and focused on being useful.

The Birds section came in three main parts: the Penguinarium was enclosed and climate-controlled with windows for viewing from outside the exhibit; the outdoor aviary, The World of Birds, a large area visitors could enter, was mesh all around and on top, except that two sides and part of the top were solid; the waterfowl pond was open, with a low barrier circling it to keep people out. A spectacled owl, a crippled bald eagle, and a red-tailed hawk were afterthoughts tucked in small cages between the pond and the aviary. Two red-headed parrots lived at the Children's Zoo.

I hadn't worked this section except for a few days when I was first hired. I thought of birds mostly as prey species for small cats or as backyard ornaments that my mother fed sunflower seeds. Getting serious about fluttery, fluffy things was going to take some work. I'd ask Calvin if he would loan me some of the books stored in a cupboard, books about penguins and waterfowl.

Left unsupervised, I referred to the diet records and carefully whacked fish into halves, quarters, and thin slivers to match a variety of appetites and beak sizes. Penguins brayed and splashed in the exhibit, sometimes coming to the baby gate to check whether I was doing it right. I took a break from fish prep to watch them over the gate.

In the water, the penguins were agile and elegant. Usually two or more synchronized their dives and turns, Olympic style. Out of the water, they waddled comically on the central "island" where the nest boxes were strategically placed. Unlike cats, they didn't have potty corners, so walking around the island was a slippery business for humans. It smelled different from Felines, of digested fish instead of digested meat. "Pretty whiffy," Calvin said each morning.

Two penguins were out of sight, sitting on eggs in nest boxes, but there would be no chicks. "Too crowded in here," Calvin had said yesterday. He had removed the real eggs, which were sitting on the counter, and replaced them with plastic eggs. The birds didn't care. When I asked why the fake eggs, he'd explained that incubating shut off egg laying. "If I don't leave them something in the nest to set, they'll keep laying," Calvin said. "They ain't chickens and it's not good for them."

The Penguinarium kitchen had the usual stainless steel counters plus a refrigerator and two sinks. One sink was for washing; one was for running cold water into a bucket of fish if the fish weren't fully thawed. A wall was taken up with shelving and one full shelf was devoted to insects. Bird keeping meant bug keeping: bins of mealworms and wax worms and a wooden box with hundreds of crickets crawling around on egg cartons. The fridge held cardboard containers of nightcrawlers. The worms and insects were for the bewildering assortment of species in the World of Birds aviary. I was determined to be open-minded.

Homey touches included a yellow Penguin Crossing road sign, a big crayon drawing of penguins done by a third grader many years ago, and a plush stuffed penguin perched on a shelf. Newspaper articles about a big oil spill off South Africa were taped to the walls, with shots of penguins so black with oil that they looked charred.

After washing fish slime off my hands, I tackled the other diets: cutting fruit, setting mice out to thaw, measuring out various grain mixes. I was short of food pans, since Calvin hadn't come back with them, and had to set out two meals on paper towels.

The only food prep left was the mix for a pair of fruit dove chicks that Calvin was hand-feeding. That didn't require a food pan. But he might want to fix it himself. Would it be better to wait until he returned? I could be the timid trainee or I could read the instructions and get the job done. It wasn't as if I'd never prepared a complicated diet.

I assembled the blender, measured all the ingredients, and blended them to an even, if unappealing, consistency. Calvin stored the stuff in a metal pitcher in the fridge. When I picked up the blender to pour the contents into the pitcher, the bottom part with the blades fell off onto the floor, where I stepped on them and slid, flailing my arms and waving around the rest of the blender for balance until I caught myself against the now-goo-coated sink. I emitted a few alarm barks in the form of profanity. When I leaned down to retrieve the blender bottom, the plastic jar with the turtle eggs fell out of my jacket pocket, where I'd forgotten it from the day before. I was bending over to pick that up when Dr. Dawson walked in.

He looked a little startled and stood a moment taking in the scene. "Good morning, Iris. Uh, is Calvin around? I'm looking for penguin fecals he was going to get yesterday."

I straightened up, setting the jar and the blender bottom on the counter, and gathered my wits. "No, he's probably over at the aviary. Let me see if they're ready." I made it to the fridge, slipping a little. No white Styrofoam plastic cup with a lid and a "fecal sample" note on it. "He's probably planning to get you fresh ones this morning. He should be back any minute." I actually had no idea what Calvin's plans were, but it was good form to try to cover for him. I grabbed paper towels and started wiping the floor. What evil alignment of planets had sent Dr. Dawson to the Penguinarium at this particular moment?

Dr. Dawson nodded. "I can wait a bit."

I marveled that he could look and act so professional—button-up blue shirt, gray pants, leather shoes—faced with a disheveled keeper flinging slop around. He stood and watched me, then took off his glasses and polished them on a handkerchief.

"Are all the cats okay?" I asked, unnerved. "Is Rajah eating?"

"Oh, yes. They're all fine." He put the glasses back on and frowned at me a little, looking lost in his own thoughts. At last he said, "I'm glad to have a moment to speak with you privately. Wallace is gun-shy right now about accidents. Possibly he overreacted. Moving you away from Felines, before we introduce the clouded leopards...Well, I might have made a different decision."

The man was full of surprises. "Thanks. I appreciate the support, especially since this isn't one of my finer moments." To say the least.

"It may be a difficult transition to Birds, but I'm confident it will turn out well eventually."

"Yeah, I'll get the hang of it—eventually." If I didn't break my neck or get fired. I wiped a goo-smudge off my cheek with my left sleeve.

"Rick's death was a loss to us all. He was a fine keeper and I liked him. He improved our reptile management quite a bit. Extremely regrettable." He drummed his long fingers lightly on a chair back.

He seemed to have saved up that little speech until he caught me alone. It was news to me that the vet had developed so much respect for Rick, probably established during their snake breeding project, but hardly surprising. Rick was good at his job and easy to like.

I, on the other hand, was a chaos generator who was offending people every day. "Thanks for coming to the memorial service. It's been tough." A penguin at the baby gate brayed demands at us. "Calvin already fed you," I told it. I threw away the soaked paper towels and made a second pass at the floor with a sponge.

Leaning over seemed slightly more dignified than crawling on my hands and knees.

Dawson nodded sympathetically, apparently still oblivious to my culinary catastrophe. "If you don't mind my saying it, this must be especially difficult, given the way he died. I understand alcohol was involved."

"It was. He told me he wanted to quit drinking and get back together. Then he tied one on that same night." I rinsed the sponge at the sink and went after another section of floor.

The vet nodded. "Alcohol addiction is powerful."

And can lead to overly simple conclusions. I straightened up. If the opportunity and the nerve to question Dr. Dawson would ever come together, this had to be it. I clutched the sponge in a death grip and plunged in. "I keep trying to figure out how it happened. Do you have any idea why he came up to the zoo that last night?"

"No, I'm afraid I'm as puzzled as everyone else." He gave a barely perceptible shrug.

"You'd think *someone* would know."

"Iris, I meant it when I said you could drop by my office any time. I'd like to help in any way I can."

I was digesting this when Calvin came in.

He took an appraising look around before he dumped a stack of food pans in the sink and turned to the vet. "I got you those fecals, just ran them up to the hospital. Thought I was saving you a trip." He went to a corner cabinet, pulled out a string mop, and handed it to me.

"I'll take a look at them later today." The vet nodded at me and moved toward the door.

Calvin followed him. "You might remind Wallace about finding a place for those yearling penguins. We're gonna have problems if we don't thin them out pretty soon."

"I've reminded him. I'll bring it up again."

"What's this?" asked Calvin, picking up the jar on the counter.

I was wetting down the mop in the sink. "Stuff from Rick's locker."

Calvin held the jar to the light and he and the vet peered at it. "Snake eggs and a shed," Calvin said.

"Turtle eggs," I corrected, "at least, that's what Denny told me. And some little tooth."

Calvin shook it out of the jar. "Looks like a deer incisor."

"Yes, it does," said the vet, his jaw twitching up a little.

I shoved the mop over the floor. "Probably something he found in the woods."

"I've got a deer jaw. I'll bring it in and we can compare the teeth," Calvin offered.

"Just the lower jaw? Wouldn't we need the whole skull?" I asked.

Calvin gave me a patient look. "Deer don't have any upper incisors. Just lower ones."

Oh.

I knew that.

Calvin put the lid back on the jar and set it on the counter. Dr. Dawson took his leave and I started scrubbing food pans, with the vet's kind words mending a little of my discomfort. I respected the man for responding promptly to animal health concerns and for his thorough research into the hundreds of species he cared for, but he'd always seemed aloof, unknowable. Now I was starting to like him.

Calvin wordlessly demonstrated how to secure the blender bottom and then inspected the diets I had prepared. "Who's this for?" he asked, pointing to a paper towel with three tiny, naked mice babies laid out to thaw.

"The spectacled owl? The chart said three mice on Wednesday?"

"Not pink mice. If that's all he gets, his stomach will think his throat's been cut. He needs three adult mice. The pinkies is for the green jays." He took a critical look at the other pans. "You got the wrong feed for the nene geese. This is the starter diet for the babies. They're old enough for the regular diet, been on it for weeks. You want the bin on the left." He spent a few minutes taking a close look at all the pans, then left without a word.

Selling furniture? Flipping hamburgers? I rifled through alternative careers, then swallowed my humiliation and dug around a second time through the buckets and bags Hap had sent, finally unearthing three gray adult mice, still a little icy. I set them out to thaw.

At least Dr. Dawson hadn't found my questions offensive. Small consolation. I hadn't learned anything either.

At lunchtime, I slunk off and found a clean jacket on the laundry shelves at the Commissary. Hap was busy unloading a produce truck. I took the long way to lunch, past Felines, intending to say hi to Raj.

Simba was posing regally, crouching with his head up and forepaws stretched out like a statue in front of a New York library. Sugar and Spice were sprawled in the weak sun, Spice on her back with her hind legs flopping, decidedly non-regal. Wallace and Dr. Dawson walked toward the Feline service entrance engaged in serious conversation, not noticing me. The tall vet shortened his stride to match the foreman's heavy pace. Wallace's voice rose on the phrase "...managing risk..." Spice lurched to her feet, stared at them through blank yellow eyes, then padded down the cement slope to the bottom of the moat. The men moved out of sight and I heard the door slam as they entered. They would be talking to Linda, not to me, about risk.

Seeing Dr. Dawson reminded me of the jar from Rick's locker. Which I'd left in my dirty jacket, in the laundry pile at the Commissary. I headed back to retrieve it, wondering why I didn't just throw it out.

Hap was moving boxes of lettuce inside from the dock, with the Grateful Dead helping. We chatted for a few minutes about his seasonal transition from BMW motorcycle to Toyota sedan, once the rains commenced in earnest. He said Benita was after him to buy her a Mini Cooper. Red, of course.

I was leaning into the dirty laundry bin with my rear sticking out when Wallace showed up, without Dr. Dawson. Hap flipped the music off as Wallace began fretting about running out of primate chow and criticizing how the produce boxes were stacked.

"What are you doing?" he asked with characteristic charm as I emerged from the bin.

"I forgot something." My jacket was the smelliest thing in the bin, which was saying something. I fumbled in the pockets for the jar and dumped the jacket back in.

Hap came over and took a look, possibly hoping to distract Wallace from his critique. "Reptile stuff?"

"Yeah, from Rick's locker."

Wallace followed him. He reached for the jar and I reluctantly handed it over. He dumped the contents onto his palm. "Zoo property. Ask the Education Outreach people if they can use this stuff." He carefully returned everything to the jar.

"Sure thing." I took the jar back and stuck it into the pocket of my current jacket.

Wallace scowled. "You staying out of trouble?"

"No worries. Calvin barely lets me go to the bathroom without supervision."

"Good strategy." He went back to inspecting lettuce, muttering that it was slimy and a rip-off.

"Going to lunch?" I asked Hap, and he was glad to escape with me.

Hap's reliable friendship bolstered my courage. I'd tended to avoid my coworkers since the Raj accident and my abrupt transfer to Birds.

We joined Denny, Arnie, and Linda huddled at a covered table in front of the café, denying the reality of fall chill. A few yards away, two education volunteers were clamping a temporary four-panel bat display to a signpost. Panels about the benefits of bats would be Finley Zoo's only nod to Halloween. Prizes for the best costumes had come to an abrupt end the year before when a man in a realistic gorilla costume strolled around the Primate building. The monkeys and gibbons had gone nuts, screaming and threatening—we heard them all over the zoo. Kip Harrison, the primate keeper, had come running, but too late. The two female mandrills had truly lost their minds and taken advantage of the riot to attack the big male. Sky, twice their size, was a bully who had it coming, but Violet and Carmine were the ones that ended up in the hospital. Kip Harrison and Dr. Dawson had ensured that costumes were banned forevermore.

Denny was chowing down what looked like walnut hulls and grass clippings as I settled in with my tuna melt and fries, Hap with two corn dogs and an orange soda. I took one bite out of my sandwich and realized that fish were falling out of the edible category for me. Too much smelt and herring in my life already.

Linda put aside her crossword puzzle and said hi. Denny began expounding to Hap on the high probability that the British royal family was the successful result of a longevity experiment involving nanobots, whatever those are. "Only one of them has died of natural causes in over fifty years," he summed up, and segued into the reasons Princess Diana was assassinated, something to do with land mines and Muslims. The diversity of Denny's conspiracy theories was a marvel.

I wondered if I should toss the tuna melt and go buy a hamburger. I'd never survive the afternoon's disasters without food.

"How's Benita's rattlesnake doing?" Denny asked Hap.

Linda looked amazed. "Benita has a rattlesnake?" she asked. "In the house?"

"Uh-uh," Hap said around a mouthful of corn dog. "In the garage. I can't have it near the parrots. She inherited it when her mother died."

"Did her mother, by any chance, die of snakebite?" Linda asked.

"Oh, no. She and her boyfriend took his crotch-rocket to the coast and he laid the bike down on a curve on Highway 53, on the way to Neahkahnie Beach. Probably a deer or something in the road. Took them both out. Great way to go. That was about a year ago. Then Benita had to keep the snake."

"Naturally."

"And that mouth thing it had?" I asked, remembering. "Some kind of fungus Rick was helping her with?" That had been weeks ago. We'd visited their place for him to examine the snake.

"She used hydrogen peroxide and cotton swabs like he told her to. It cleared right up. Eating great."

Arnie spoke up, derailing me from starting to obsess about Rick. "Hey, Iris. How's it going at Birds? Silent Cal treating you right?"

"He hasn't kicked my butt out of his area yet."

"He's mighty particular," Arnie said.

Arnie probably found most people he worked with to be mighty particular.

No one brought up tiger attacks or sudden changes in assignments. I breathed a silent thanks to Benita and her venomous family heirloom.

Linda peered at the name sewn onto my jacket. "Why are you wearing my spare jacket?" she asked.

"Because yours was the only clean one that fit me."

"My pleasure, I'm sure."

"I messed up mine and didn't have a spare. I'll bring it back clean tomorrow. You don't mind, do you?" It came to me that I'd taken her jacket instead of, say, Arnie's as a way of reasserting our friendship.

She seemed relaxed, our uncomfortable discussion about whether she'd let Raj out on me forgiven if not forgotten. "No problem. I'll take it out in trade when I need dry socks. I know where you hide your stash. Hey, Wallace wants to get ready to put the clouded leopards together, probably in a week or so. Losa spent most of yesterday lying in full view outside. She's settling in. Dr. Dawson wants a twenty-four hour watch on them for the first month. Wallace says it has to be volunteer time, no pay."

"I can do Wednesdays or Thursdays. Those are going to be my weekend, but I'm not sure when Wallace will switch me over. I'll get back to you in a couple of days." The luxury of real weekends off would end after my two weeks of training. Saturday and Sunday were Calvin's days off and therefore not mine.

Linda's offer of a legitimate reason to hang out in Felines again sounded wonderful, catching up with the cats and returning to a place where I wasn't incompetent.

Hap and Denny argued about hybrid cars and whether global warming was really happening while Linda and I talked through the whole feline string. Somehow I ate the tuna melt without noticing. She and Spice were having a good time with lessons. She could get the lioness to open her mouth reliably and hold it open for a few seconds. I urged her to start training the other cats and to continue the enrichment activities: big bones, catnip, various scents such as perfume and spices, all to add some variety and sensory stimulation. She wanted to try hiding food in the exhibit for the lions to search for.

"Watch out they don't fight," I warned.

"I'll keep an eye on it." The patience in her voice reminded me that I wasn't the cat keeper anymore. She left and Denny followed, leaving me wondering if my longing for my old job was pathetically obvious. The comfort of talking about cats oozed away.

"It's freezing. Why don't you guys eat where it's warm?" Jackie, the administration secretary, pulled out Linda's chair and yanked her black coat closed. Hap and Arnie shrugged. Jackie was in her forties, divorced and living alone, a tense, bony woman with jet black hair and a nasal voice. Long red fingernails clutched a cigarette. She blew the smoke out of the corner of her mouth, an ineffective concession to purists. Often Jackie was fun, her gossip and cynical wit brightening dull days. Other days her drama addiction was repellent, more like picking at a carcass.

"It's a miracle Raj didn't do you like those lions did Rick," she said. "I hear you're on Birds, thank god, where you can't get yourself killed."

A chill breeze cruised through the hole this left in the table's conversation.

If I insisted that someone let Raj out, would anyone believe me?

"Paper said Rick was really smashed when the lions got him," she added, since this topic was going nowhere. "You guys go out drinking after the party?" She eyed me sidelong, waiting for my answer.

"No. I don't know how or when or where he got drunk." I finished off the fries, eager to flee. "But I would like to know what happened that night." I looked at her, then at Hap and Arnie. "Any idea why he was up here? Or how it happened?"

They shook their heads.

"It was an accident," Hap said, gruff and certain. "Happens to everyone—your number comes up." He shrugged acceptance of the unpredictable.

Arnie nodded. Jackie looked resigned to a disappointing reality.

"Accident? Rick wasn't stupid and incompetent, even drunk." The conviction in my voice surprised me.

Arnie and Hap gave me identical startled looks. Jackie cocked her head at me, her bright eyes evaluating.

"You guys can't really believe Rick would die like that." My voice was getting shrill. "You *knew* him."

"Police *said* it was an accident," Jackie insisted. "Everybody knew he was drinking a lot."

Everybody knew because I'd mentioned it to Jackie weeks ago.

"It's been real hard on you," Hap said cautiously.

Arnie looked confused.

The dust was settling: Rick died because he was incompetent. I was incompetent *and* a nut case. Dismayed, I tossed my garbage into the can and left without another word.

Chapter Nine

Sleeping in on my day off didn't work out. Bad dreams sent me to the kitchen table at seven o'clock Saturday morning. I took stock over a second cup of coffee. It was a gray, cold day, with rain likely. The house was not great. Dirty dishes in the sink, a thin layer of dog hair on the floor, mail piled on the table like molted feathers. Rick had been the one who knew how to keep the bathroom functional. I was showering in a couple inches of water already, not the ankle-deep swamp it was before Rick, but getting there. The toilet was picking up an attitude also.

It would be foolhardy to let Marcie or my mother see me slipping in the housekeeping arena. I didn't need my best friend and parents to decide I required intervention.

Another slug of caffeine failed to generate the energy I needed to tackle the list. Going back to bed was enticing, but I didn't have the verve even for that. A week of working as hard as I could while sleeping poorly left me feeling like an old caribou exhausted by migration, mosquitoes, and parasites. The wolf pack should be showing up soon.

Instead, the domesticated wolves came in from the backyard. Winnie stuck her nose in my hand and shoved. Range nudged my thigh, lips bulging with his tennis ball. There'd be no peace sitting in the kitchen.

I wiped dog snot off my hand and onto my jeans, put on a jacket and grabbed a couple of plastic bags for poop-scooping.

The dogs bounced around in a frenzy, seriously worried that I would change my mind. They bounded into the back of the Toyota, I snapped on the short leashes attached to the truck bed that kept them from falling out, and off we went.

In ten minutes or so, we left the freeway and wound down a curving, tree-lined road into Leverich Park. It has the usual signs and rules, among them clear prohibitions against letting dogs run loose. So call me an outlaw. It was raining, 7:20 in the morning, nobody but another outlaw was likely to be there, and a walk on a leash is a pathetic form of exercise for a healthy dog. I unclipped Winnie and Range and they leaped ecstatically from the truck and galloped off into the drizzle.

I carried leashes in case the canine paddy wagon showed up. Winnie's chain was heavy in my pocket since she would chew through a $15 nylon leash in seconds. Range would never do such a thing, maybe because his retriever ancestors were bred for soft mouths.

The dogs dashed across the creek, spray flying, and went in a big circle through the meadow and off to the trees, fading in and out in the uneven mist. Winnie was lithe and graceful, her flexible back arching as she poured on the speed and skidded through the turns. Range thundered along powerfully, not as fast, but cutting corners and catching up now and then. Few sights are prettier than your own dogs romping with all their hearts.

Rick used to throw a Frisbee at the park for the dogs. I hadn't thought to bring one. He would flick it in a high arc over the lawn, then sprint after it. Range loved the competition and never tired of winning. Two perfect male bodies playing, all vitality and grace...

After an hour, other people began to show up and it was time to go. Happy dogs with long tongues and short breath hopped back into the truck. I dried them off with an old towel, and we went home.

The house was still looking neglected, much as though someone really depressed lived there. I set the radio to aggressive rock, vacuumed the floor and sofa, and gave myself a handful of chocolate covered peanuts. Changed the sheets. Emptied the wastebaskets. Cleaned the iguana cage while Bessie tried to bite me. More candy. Washed the dishes.

Hostile rock had grown tedious, so I put on a couple of Rick's blues CDs.

My blues CDs.

Plumbing seemed the next easiest place to start. The instructions on an old can of chemical drain cleaner were terrifying. A manual plunger seemed low-tech, but far more benign. I gingerly poked at the toilet's maw, then got into it, sucking and shoving to Sonny Boy Williamson. "Flush when I say flush," I warned it. "Or it's poison for you." It eventually did so with civilized vigor; I chalked one more up to progress, and dug a wad of hair out of the shower drain for good measure.

I thought about the next challenge over a second cup of coffee and a few more chocolate peanuts, for the protein. The dogs came in from the backyard, tracking mud on the clean rug. They got doggy cookies for clearing squirrels out.

The way your smile just beams
The way you sing off key
The way you haunt my dreams
No, no they can't take that away from me.

What had I been thinking to put that album on? It was only another song, no reason to cry. It wasn't going to derail me. I made a fuss over the dogs and wiped off their feet with a rag, not listening.

Money was next on the list. The zoo had turned over Rick's last paycheck and eight days of vacation pay. Paying off his credit card bills would take most of that. I hadn't had a housemate until Rick moved in, except for Denny, who didn't count because he spent all his money on fancy comic books and fixing his van. Rick had saved me from confronting the fact that I really couldn't swing the rent alone over the long haul. I would need to find a roomer.

Truck payments were another problem. Rick had been a salesperson's dream, ready to reach out and grab the good stuff, fearless about debt. The truck ran well and it looked great, but it was a Dodge Dakota with all the fixin's: a CD player, big tires, fancy stripes, and big, fancy payments. No way could I afford it. My old Toyota was paid off and it ran fine.

I fired up my computer and dug up a selling price on the Internet. A call to my dad confirmed that it was in the ballpark and another call set up a newspaper ad for Sunday of next week. If I got the price, the truck loan would be cleared, with a little left over. I celebrated with a bag of chocolate chip cookies, picking out the chocolate chips before sharing one each with Winnie and Range. Chocolate's not good for dogs, but it's dandy for me.

I suited up in work boots and a rain jacket and went outside to prepare the truck for sale. As usual, the gravel road in front of the house was deserted and there was no sign of the neighbors. The lawn was high, but too wet to mow. After washing the outside of the Dodge, I climbed inside, out of the wind, and rounded up gas receipts and candy wrappers, removing the last traces of Rick. The stack of CDs contained some puzzlers: Carlos Nakai playing flute in a canyon, Buffy Saint-Marie, a sampler of traditional Native American drumming. Indian music wasn't in Rick's usual area of interest. The blues were his staple, but he would seek relevant music for any new interest. We had a couple of bagpipe CDs from his get-in-touch-with-his-Scottish-side phase, one of frogs croaking in a Georgia swamp from research-ing amphibians, German drinking songs for microbrew…

These were still shrink-wrapped, so probably purchased a day or two before he died.

I recalled the brown mailing envelope he'd had in the truck the last time I'd seen him, but it wasn't there.

After a quick late lunch, I decided to drive the Dodge over to the folks to use their canister vacuum cleaner. My upright wasn't designed for the job. The dogs were keen for another ride. They'd been housebound all week and I yielded. We caught the freeway and drove south, then crossed the bridge over the Columbia River to Oregon. Pricey little boats bobbed at the moorage below. The neon horse at Portland Meadows racetrack galloped and galloped in place. An accident had tied up the right lane and I slowed to let a trapped van escape into the left lane. The van driver repaid the courtesy with the traditional Northwest thank-you wave. A few more miles took us to an exit for southeast Portland. This was where my roots were, a neighborhood of lawns and old wood-frame houses, with a few new fourplexes thrown in. Old maples in the parking strips arched branches across the streets and gilded sidewalks and gutters with glowing yellow leaves.

I parked in the folks' driveway in the chilly late afternoon. A new neighbor on the north side, a woman I'd met once or twice, was huddled in her parka, leaning over her fence staring into my parents' backyard. I followed her gaze and walked to the back gate. The garden was overflowing with wet green things and a few bright blooming things, even in winter. Mom got the plant gene; I got the animal gene.

She had her back to us and was doing a little dance, stamping up and down, rather crane-like. Then she poured something onto the brick walkway and a cloud of steam rose up. She looked perky, in jeans, sneakers, and a bright yellow sweatshirt, with her curly hair bobbing. The hair was definitely getting gray. She stamped a couple more times, then more steam from the bricks. This time I glimpsed the teakettle in her hand. The neighbor—Lucille? Lucy?—turned to me and said dryly, "Yesterday she was hurling apples at squirrels" and clomped back into her house.

"Mom? What *are* you doing?" I inquired as I opened the gate, wary of getting scalded.

"Oh, it's you! Good! Your dad's gone to the shop."

"Mom, *what* on *earth* are you doing?"

She looked a little offended. "I'm killing off Scotch moss that's doing entirely too well. It wants to take over this whole walkway. It's not really a moss, of course, it's a flowering plant. True moss is nowhere near that invasive. I figure boiling water is a good way to kill it without a lot of work. And it's still organic gardening."

"So, Mom, why the little dance? Part of the ceremony?"

"Ceremony? What an imagination you have! Big earthworms, nightcrawlers, live under these bricks. I'm scaring them deeper so they don't get cooked." Her tone said that any fool should have figured that out. Well, I'm not just any fool.

I'd have to remember to tell Lucille. Or Lucy.

Mom patted Range and Winnie politely, with a reminder to stay the hell out of her flowerbeds. I told her what I was there for.

"Don't forget to pull up the floor mats and vac underneath. And remember to check the glove box."

I dragged out the vac and found a long orange extension cord in the basement and went at it. That done, I stood back to admire my work. The hubcaps gleamed; the stripes flashed. "Vinyl," my father had sneered, not in Rick's hearing. "Factory job." Sign painters reserve their respect for hand striping. No matter, the truck looked sharp.

Dad came home soon after, tall and competent, solid in jeans and a heavy green shirt. I get my height from him, and my brown eyes. The curly hair is from my mother's side.

It wasn't that hard for them to persuade me to stay for dinner. We had, it turned out, an unspoken agreement not to talk about Rick or my emotional state, and I was grateful. After meatloaf, baked potatoes, and fresh-picked chard with a speech from Mom about the perfidy of leaf miners—a bug, I gathered—and their inroads on the chard crop, we ate a little blueberry shortcake and I felt the best I had in some time. Full stomach, happy dogs underfoot, clean house to go home to.

"How's work?" Dad asked.

"Um, I switched over to Birds. It's interesting. I work with a guy named Calvin. What's on TV tonight?"

My parents exchanged one of their content-dense glances— "thank heaven" plus "she didn't tell you either?"

"You mean you aren't working with the lions anymore?" Mom asked cautiously.

"Right. Penguins, ducks, hawks, like that. I've always liked birds." My voice was calm, casual; so far, so good. I went for a second helping of shortcake.

"Humm," said Dad.

Mom said, "I'm glad you finally got out of there. Good thing your boss had another spot for you."

Dad put his fork down and set his wrists on each side of his plate. He looked at me and waited. He doesn't do that often.

"What?" I asked.

"About this job change." He waited, watching me. He was good at waiting. It always works.

"I had a little episode with Rajah, the tiger, nothing serious." I was an adult; I didn't have to do this. But the shortcake had weakened me. "I think somebody let him out when they shouldn't have. Wallace thinks I was too distracted to pay attention and didn't lock the doors properly. Anyway, nothing bad happened, but I had to leave Felines. I'd really rather not talk about it anymore, if you don't mind."

Dad looked startled and a little white around the lips. Teach him to pry. He shared a quick glance with my mother, but dropped the subject. We cleared the table in silence.

After the TV show, something with cops, car chases, and young women in swimsuits, Dad lurched out of his recliner and headed toward the kitchen to deal with the dishes. Mom flipped to the middle of a movie. A taxi driver in a Hawaiian shirt was haranguing Nicholas Cage. When a commercial came on, she thumbed the mute button. "Iris," she began, using her reasonable voice, "have you given any thought to a fresh start, like going back to college? This might be a good time to think about your future." Her disappointment when I quit college was still vivid, as if it were her personal failure.

"We've had this same conversation for years," I started, vowing *not* to lose my temper, just to make my position clear until she dropped the subject. "I like my job. I'm on emotional overload because of Rick's death and it's actually a really bad time for me to make any major changes." That came out well, I thought.

"You never gave college a fair chance. You're older and you might like it better." She leaned forward—earnest, hopeful, relentless—in the gray wing chair. "You have the brains, if you want to use them."

"I like what I'm doing. I use my brains plenty on the job." I got up out of the rocking chair. Time to get gone before this devolved into another yelling match. I called the dogs and found my jacket.

Mom insisted I take a bag of leftovers. "It's not like you ever cook," she muttered under her breath, so that I wouldn't think she was going soft. I was careful not to hear it.

The argument with Mom faded on the drive home, eased by a full stomach. Our wrangle was even comforting, in a familiar, irritating way, like the mild rain speckling the windshield. Maybe it was the shortcake, but I was feeling good. The dogs shifted around on the passenger seat, too crowded to settle down, but I didn't want them out in the wet in the truck bed. I'd wipe the seat down before potential buyers checked it out.

I reached for a CD, but there weren't any. I'd cleared them out. What was up with Rick and the Indian music? The blues were always in favor, but he'd had his songs-about-cars phase and a fling with the Japanese shakuhachi flute. Maybe the Vultures' Roost, Rick's favorite tavern, had featured Native American music recently and gotten him interested. Probably that was where he'd started drinking after the party. Was it open that late?

The last of a week's supply of self-discipline brought me to the Roost's parking lot, north of downtown, between my house and the zoo. I'd take care of this, then go home to clean sheets and the sleep of the virtuous.

The hours on the front door confirmed that it was open until 2:00 AM. Rick could have left me at midnight, gotten loaded here, and driven to the zoo. The Roost was jammed, not a good night to talk to the staff. All the knotty-pine booths were full. I waited for a stool at the counter and ordered coffee. No live music tonight, instead, a disorienting alternation of indie rock, Celtic wailing, and vintage country, incompatible tastes warring at the jukebox. I didn't see anyone I knew. The crowd was my age or older, jeans and parkas for the most part. The seat next to me at the counter opened up, and a guy in a black knit shirt and black jeans slid in. Thin face with a sharp nose, dark hair mowed down to a stubble, a big chrome wristwatch that looked to have a zillion features.

"Buy you a drink?" He waved his beer glass at me.

I shook my head. Where was the coffee?

"I know a place that's got more happening," he offered. "Comedy hour and killer buffalo wings." He had an indoor pallor, probably from a job that required a lot of keyboarding and many obscure technical terms.

I gave him the minimum polite smile and turned away. A touch on my elbow startled me.

"You came in with Rick. You his wife?" It was the head barkeep, a big woman I remembered from my last visit months ago.

"Yeah. I'm surprised you remember."

"I remember everyone. He came around a lot, for awhile."

"He liked it here. Better than home."

"Yeah." She leaned an ample hip against the bar, straight blonde hair falling around her shoulders and chest. She wore a tight pink vest with a zipper, a generous scoop at the cleavage, and billowy purple pants tight at the ankles. "He was a regular. But it didn't last, you know? What he told me was so long, wouldn't be seeing me anymore."

"When was that?"

"Well, I don't remember exactly. He said he had another woman, had to choose. It was a joke, see? Wasn't anything between us. He was talking about you, or me and the brew. He was getting a little too into it, you know? He was a good guy— fun—so I was sorry he wouldn't be around. But he figured he had to take care of business."

"He showed up the night he died?"

"No, must have been a couple of nights before. He was a great guy. I really liked Rick, you know? I'm so sorry it ended like that." She gave me a half-hug with an arm as big as my thigh. She smelled of roses and hair spray.

"You're really sure he wasn't here the night he died?"

"Honey, wouldn't I remember a thing like that? We were all talking about it when it came out in the papers."

The guy on the next stool leaned toward me. "Look, if you want to talk about it, I'm a great listener."

The big woman said "Git," without raising her voice.

He studied her, checking that she really meant him. Drained his beer to show he couldn't be buffaloed. Got up and left.

She patted my arm and sailed into the crowd like an elephant matriarch through a flock of guinea fowl.

A harried young man with a ponytail slammed my coffee on the counter and turned away. I grabbed his wrist.

"Hey, you ever have any Native American—Indian—music here?"

He curled his upper lip in amazement, shook his head in pity, and was gone.

I dropped two dollars on the counter and escaped, but not before confirming the lack of whiskey, rum, and vodka bottles behind the bar. The Vultures' Roost dispensed only beer and the odd glass of wine, not scotch or other spirits.

The rain had picked up. The truck cab reeked of dog breath. I backed out and pointed it home, wondering at the comfort of the big woman's hug. Rick told her that he chose me over alcohol, exactly what he'd said to me.

Tears lurked at the back of my throat, softer ones than usual.

At home, I pulled up next to my own truck. I let the dogs out, unlocked and opened the front door, then stood baffled on the little cement porch with rain tapping my hair. Smoke drifted out; the dogs clustered close to my knees. I reached in to flick on the living room light and confirmed that my house was on fire.

Chapter Ten

The living room was oddly dim, the ceiling light thwarted by thick smoke. Flames flickered red and yellow. I couldn't believe it. Someone had broken into my house and set it on fire. It was going to burn up, along with all my stuff, whatever hadn't been stolen. Through the smoke, the room looked seriously disheveled—sofa cushions on the floor, CDs stripped off their shelves and strewn around, books sprawled open on the rug. I made out something more significant across the room: newspapers dumped out of the plastic recycling bin and heaped up against an inside corner of the living room. The source of the smoke and flames.

Impotent rage held me rooted on the porch until the smoke drove me back. Movement restarted my brain.

Call 911, that was the obvious step. My keeper's salary required choosing between health insurance and a cell phone, and I was thinking I'd made the wrong choice. Rick had a cell phone, but it hadn't survived his last night any better than he had. I looked around at the neighborhood. All windows dark; nobody home. Okay. Get back in the truck with the dogs, drive to the convenience store two miles away and make the call. I started toward the truck and stopped.

Bessie Smith.

Damn.

The smoke was probably enough to kill the iguana trapped inside. Ten minutes to get to the store, who knew how long for the fire department to arrive…

A car engine started up down the street out of sight and faded into the distance. I listened and wondered, tamping down a flicker of fear.

I turned back to the house, stopped now by the smoke drifting out the front door. I crept up and peeked inside again. It wasn't that big a fire, not yet. Still, I didn't want to go in there. My house had become an alien place filled with dangers. Why couldn't Rick be here and save his own iguana? But Rick wasn't here, not even Rick's cell phone, and Bessie Smith wasn't going to make it if I didn't act.

I ordered the dogs to stay on the lawn, grabbed a deep breath, and charged. It took broken field running, football style, to dodge around the obstacles. I slipped on the phone book and nearly went down.

The lid to the iguana's cage was ajar. I checked; she was still in there and still moving. I secured the lid, yanked the cords on her special light and heater, and heaved the big acrylic and wood box up off the little table by the kitchen door. Staggering outside, I put it down on the lawn and stood panting. I lifted the lid off and used it to fan the inside, trying to flush out the smoke. Bessie could move fast, so ventilation had to be balanced against the risk of escape. Winnie and Range shoved their noses at her, trying to satisfy their long-standing curiosity about iguanas. I shooed them away and resecured the lid. It was too cold outside for her, but there wasn't much I could do about that.

I straightened up from Bessie Smith's habitat and turned back to the house. My quick close-up of the fire had indicated it was still in one corner, but that wouldn't be true for long. Flames were clawing for a toehold on the walls. Driving to the store would give it more time without interference. I wavered—do the sensible thing, risking all my stuff, or deal with it? It took a second to decide again that I wouldn't be ruled by fear. I'd faced situations far more dangerous than a little bonfire.

Again I inhaled largely and jogged into the house, through the living room to the kitchen. All the drawers and cupboards were open, everything dumped on the floor. The smoke alarm was disemboweled, its battery ripped out. I found the phone and, blessedly, a dial tone. I croaked out my address and the nature of the disaster to the 911 operator. He promised a swift response but asked me to stay on the line. That was clearly impractical, so I hung up and ran back outside. Next time I'd pick a house with neighbors who were home in the evening.

I waited on the damp lawn, gnawing my lip and picturing my worldly goods charring. Why me? Who had done this and for what possible reason? And, come to think of it, why was I assuming that the perpetrator was gone? The rain continued in gentle, pervasive droplets. I tried to get the dogs to patrol the perimeter and let me know if an arsonist was still on the premises, but they were fixated by the fire and intended to stay close to me. I was starting to get creeped out.

No siren. The front door was still open. I paced around, peering in now and then. The fire wasn't growing all that fast, not really.

I couldn't stand the inaction. The roof wasn't going to collapse—the fire was nowhere near the ceiling. I'd been in and out twice with no harm. I had a right to protect my stuff, didn't I? I looked briefly for the garden hose I was pretty sure didn't exist. Rick and I hadn't been much into yard maintenance.

"Cover me," I told the dogs. "I'm going in." I took a deep breath.

In the kitchen, I opened the back door for a quick escape route and set a pot under the faucet. That was too slow, so I tried the refrigerator. Half a gallon of milk splashed on the liveliest corner slowed down the fire's assault while the pot filled. I raced back and forth from the kitchen to the living room, filling and dumping, sticking my head out the front or back door for fresh air. As the fire truck wailed and rumbled into the driveway, I stamped out the last flickers, leaving an unappealing slurry of ash, wet newspaper, and dairy on the floor and my shoes. Tendrils of smoke curled lazily in the corners of the room, but the supply was cut off.

Firefighters emerged from the truck. Pumper? Hook and ladder? Whatever, it was huge and red and carried hoses and ladders. As the crew hooked up to the hydrant half a block down the street, I leashed the dogs, who were too intimidated by helmets, boots, and flashing lights to even consider defending the property or me. The fire professionals toured the house cautiously, stirred the embers, hosed here and there, and emerged to share their deep disapproval of my self-help efforts. The lead firefighter's lecture on death by smoke inhalation, ordinary common sense, et cetera, halted only when the police arrived. He gave up on me, briefed the two police officers, and ordered his crew to pack up. They drained and coiled their hoses as carefully as zookeepers. The lead firefighter stood aside, now talking steadily into a cell phone.

The reprieve from humiliation allowed me to remember my priorities. "Help me get this inside," I said to the police persons, both male, waving my hand at Bessie Smith's habitat on the lawn.

"What is it?" one of them asked.

"A green iguana. She won't hurt you." Not unless she got the chance. The rear twelve inches of Bessie was a long thin tail, green and unarmed. The front twelve inches was bulky and ended in a large mouth with many teeth. The front end also contained a tiny brain with the personality of a meth addict. Why had I risked my life for an animal that hated me?

"In a minute." The police had other priorities. They searched all the rooms, then outside the house and the garage with big flashlights while I waited on the lawn. The dogs were still dismayed, but tried for normalcy by barking and growling at the cops. Bessie Smith kept her mouth shut. I was about to give up and risk all my disks and vertebrae to get the iguana inside when the cops wandered back. "Can you give me a hand?" I asked. "It's really heavy and she's too cold out here."

It wasn't in their job description, but the shorter officer finally helped me carry Bessie Smith's home back onto the little table while the other one reluctantly held the dog leashes. I plugged in her life support system. She looked the same as always—no weepy eyes or gasping mouth.

"You know, you're not supposed to run into burning buildings," the officer with the dogs said, handing me the leashes. "Especially for pets."

"Yeah, so they told me. Fire truck took forever." Pet? Bessie Smith was more like a nasty relative or maybe an abscess, something unpleasant you couldn't get rid of.

We confirmed that the back door had been kicked in. "Looks like robbery and arson," the shorter one said.

"What do you think they were looking for?" the tall one asked me. Officer Frank Chester, per his badge.

"I don't know. I don't have any money or expensive jewelry. Is the DVD player gone?" It wasn't. I tied the dogs to the bedroom doorknob, freeing my hands to sort through the wreckage.

The shorter one, Officer Gonsalves—a really good-looking guy, now that I'd calmed down—followed me into my bedroom. It was in the same condition as the living room and kitchen, but with less smoke damage and without the water. It was hard to tell whether anything was missing. He double-checked window latches and nudged stuff on the floor with his foot. My scattered cotton underwear embarrassed me, but it wasn't clear what style of undies would be appropriate for the situation. An intruder pawing through my clothes…I pushed the dismaying sense of violation aside, aware that it would be back.

"Frank," Gonsalves said, "you think this is tied in with those break-ins closer to downtown? Could be our guy was loaded on something when he did this one. Flipped out when he didn't find anything good and fired the place?"

Frank shook his head. "He knows what he's doing. Even ripped. This one is a bozo."

"Bozo?" I asked.

"Amateur. Look at the dresser drawers. He started at the top and messed the stuff up too much to close it all the way. He had to haul the drawer out and dump it on the floor to get to the one below. A professional starts with the bottom drawer and leaves them hanging open."

"Do you think he'll be back?" I asked.

They pondered and shrugged. "Depends on why he was here in the first place. You have any idea at all?"

Nope.

They doubted fingerprinting would yield anything useful. Assuring me they would check on the house a couple times that night and warning me not to touch anything until the arson specialist took a look, they climbed into their cruiser and departed. The fire truck followed them out, leaving me alone.

Don't touch anything? I sighed and called my parents. It was 1:00 AM and they were asleep, but once I'd said the word "fire" a few times, they kicked into emergency mode. I hung up and set the kettle on the stove for tea and coffee. For a few minutes, the house was silent. Was this fire my next lesson in how fast life can change? A stranger pawing through my things...Since I didn't know what he was looking for, I had no idea whether he would return. None of it made any sense, and I was sure the house would never feel safe again. I surveyed the chaos, unable to imagine what the next step was.

The arson specialist showed up before my folks. The dogs, who were loose and nosing around the mess, erupted into a frenzy of intimidation when she knocked. I snapped on leashes again and asked to see her ID, which I couldn't read in the dim porch light with the dogs seething and yelling around my knees. For some reason, she hesitated to step in. I considered shoving the dogs out the back door, but the latch was ruined and the door wouldn't stay closed. I tied them up to the doorknob instead.

A small, frowning woman maybe forty years old, she was appropriately attired in a beige trench coat. "You really should not have gone into the house once you knew it was on fire," she said. Everybody knew that but me...She pulled up the carpet under the most charred corner and had a cool little machine to check for gasoline sloshed about. The machine seemed to say there wasn't any. She wanted to know the color of the smoke and whether I'd seen anyone flee the scene.

She was asking about renter insurance (none), suspects I could think of (none), and relationships gone bad (yes, but irrelevant) when my parents arrived. I made the introductions as we stood around the living room in puddles. Mom immediately walked to the kitchen and emerged with four cups of tea, her reflex strategy in any crisis. I expected points for having the water boiling. She returned for milk and the sugar bowl, and I explained why I was out of milk. She and the arson specialist gave me the same unbelieving look. I looked to my dad for support, but he was gazing at the charred corner.

The arson lady poked around and took pictures, then told us that this looked like an impromptu job and didn't seem to be linked to the series of fires she was focused on. My impression was that normally she wouldn't have gotten out of bed for my unprofessional little house fire. I asked, and she said she had no idea what he was looking for or whether he might come back.

"Why burn the place at all?" I asked.

"Maybe to hide his tracks, maybe revenge for something. Could be lots of reasons. You live here alone? I don't think I'd be too comfortable with that."

That was enough for the parents, who insisted I come home with them to spend the rest of the night. "If he does come back, all I'll find in the morning is a pile of charcoal," I said, but that didn't convince even me.

The arson specialist left, saying I'd be hearing from her later and that it was okay to clean up. I loaded the dogs in the truck and back we went to Portland.

The next day was Sunday, also a day off. We slept in, ate breakfast, and drove back to clean up. The house was not a heap of ashes; Bessie Smith had not expired. It was the same mess we'd abandoned the night before, except that the puddles had drained.

My dad set up fans to dry out the living room, and we started picking up and trying to determine what had been stolen. Rick's computer was missing, but he might have taken it with him to Denny's. I'd have to ask.

Leaving Mom at the house to finish putting the kitchen back together, Dad and I drove to the hardware store on Vancouver's Main Street and loaded up on security gear. I drew the line at a motion detector, what with the dogs, but we got locks, latches, and bars for windows. They had pepper spray, too. We picked up groceries since most of mine were ruined.

Back home, the air smelled of cleaning supplies, stale smoke, and scorched milk. I fed Bessie her greens and veggies. She ate, so she wasn't at death's door, but she lacked her usual vigorous hostility. Maybe she appreciated that I rescued her. Fat chance. Rick was the only person she had ever tolerated.

At Mom's suggestion, I checked in with the neighbors to see if they had noticed anyone prowling around. The house on the west side was vacant. The house on the east was inhabited by a scrawny young man who worked night shift and was sure he knew nothing about anything. No one was home, as usual, at the houses across the street.

I called the landlord and got his wife. They were Russian immigrants and it was not at all clear that her English was up to "burglary" and "arson." However, the word "fire" produced a flurry of unintelligible words. I agreed with whatever she'd said and ended the call. I'd done my duty as a renter—if the landlord wanted more information, he knew where to find me.

For awhile. Moving was looking good to me.

Mom climbed a stepladder and washed the living room walls to remove the smoke grime and the smell. She left reluctantly to prepare for teaching her high school classes the next day, eager to assist with house shopping in a better neighborhood. My dad spent most of the day installing the security devices, and I spent it vacuuming and mopping, bitter about doing that twice in one weekend. We didn't talk much, but now and then one of us would try out an explanation.

"Probably thought you had money hidden," was Dad's first effort.

"Why? It would make more sense to look in an expensive house than a little rental."

"He was an amateur."

"But very, very thorough. He took off Bessie's lid and the toilet tank top. He must have been tearing up the house for a couple of hours."

"Maybe he thought you were someone who keeps drugs around."

None of our theories was promising.

The landlord, a thin, mournful man, dropped by. He shook Dad's hand with an appraising look, and I felt it necessary to explain that my husband had died and that this truly was my father and not my sugar daddy. The Russian viewed the damage and said he'd talk to his insurance agency about repairs. He left me with the feeling that he wouldn't trouble about the lease if I wanted to move out soon.

We returned to installing security features. "I should have done this the day you moved in here," Dad muttered. I remembered he had planned to upgrade the locks, but hadn't because Denny moved in with me shortly after I'd rented the house. Dad was always leery of Denny. Then I kicked Denny out and soon Rick was sharing the place. I'd felt safe living with Rick, physically at least.

"I should have done it myself," I told him.

Dad wanted me to get rid of the doggy door. No way. I couldn't run home every day at lunch to let the dogs out. "It's not that big a door, anyway. Only a junior burglar would fit. The dogs and I can beat up a junior burglar." I'm a lot braver in daylight.

Dad stalled until evening and was reluctant to leave, even after the house was as secure as it was ever going to be. I elaborated on Winnie and Range's ferocity, pointed out the police cruiser passing by, and accepted a pipe wrench he provided from his truck. I'd be fine alone. Really.

That night, I had second thoughts as I lay in bed listening for Bad Guys, pepper spray beside my pillow. Range licked his privates noisily; Winnie snored in a genteel way. Would the intruder be back? Was the fire set to destroy whatever the intruder couldn't find? What *was* he looking for? Surely it had to be a man. A woman wouldn't have been that messy.

Things moved around outside, ignored by my unreliable canine guardians. The kitchen faucet dripped, or maybe the bathroom faucet. Bessie scrabbled in her cage, little scraping noises.

Chapter Eleven

Monday morning, I awoke early, nauseated from bad smells and bad dreams. The faint beer smell had been bothersome, but this was worse. My mother's prescription—paint everything—required more effort than the rental was worth. I looked forward to some sympathy at work and maybe help in locating new housing.

If there was any justice in the universe, my second week at Birds would go better than the first. Work hard, pay attention to details—it would pay off eventually. Calvin didn't need to be my new best friend; all I wanted was a comfortable working relationship with a little respect.

Finding Arnie settled comfortably in the penguin kitchen, in the chair that wasn't Calvin's—in *my* chair—curdled good intentions into irritation. Apparently it didn't take much time for me to start feeling territorial. Calvin was bent over hunting around in the cupboard left of the sinks.

"How'ya doin', Iris?" Arnie's purple cowboy hat sat damply on the table, mottled by rain.

"Just ducky, Arnie. What brings you to our avian paradise?" Arnie was not the audience I had in mind for my domestic crisis.

"Oh, Calvin asked me to drop by and help him catch up the eagle. He's got to fix that leak in the roof where she likes to sit." He beamed amiably at me.

I suppressed a scowl.

The eagle was a big, powerful bird who had collided with a power line years ago. A permanently droopy left wing and life in a cage were the results.

"You might clean up the kitchen and tend to the bugs," Calvin suggested, his back to me as he set out two pairs of heavy leather gloves. "We'll be back in an hour or so."

I bristled. "Hadn't I better help out so I learn how to do it?"

"Well, I wouldn't want anybody getting hurt," Calvin said slowly.

"Bald eagle's a lot of bird," Arnie added, with a hint of condescension that made me want to yank the mustache off his face. "Those things got strength in their feet like you wouldn't believe. They bite, too. It's better not to have people crowding around when you're working with them."

Calvin seemed to accept that as summarizing the situation. He handed Arnie one of the pairs of gloves and a net with a four-foot aluminum handle. He carried the other gloves, a hammer, and some nails. The senior male and his favored subordinate set off to conquer the eagle, leaving me in the kitchen.

I said a lot of bad words about macho exclusionism and cursed myself for not knowing how to nip it in the bud. After banging food pans around for a couple of minutes, I swore at myself again for letting them shut me out and headed down to the birds of prey area.

By the time I got there, they had the bald eagle on the ground tangled up in the net. Both men were jammed into the exhibit. The door, wire mesh on a pipe frame, was wide open. The eagle was not going gently; the net heaved as she tried to flap her wings and strike with her feet. One long dark wing feather was broken and sticking out of the net at an angle. Calvin was bent over maneuvering to grab her legs while Arnie held the net. Calvin grabbed one yellow leg that ended in talons with two-inch claws. The eagle slashed at his glove with the other foot, whickering shrilly. Finally he grasped the second leg and stood up, a leg in each hand, the eagle bashing her wings against his face. The net was still draped over her with wing tips poking through. Arnie tugged at it, trying to disentangle net and bird.

It was not an elegant performance.

"Arnie, get that net off and grab her wings. She's going to bust every feather," Calvin barked. Damaging a bird's feathers was a significant misdemeanor since they wouldn't be replaced until the next molt.

Arnie fumbled around with the eagle's wings, finally disentangling the net. The bird turned her attention to Calvin. His voice got louder. "Get her behind the head, Arnie, she's going to bite. Get in there and grab her. Do it, Arnie."

Calvin couldn't do anything besides hold the legs. The bird was excited, flapping vigorously, and her yellow beak was huge. Arnie reached cautiously for the back of her white head and pulled back when she bit at him. That was not the right move; she struck at his thumb and hung on like a feathered bulldog. Arnie yelled and did a little dance. Perhaps the gloves weren't quite thick enough. Finally he yanked his hand away, out of the glove. The glove dangled from the eagle's beak for a few seconds, which kept the beak occupied, but Arnie didn't move to grab her head. Instead, he had a few words to share with the bird. I found them educational and was glad no visitors were within earshot.

Calvin was getting angrier and not at the bird. Arnie picked his glove up off the ground and tried to grab her head again, with more success.

I might not know much about birds, but I knew chaos when I saw it. If the bird hadn't been so upset, I would have savored watching the skilled professionals in action. Clearly there was no role for me in the situation; another person would only make it worse.

Calvin got both legs under control and the bird's wings tucked under his arm. Arnie finally slipped a dark cloth hood over the blazing yellow eyes and fastened it around her neck. Her cries shut off and both men relaxed. The eagle no longer struggling, Calvin muttered apologies and carried her out of the exhibit. "Get going," he barked at Arnie, who went to work with the hammer.

The fun was over and I was discouraged. I thought rodeo-style animal handling wasn't supposed to happen anymore. The other areas at the zoo had succeeded pretty well in training the animals to shift to a holding area. I couldn't see any way to do that with the eagle, given the cage construction. Still, there should have been a better way, something a lot less stressful for the eagle and the keepers. My enthusiasm for learning how Calvin managed eagle restraint was gone. I should have stayed in the kitchen.

Calvin was snapping instructions at Arnie about the repairs when he noticed me as I turned to leave. I didn't say anything and neither did he. His face reddened. I expected him to yell at me for not staying in the kitchen as ordered, but he didn't. Walking back to the Penguinarium, it came to me that he was embarrassed, not mad. Prospects for a relationship based on mutual respect were looking poor.

I hustled through the kitchen chores and lugged feed down to the waterfowl pond, strategies that kept me out of his sight. When the ducks and swans had finished bolting their food, it was time for my own lunch.

I grabbed a hamburger at the café. Everyone else had eaten and left so I lacked an audience for my dramatic episode of burglary and arson. On the plus side, Calvin wasn't there either.

I drifted to the office to share my disasters with Jackie and found Dr. Dawson emerging from the Administration building.

"Ah, Iris. We're moving forward with the clouded leopard introduction in a few days." He led me a little away from the building, out in the open.

"Linda said you were about ready to give it a try."

"Yes, somewhat against my better judgment. Waiting at least another two weeks would be better, but Mr. Crandall is anxious to report progress to the zoo board. This process is too subjective for me to marshal good arguments in favor of delay, so we go ahead. Don't take me wrong—the protocol you developed is working well. You did a nice job on the research."

He really didn't think I was a hopeless bungler. I felt like a desiccated houseplant plunged into a big tub of water.

Dr. Dawson glanced back at the Administration building. "I'm not optimistic, but we'll take all reasonable precautions. I trust things are going better at Birds?"

"Not too bad."

I watched him stride long-legged and erect toward the Commissary, unsettled that I was so pleased by his comments. What word would Marcie use? "Needy" perhaps? That did not fit Iris Oakley at all. Still, his words were balm that fortified me to face the rest of the day. I decided to pass on a chat with Jackie and headed back to work.

Arnie was gone from the Penguinarium and Calvin was no more or less talkative than usual. He sat at the kitchen table with a stack of rumpled daily logs in front of him.

"You do the afternoon feed at the aviary," he said. "I've got to get these report summaries caught up."

This was the first time he'd trusted me to do this alone. Or maybe he didn't want to be around me right now. I moved around the kitchen fixing the afternoon pellets, fruit, and bugs while his head stayed bent over the paperwork, ballpoint pen in hand. I piled the food pans into a green two-wheeled garden cart. Maybe I should ask him where we stood, let him yell at me, yell back that he wasn't such a hot-shit bird keeper either. But words didn't come, and I left with the silence still intact.

It was a weekday and cool; visitors were few. I had the World of Birds to myself, people-wise. The big aviary was heavily planted with shrubs and a mix of live and artificial trees. A little stream ran through, with an arched bridge over it. You could wander the path and play "Where's Waldo?" with birds above and below.

Entry was through a door into a little anteroom, then through another door. Laden with food pans, I pushed my way in. The nenes hissed at me from the ground. Little teals paddled in the stream like expensive toys while bright bits of green and red and blue flickered in and out of the foliage, clucking and trilling. I set out the duck chow and stood on the cement path beside the little stream and waterfall, watching. Small ducks in rounded shapes and subdued browns and grays; jays and starlings and tanagers gleaming in extravagant colors: they were all beautiful. I wondered if I'd ever learn the two dozen species that lived there and couldn't imagine telling individuals of the same species apart. But Calvin could do it, so maybe someday…In the meantime, what a peaceful place to stand and watch and listen. Arsonists seemed remote and irrelevant.

After all the food pans were distributed, I made a careful tour, tidying up leaves, visitor trash, and spilled food, the way Calvin did. I salvaged a couple of bright feathers and stuck them in my breast pocket.

On the bridge over the stream, I noticed that a heat lamp was burned out. The enclosure wasn't heated, so warm spots were important. Multiple heat lamps provided options so weak or unpopular individuals couldn't be shoved out in the cold. Each was tucked inconspicuously into foliage, with perches underneath.

Maybe the bulb was only loose. That would save a trip back to the kitchen for another one. It was easy enough to check. I put a hand on the iron guardrail and leaned over the stream, weaving the other hand up through twigs, around a food platform, and past the larger branch that served as a perch. My wrist brushed the rim of the metal reflector that housed the bulb.

The jolt knocked me flat on my back on the bridge.

Stunned, I lay there, mind and body both out of order, staring at palm fronds.

Nothing happened for a couple of minutes, except my heart lurched unevenly and body parts reported for duty by starting to hurt. A Mexican green jay landed on the railing and inspected me. A bird I couldn't identify gave a loud, rattling call from the far corner.

When a nene waddled over and evaluated the possibility of pecking out my eyes, I tried sitting up, with some success. The jay flew off; the goose hissed at me without retreating.

What the hell?

My heart was still pounding and my breath came short. There was something familiar about this. Ah, yes, the same as when Raj almost nailed me. Raw terror.

I lurched to my feet, shaky but unwilling to touch the rail, and tried to figure out what had happened.

It wasn't that hard.

The metal reflector was charged; I had touched it and the iron handrail at the same time.

I took a shuddering breath, then limped off the path. The goose sneered and hopped off the bridge into the water. I followed the electrical cord to the outlet hidden in a corner. My hand trembled as I yanked the plug out of the socket.

Now what? Take the time, think it through.

Having the daylights scared out of me didn't count as damage. My ass was bruised, and I had a lump on the back of my head and a burn mark on my wrist. Nothing seemed to be broken and I hadn't been actually unconscious. Was this a big enough deal to report to Wallace? Keepers banged themselves up all the time. Working Birds had already given me a new collection of bruises, cuts, and scrapes from unfamiliar obstacles.

If I reported it, Calvin might get in trouble for allowing a safety hazard, making my prospects as a bird keeper even dimmer.

If I kept quiet and Wallace found out, it might terminate my prospects as any keeper at all.

Then there was the "Iris the Idiot" factor.

This, too, was familiar.

My brain must have taken a bigger hit than I realized. Keeping quiet and avoiding a thorough investigation risked a repeat, possibly jolting Calvin or a visitor.

Sighing, I sucked it up—again—and trudged painfully to the Administration building. By the time I got there, I'd realized that telling Calvin first was a good idea. I pushed on the door to the Administration building and it flew open, yanked from the inside by a big middle-aged man whose pink polo shirt clashed with an unhealthy red face.

"No one talks to me like that. No one gets away with that," he insisted over his shoulder as he shoved past me.

At my raised eyebrows, Jackie said only, "Denny." She listened in as I called Calvin and delivered the short version of what had happened. I started toward Wallace's closed door.

"No sunshine in there today," Jackie warned.

I stopped. "What did Denny do this time?"

Jackie scanned the office for witnesses. "That jerk threw his popcorn bag on the ground next to the trash can. Denny asked him if he shits next to the toilet."

A grin surprised me by burbling through the day's traumas. I straightened out my face.

"And," Jackie went on, "Wallace got the estimate for resurfacing the Children's Zoo asphalt after it got wrecked by the flooding. It's twice what it was last time. *And* two of the petting zoo goats are having a pecking order issue. They were slamming their heads together and one backed into a preschooler and tripped him and he knocked out a tooth. That was about an hour ago."

Oh, boy.

Wallace glowered at my news and decided he had to make a personal inspection of the accident site. "When things are bad, I can always count on you to make them worse," he snarled as we walked back to the World of Birds.

Calvin met us there. He'd called Maintenance, but no one was reachable. The three of us eyed the heat lamp and its reflector. Calvin first traced the cord to the outlet to be sure I really had unplugged it, then bapped the reflector with his finger a couple of times to confirm it really wasn't charged. That knocked loose the cord, which had been draped over the reflector and hidden by foliage. He inspected the cord. Two inches of plastic covering were melted, bright copper showing. We all nodded thoughtfully. Cord fell over reflector, which was hot from the bulb. Insulation melted, wire touched reflector, reflector was charged.

"This could of killed you," Calvin said.

"The bulb was burned out," I said, not sure what my point was.

Wallace took the cord from Calvin and looked at the damaged section. "The bulb isn't necessary—you completed the circuit. Did you get burned?"

"Nothing to bother with." They both seemed to know about electricity.

Wallace turned to Calvin. "You aren't using the right wire and you shouldn't have this where visitors can get at it. This setup is an accident waiting to happen. We got a big surplus of accidents and don't need any more."

His voice wasn't quite that of a foreman chiding an employee. There was a faint note of triumph, of evening a score.

Calvin's face shifted from puzzled to truculent. "You hold on a minute. This don't make sense. I never put a heat lamp that low—it should be three feet higher, the food platform too. And those cords don't melt that easy. What was it doing draped over the reflector anyhow?"

He didn't sound like an employee being chided.

I'd never seen them interact before except in keeper meetings. What was up with those two?

Wallace's face was stony. "So you think Iris fooled with your setup?"

"I did not!"

"Coulda been a visitor." Calvin didn't sound convinced or convincing.

"Work with Maintenance to get something better. I want all of these replaced by tomorrow," Wallace said and left, muttering about accident reports.

Calvin stayed in the aviary. He went to the tool shed hidden in a back corner and pulled out the stepladder. He inspected the World of Birds thoroughly. None of the other heat lamps was reachable without the ladder. Lacking any instructions, I stood and watched. Finally he removed the defective fixture and pushed the food platform higher up the pole that supported it. He examined the pole, and shook his head. Insisting I hadn't messed with it was futile and possibly humiliating, so I kept quiet. On impulse, I took the damaged fixture from him, removed the bulb, and climbed the stepladder to try it in another fixture. It lit up. It had just been loose, not burned out.

"Teenage boys messing around," Calvin finally diagnosed. "Pulled the food platform and heat lamp down, left the cord touching it. Seen visitors do a lot of strange things but not this one."

I couldn't tell if he was covering his own rear or if he really believed that.

I wondered if I had seriously underestimated how dissatisfied he was with me. Enough to set up a nasty practical joke, possibly a fatal one? Then I thought about the accident with Raj. Was something really malicious going on that had nothing to do with Calvin? If so, who and why? But it was possible I was at fault for Raj getting out. Maybe I was unbelievably accident prone. Someone had pawed through my clothing and set my house on fire…

We went back to finishing up the daily routine, my head aching with bruises and questions.

Calvin usually said, "Time to head for the barn" at 4:00 PM. Today he hadn't even that many words.

Wallace had left a note on my time card. Instead of punching out, I had to hobble to the Administration building again, plenty of time to consider the possibilities. Wallace thought I'd screwed up the light fixture myself and hadn't admitted it. I was about to be fired or invited to resign. Calvin had complained about me and I was being transferred to Children's Zoo or the gardening crew. Or maybe a thorough reaming out with threats of what would happen next time. That sounded like the best-case scenario. I gimped into Wallace's office with my jaw clenched, vowing to keep my mouth shut and not make a bad scene worse.

Nothing good ever happened in that room. Wallace rummaged around on his desk, not looking at me, and pulled out a piece of paper. "L.A. Zoo's looking for a keeper with carnivore experience. This is the ad. You got the qualifications." He met my eye, apparently with some effort. "Now I don't want you to think I'm trying to get rid of you or anything. None of you keepers ever believe I could be on your side, but the truth is, I'm thinking you might want to get back to the cats and start fresh at the same time. I'm thinking of what I might want in your position, and if it isn't what *you* want, forget it." That said, he squared his shoulders and waited.

Instead of responding to this little speech with a heartfelt "Huh?" I mumbled something about thinking it over and stumbled off. Wallace called me back to hand me the ad.

I was so flummoxed that I forgot to worry about another break-in until I was nearly home. But I found an undemolished house and unpoisoned dogs. After feeding the dogs and Bessie and eating my chicken potpie, I sat on the floor for some canine consolation. Range seemed less depressed about Rick's disappearance and more resigned to getting his affection from me. Winnie wanted a walk, as always, but I didn't feel like strolling around my neighborhood in the dark.

Buffered against near-death willies by loyal companions, I considered the incident in the aviary. Dr. Dawson said Wallace was concerned about accidents. No surprise the foreman had lit on the L.A. job as a way to ease me out. From his perspective, I was the straggler in the herd. "I can count on you to make things worse." That hurt worse than the bruises.

My second week on Birds was not going well.

I set aside all the other mysteries and considered the puzzling dynamics between Wallace and Calvin. I didn't know much about Calvin before I started working with him, and I didn't know much now. Aside from the clumsy incident with the eagle, he was hard working and conscientious. He clearly wanted the best for his birds. Wallace seemed to give him a free hand, maybe because Wallace didn't give Birds much of a priority. Who could tell me about Calvin and his relationship with the foreman? Jackie and Hap came to mind, mostly because they would talk to me. Kip Harrison, the head primate keeper, and Sam Bates, the hoof stock keeper, both knew Calvin better, but they weren't likely to share gossip with me.

This transition to Birds was exhausting and nerve-wracking. Which was most at risk—my job or my life? The more I thought about it, the more significant that question became.

On the other hand, Rick was not the same festering wound in my heart that he had been. The wound hadn't healed, but it had changed, become sadder but less crippling somehow. I couldn't forgive him, but I didn't hate him anymore. And I missed him. If he were with me, at least I could yell at him, demand to know what he thought he was doing that night, tell him how bad this was for me.

I pushed the dogs aside, checked the locks on doors and windows, took a hot shower to ease my aches, and gave it up for the day. I never had gotten to share the story of the house fire with my coworkers.

Chapter Twelve

"Did they steal any of your ID? Your checks?" Jackie had sunk her teeth into my housebreaking. She was mumbling around a mouthful of Polish sausage with sauerkraut, her ruby nails digging into the bun. It was too wet for sitting outside; we were camped in the café. Peacocks wandered disconsolately outside, deprived of their opportunities to mooch.

"I don't think so. No, the police asked about that. The checks were dumped out, but they were all there. My ID was in my wallet with me."

"So what *did* they take?"

"I don't know. I'm still getting everything straightened out. They left the TV and DVD player."

"You might want to change your bank account."

"Police said it was an amateur, not anyone good at robbing houses."

"Sounds like rotten kids looking for drugs."

I didn't think so, but my guesses weren't any better.

I gnawed on my own sausage and winced as Jackie squirted more catsup on hers. Catsup and sauerkraut? Gross. I had arranged an early lunch for the two of us, using my break-in story as the lure. Two elderly women were the only other customers in the café.

"Jackie, I don't get why anyone would break into my house and I don't understand Calvin either. Tell me about him." There, the transition was inept, but the question was nicely nonspecific.

Far better than "Does Calvin like to set lethal booby traps?" or "Does he hate women?"

Jackie considered the matter. "He's always kinda cranky, not much fun. And *so* straight-arrow. No bad words. No bad *thoughts* as far as I can tell." She shifted in her seat and tried another approach. "His wife died a few years ago. He wasn't such a grump when she was around. I suppose he blames Wallace."

"Huh! *Major* bad blood. Why?"

"Not bad blood *between* them exactly. Just bad blood from Calvin. Wallace doesn't hate Calvin, only the other way around. I think."

"So why?"

Jackie picked at strands of sauerkraut, taking her time. "Well, back when I first started, about four, five years ago, Calvin had his daughter, Janet, working in the office, and didn't she think she was something special." Jackie's lips thinned. "She got hired as the bookkeeper. Mr. Crandall thought the world of her. Then she and Wallace started dating and there was no living with her. She was forever having a better idea how to do things in the office. She'd yak about it until somebody made us do it her way. The queen bee for sure. But she got hers." Jackie delicately licked her fingertips. "I mean, who would have thought she'd have her fingers in the till? She was such a little do-gooder, Christian and everything. But she had sticky fingers and got caught and fired. That was the end of marrying Wallace."

"Marry Wallace? God, what a narrow escape!" Wallace in a romance? Sounded like a rhino taking up ballet.

"Probably got the job 'cause of her dad and she was short and perky. Mr. Crandall loves that kinda woman. Maybe she had a drug problem and that's why she took the money." Jackie brightened at the thought. "Anyway, we had this bomb scare so we all cleared out of the building." She finished her sausage and sipped her diet cola. "This money was sitting around from a special Easter egg hunt the zoo set up to get all these kids in. It was awful, millions of them, crawling all over the grounds for these fake eggs in the rain. But it brought in some extra gate receipts. She was going over it at the end of the day when we got the bomb call. So we all had to stand in the rain for, like, hours while the bomb guys went over the whole building. They should have sent us home." Jackie pulled out a cigarette and tapped the butt on the table, still bitter.

"And?"

"Oh, the till was empty when we got back in. Wallace asked everybody, then he called the police. We had to let them search us and they found the money in Janet's purse. Nobody could believe it, at first. She was crying, saying she didn't do it. Said she was set up. Yeah, right. Mr. Crandall went all fatherly to her, but he made Wallace fire her. He wouldn't fire anybody himself. She never did admit she took the money."

"Calvin thought she was innocent?"

"Well, yeah. I mean, she was his little darling. I heard him yelling at Wallace to be a man and stand up for her. He figured Wallace wanted to break up with her, so he framed her. Framed her. Just how likely is that, I ask you?"

It was easy to picture Jackie hovering outside Wallace's door, head cocked like a serval listening for a mouse.

"So anyway, Janet disappeared, thank God. The zoo got the money back, and Calvin stayed mad at Wallace. Like he thinks Wallace was unjust 'cause he can't face his daughter being a thief."

"Jackie, you know everything," I said.

"Oh, not really. I just keep my eyes open," she said, crossing her legs modestly. "Anyway, then his wife died. So I figure he blames Wallace for that, too." She piled up her trash, ready to leave.

"I'm still stunned at the idea of Wallace having a girlfriend."

"Janet wasn't the only one, but none of them worked out. Can't seem to keep a woman happy. Mr. Crandall could teach him a thing or two about that." She gave a knowing nod.

"That old goat? He's married, been married for a hundred years."

"Sure, he's got this crabby wife in a wheelchair. Maybe he found somebody more fun."

"Like you?"

"God, no!" Jackie looked around nervously, and gathered herself to go. She saw Hap and Denny coming in, changed her mind and settled back. She had my burglary to share.

I stood up to go back to work. Jackie had given me plenty to think about.

"You got good locks on your house?" she asked.

"Yeah, my dad put better ones on, but I've got to move. Look, don't tell Denny about the housebreaking, or he'll drive me crazy with fifty theories."

"He'll find out. Everybody at Finley knows everything eventually."

I snorted. "I thought so, too, but no one can tell me the important stuff. Like why Rick came here the night he died."

Jackie started digging around in her black purse for her lighter. "I got a theory." She looked at me sidelong.

"Yeah? I could use a theory."

"You won't like it much."

Hap and Denny were still in line ordering food.

"Try me."

"Here goes," she said, leaning back in her chair. "You two break up. There he is, good looking, straight, maybe not going to be married much longer, right?"

"Jackie, we were separated for one week. One week."

"Yeah, yeah," she went on, ignoring the warning rattle in my voice. "So anyway, why would he come here except to meet someone? He came to meet a woman. That's what I think."

Calm vanished in an eye blink, swamped by a caustic mix of anger and grief. "And exactly who might that be?"

Jackie dropped her gaze. "It wouldn't be right to toss names around. He was friendly with plenty of women."

"Meaning you don't have any idea. Good, because you're right. I don't much like your theory. I think it's a crock of shit."

"Well, you're the one that asked..."

I was gone, striding fast away from more ugliness about Rick. Served me right for pawing through Jackie's opinions and observations. From her packrat midden of gossip, a rattlesnake had struck. Marcie and the bartender had persuaded me that Rick wasn't a lying jerk, but Jackie had contributed a whole new dimension of betrayal. My stomach lurched and my eyes blurred. I took a shaky breath. Jackie's fantasies had to be the product of an overactive imagination and a boring job. But part of me was sick—certain that the worst had to be the most true.

How many ways, exactly, could Rick break my heart? One more? Yes indeed, they certainly could take that away from me.

I tried to focus as I scrubbed and hosed out the pond in the World of Birds, distraught but still wary of all things electrical. Calvin worked on the wire mesh at the other end of the exhibit. He hadn't let me do anything alone all day. It wasn't clear whether he feared another accident or he didn't trust my work. He would no doubt be very pleased to swap me back for Arnie.

Jackie's lurid scenario might be right, no matter how painful. No point in asking questions if I couldn't face up to the answers. I hooked up the hose and started rinsing the pond.

If only I could ask the lions what had happened. They probably wouldn't tell me, although Rajah might. What woman could it possibly have been, anyway? Too late, I remembered to put the little screen back over the drain to catch leaves and feathers.

Wallace marched into the aviary as Calvin was squatting by the drain poking at it scientifically. He kept a long piece of coat-hanger wire hidden in the exhibit for just such problems. I'd already tried that and failed, which meant I'd had to ask for help. I was standing around since I couldn't finish cleaning until the drain was cleared, and it felt cowardly to leave and do something useful elsewhere.

"L.A.'s ready for those Africans," Wallace announced without preamble. "Took weeks to get off their dime, and now they want the birds yesterday."

Dr. Dawson must have reminded him about the excess penguins. Wallace waited to see whether Calvin would go for this plan.

"Fine," grunted Calvin, still crouching and focused on the drain. "When?"

"Soon as Jackie can make the arrangements." He shifted toward the exit, done. "L.A.'s just going to hold them for that new aquarium opening up."

Calvin looked up at him. "Somebody's got to go with them."

Wallace paused. "I don't see why. The airlines know what they're doing."

Calvin's knees creaked as he got to his feet. A couple of decades older, two inches shorter, and many pounds lighter, he faced Wallace like an old lion who'd seen everything. They looked equally matched to me.

"Airlines make mistakes," Calvin said, "and we'd never know about it until the birds turned up dead in Minnesota or some-wheres. Somebody's got to see they get there all right."

Wallace looked stubborn. "I don't have the budget to ship keepers all over the country. Or pay for hotels and meals."

"Aren't they paying for these birds? Seems like we could use some of that."

Wallace shifted his weight impatiently. "Day trip only, no hotel."

"Day trip's fine. Send Arnie. I hate travel." Calvin got back on his knees and reached deep into the drain, pulling out a soggy handful of leaves.

Wallace looked peeved. "I need Arnie." He stared at Calvin's back for a moment, then turned to me. "You're going. You can interview for that carnivore keeper job. I'll set it up."

My brain locked up. "Not a good time." I searched for rea-sons. "My house was broken into last weekend and he might come back. I've got the dogs. I...I..." I didn't want to interview for that job—the beginning of a greased slide out of Finley Zoo. And I didn't want to be pulled off the trail of understanding Rick's last night.

Calvin's face seemed to say, "Safe to send her. She can't screw this up."

"Friday if Jackie can get the reservation," Wallace said, ignor-ing my sputters. "L.A. people will meet you at the airport." He hesitated on his way out. "I'm not paying overtime for this," he said over his shoulder.

Calvin went back to work with the piece of wire.

"Got it!" he said. Hooked on the end of the coat hanger was a broken necklace made of plastic beads, still recognizably pink and purple. Something plastic dangled from it, dripping wet feathers. A tiny purple dragon with big eyes. "Some little girl's probably cryin' for this," he said softly.

"It looks like it's been there a while." Not my fault the drain clogged. Not entirely. I put the screen back in place and finished up the hosing.

Wallace needed feckless Arnie. He didn't need me.

Chapter Thirteen

Early Friday I was at the zoo in civilian clothes with a novel in my backpack, loading two portable animal kennels into my truck. A penguin shuffled nervously inside each kennel while Calvin fussed nervously outside. He gave me advice on plane trips, several emergency contact numbers, and pounds of paper to hand off to the Los Angeles Zoo keepers. He reviewed each page with me in detail, complete instructions for nurturing these particular birds.

At last the penguins and I escaped to Interstate 205, aimed south toward Portland International Airport, sharing the long curving bridge across the Columbia River with commuter traffic.

The night before I'd dropped Winnie and Range at my parents since I'd be back late. The folks both thought a free plane trip was a grand bonus. I hadn't explained that it was a clear signal that my boss saw me as surplus at best and a liability at worst. Whatever. It would be cool to see the Los Angeles Zoo. This was an adventure, not a trial run at exile.

Sure it was.

But truly, the new bridge, "new" as of 1983, felt wide and open, free of the struts overhead that bound the ninety-year-old Interstate 5 Bridge I usually took to Portland. Trees in splashy fall dress dotted the riverbanks. A seagull drifted across six lanes, wings set at the perfect, effortless angle. I really could shrug off my troubles. So long, gray skies and unanswerable questions; hello, California sunshine.

In good time my truck was in long-term parking at the Portland airport and the penguins were in the hands of the airline, to be tucked somewhere in the plane where they wouldn't freeze. African penguins are from the southern tip of Africa, not Antarctica, and don't take well to frost, especially when they are used to indoor living.

I punched in a code at the ticket kiosk to get my boarding pass and discovered I was going to Burbank, not Los Angeles. Close enough. On the way to the security line, a sign outside Tina's Lounge and Grill assured me that "there is always a reason to have a drink at the airport." Not the best omen. My positive attitude faltered.

Security personnel scrutinized an X-ray of my backpack, shoes, and belt, and waved me through with indifference.

I had requested a window seat so I could survey the West Coast from above, a view I hadn't seen since my parents took me to Disneyland years ago. A woman in a black pantsuit took the aisle seat and shoved a briefcase under the empty middle seat, ignoring me. Once everyone had wrestled luggage into the overhead bins and obediently fastened their seat belts, the plane turned toward open space and stopped. It sat and roared to itself for a moment, then floundered down the runway like a loon striding and flapping on a lake surface to gain enough speed for takeoff. As the ground receded, it came to me that this was a heavy hunk of metal, and we are not a species meant to fly.

The plane steadied itself as it leveled out. My row mate hauled out her briefcase, fired up a little computer, and got to work. I dared to peek out the window. Far below a silvery river was a thread among uneven dark forests. Snow frosted the hills, and clear cuts made patterns like a badly designed quilt thrown over the entire western half of the state. Clouds hovered at eye level and below, gray lumps of thick fog.

The clouds closed in to make a tight visual barrier stretching flat and monotonous in all directions. I pulled the novel my mother had provided out of the backpack. The jaguar in the title turned out to be a metaphor and the lead character was mean-spirited to friends and enemies alike. The airline magazine celebrated vacations and promoted gadgets I could never afford, and the crossword puzzle stumped me on a German river, then on Thai currency. I put it away and looked around, jumpy and impatient. Everyone else seemed calm. Bored, even.

A flight attendant, a cheerful woman about my own age, offered coffee. Weak, but hot and welcome. The oatmeal breakfast bar had a lot in common with monkey chow, without the crunch.

The plane droned on, chewing through a dull, thick fog. The view stopped a dozen feet outside the window. My row mate stayed focused on her laptop. I was caffeinated, safe, and immobilized. Thoughtful reflection was inescapable.

What would the wasteland of my life look like from 30,000 feet? I flinched away from the emotional Grand Canyon named Rick that dominated the landscape, then dragged myself back. Marcie believed putting words around things gave them handles.

Anger…grief…humiliation…self-doubt…abandonment… loss loss loss…

And bewilderment. What was Rick + Iris all about? Why did Rick die the way he did?

Answers were not forthcoming.

As for the rest of my pathetic little life—

Evicted from Felines, faltering in my new role at Birds, urged by the boss to take a job elsewhere. An accident-prone incompetent. No place felt safe—not my disaster of a house, not my job.

If putting words to feelings gave them handles, the handles were sharp-edged and red-hot. I sank in my seat, wishing codeine was available for wounds of the heart and that caffeine could counter emotional exhaustion.

So many questions without answers. I wasn't good at this. Despite asking other keepers and wondering hard, I'd learned no more than I knew the day Rick died. Baldly stated, he had gotten drunk an hour or two after promising to stop and stumbled over the guardrail into the lion moat and to his death. Dr. Dawson had to be right, alcohol addiction was powerful. But today, that simple explanation didn't *feel* right. Where did he go to drink? Would he really switch to whiskey so that he could keep his word about not drinking beer? I had to concede that was too twisty and tricky for Rick.

Friends who should be saner and more sensible than I remained convinced it was an accident.

Like Raj getting out was an accident. The little squeak of the cat door being raised...

Like the heat lamp accident. That one stank of booby trap—I didn't buy the teenage vandal theory. Calvin hadn't warmed to me as a coworker, but he simply wasn't vindictive. I couldn't believe he'd done it.

Who was the booby to be trapped? It could have been Calvin just as well as me. Whoever had set it was willing to risk hitting the wrong target. Was it meant to kill or only to frighten? A reckless prank?

Why would anyone have it in for Calvin? Nothing much had changed there for years. He took care of Birds and kept to himself. He and Wallace didn't get along, but according to Jackie, that was of several years' standing.

I was what had changed in Calvin's world. I was displacing Arnie, insisting someone had let Raj out on me, asking about Rick's death.

Arnie as the perpetrator, wanting Birds back? Arnie hadn't the wits or the initiative to set a clever trap.

Who, then? And why?

Too many accidents. It didn't add up. Something was going on.

I stared unfocused at the seatback in front of my face. Intuition struggled through acid sorrow and weary uncertainty to the surface and hardened into conviction.

Someone had killed Rick and was trying to kill me to hide it.

"Flying scare you?"

I blinked at the businesswoman across the empty middle seat. I must have made a noise.

"Flying is much safer than driving." She smiled in sympathy.

I nodded vaguely. "I'll be fine."

I'd been too angry and sad, too rattled by accidents and change, to listen to fitful whispers from my subconscious. Stilled by a seat belt and the unvarying rumble of jet engines, I opened to another version of Rick's last night. The blood alcohol level was a lab mistake or had been faked. He hadn't been at the zoo to meet another woman, but for an innocent work-related matter. And someone, on purpose or by accident, had killed him.

This version was blessedly devoid of bitterness, unstained by betrayal. It left Rick whole, not a liar or a weakling. And me not a fool for loving and trusting him.

Rage jolted me like the heat lamp. Someone had killed my husband.

He was not going to get away with it.

The flight attendant brought around more coffee; my neighbor typed and moused. The plane bucked twice and shied a little. The captain suggested we all put our seat belts on.

Cold reality percolated through hot anger. If I tried to track down his killer, I remained a target. Staying at Finley Memorial Zoo would require dodging more fatal "accidents." Or I could leave. The job at the Los Angeles Zoo might be all that stood between me and ending up like Rick.

Wallace or not, I wanted to work at Finley Memorial. The little zoo was on a rising curve, given the bond money for upgrades. I could make a difference at Finley. Besides, I was a Northwest girl; L.A. was not my town. Too big, too flashy, too far from tall trees, vacant driftwood-littered beaches, shady mountain trails. No Marcie, no parents. Bad air, bad traffic. Way too much change for me to handle now.

I would never cut and run. I'd get to the bottom of what happened with Rick. Then salvage my job.

How, exactly, would I accomplish all this? My track record was not good.

Metallic whining noises issued from the plane's belly. Clanking and a jolt. Startled out of my thoughts, I hoped that meant the landing gear was deployed and not that a critical piece had fallen off. We seemed to be sloping toward earth, where a mosaic of roads and housing developments grew larger and more detailed. I could see for miles and all I saw was pavement and buildings. I packed up my neglected book and ugly new convictions.

The flight was fifteen minutes late and I worried about finding the Los Angeles Zoo staff. I needn't have. Two beautiful people in khaki shorts and shirts awaited me, the L.A. Zoo logo on their shirts: silhouettes of snake, condor, rhino, gorilla. He was dark and handsome; she was blond and pretty. Their pockets identified them as Ben and Cindie; their knees were tanned. I felt like Sasquatch lumbering out of the Northwest, too big, too pale, and still stunned by harsh conclusions.

We hung around until the penguins were unloaded, shepherded the crates into the zoo van, and took off through vivid sunshine, Cindie driving. Interstate 5 was a familiar landmark, although with more potholes and patches than up north. I set my fears aside, gaped at palm trees and started peeling off layers of winter clothing, down to jeans and a T-shirt.

At the zoo, we went in through a service entrance and drove to the quarantine area. Fresh paint and good equipment made me want to weep. I felt a new kinship with Mr. Crandall and his ambitions. We put the crates in a quarantine room with its own pool, then opened up their little front doors. The penguins crammed themselves as far back in the crates as they could. I reminded them that they hadn't wanted to be in there at all a few hours ago. We went off, leaving them huddled in their little prisons-turned-refuges. The idea was that they would come out when they settled down and felt secure. But it had to be by 5:00 PM because that was when I needed to head back to the airport with the empty crates. Lucky little dudes. Eventually they would reside in a bigger, better exhibit than they would ever live to see at Finley.

Ben and Cindie gave me the short version of the insider tour of the Los Angeles Zoo. We strolled among visitors, many speaking in languages other than English. My mother would have swooned at the plants, beautiful botanical specimens with neat labels. I glimpsed animals I'd never seen before including meerkats—a type of mongoose, looking like cute weasels—and capybara, sort of a hundred-pound guinea pig.

For minutes at a time I was free of wondering which person I thought of as a friend might have killed Rick.

I stopped dead at the gerenuks, African antelope that apparently the Disney Imagineers had designed because Bambi wasn't cute enough anymore. They were wonderfully slender with long elegant legs and necks. Big dark eyes were ringed with natural eyeliner. A fawn nursed vigorously, its ears flapping as it bunted the mother's udder. The mother stood stock still, except that she switched her tail rapidly and stamped one foreleg delicately, over and over, like a film loop. Another doe stood straight up on her hind legs to nibble shrubbery eight or ten feet above the ground. The adult male, presumably the father of the fawn, walked up to the high-reaching female and waited until she dropped lightly back to all fours. Just as weightlessly, he reared up and mounted her back. She casually walked out from under him, not interested today. No hard feelings on either part that I could see.

This place made Finley Zoo look like a backyard menagerie. I had a wonderful time, except for fear and anger about the quagmire waiting for me at home bubbling to the surface every quiet moment. Joy would slip off like an unbuttoned cloak, leaving me chilled.

We ran into Ben's boss, whose exact title escaped me. An athletic guy with wraparound sunglasses, a gold earring, and a sexy little beard, again the shorts and tanned legs. Greg something. Ben explained my mission.

"I've heard of Finley Memorial. Thought it was in Canada. I know a guy who worked there. Is Neal Dawson still around?"

"Yeah, he's still the vet." Greg wasn't the first person to overlook Vancouver, U.S.A.

"We were in school together for a year, UC Davis. He stole my girlfriend."

Dr. Professional in a fevered love triangle? I gaped.

Greg laughed. "Yeah, he doesn't seem the type. I think it was the contrast effect, Mr. Distant coming on to her. I thought he was stuck up and bad tempered, so it caught me off guard. But she thought he was shy and lonely." He shook his head, shaking off regret. "Man, was she ever hard to write off. Perfect body, a smile to light up a city…"

"*I* had no idea he was married. Seems like the classic bachelor."

"I wish. Hey, maybe she left him. That would be fantastic. Got divorced myself a year ago."

"Again," said Ben.

His boss shrugged that off. "Man was not meant to live alone. You tell Dawson you met me, and I was incredibly hot and have an awesome job, okay? And if you find an address for Winona, send it to me."

I couldn't help but laugh with him. He *was* pretty hot.

He gave my upper arm a tiny squeeze and the sunglasses probably hid a wink, then he was off down the path. Cindie rolled her eyes at his back.

The beautiful pair of keepers—I tried not to think of them as prime breeding stock—left me to finish the tour by myself. They gave me their work phone numbers on a scrap of paper. Cindie dotted her "i"s with circles, but didn't turn them into smiley faces. They promised to try to connect later and show me around some more if there was time before my flight.

I had two hours before my job interview and made slow progress through more of the zoo. The black rhino was hypnotizing—quick, agile movements in a burly shape that should have been cumbersome. The horn on the tip of her nose was improbably long and sharp, with a shorter horn closer to her eyes. She had something on her mind and was pacing from one end of the enclosure to the other, raising her weirdly shaped head to peer and sniff every few minutes. Her skin was reddish brown, hairless like a person's. Her eyes were dark and suspicious.

"I like a big girl who drools," said a voice behind me.

I turned to see Greg, still in the sunglasses. "She's worth drooling over," I said.

"Not you—her." He grinned.

The rhino was indeed drooling a little.

He leaned against the rail next to me. "Lunch coming up. She's on a diet so she's hungry." Aftershave lotion and a hint of fresh sweat awoke a primitive part of my brain. "Hey, did you leave a husband in Portland or are you free for dinner?"

Interesting way to phrase the question. "No husband, but I've got a plane to catch. Sorry."

"Lunch then?"

"Uh, sure." I nodded and produced a cautious smile. I could use a few friends at this zoo, and I was hungry.

White teeth showed when he grinned, a dominant, confident lobo. "Let's go to my apartment. I'll fix you something special. Gourmet chef is one of my many talents. Parking lot's this way." He took my elbow and started off.

I balked. "A restaurant would suit me better." He wasn't *that* charming.

"I make a mean spaghetti carbonera. Got some white wine in the fridge, a nice salad. Show you a little California hospitality." There was the grin again, and the pressure on my elbow.

"Hey, back off. I'm not going to your apartment for a nooner. And let go of me, damn it."

He stepped back, hands held palm out. "We're talking *lunch* here. Just a little hospitality." The smile was gone.

I felt off balance and klutzy. Was there a worse way to turn down a pass? Now his pride and feelings were hurt, a potential ally lost. "Look, I'm not up for this. My husband died a couple of weeks ago and I'm…not up for this."

Greg's eyes were hidden behind the dark glasses. The rest of his face shifted from resentment to curiosity. "No kidding."

A pause. "You're from Finley Zoo? They lost a keeper recently, right? I saw a newspaper article."

Sigh. "Right."

"A cat keeper. Was that your husband?"

"Reptile keeper, not cats," I said, trapped. I had never used Rick's last name and had been counting on that to shelter me from talking about his death.

Greg thought about it. "Rough situation. Don't miss seeing the bongos."

And he was off, head up, arrogant stride, saving his charm for a more likely prospect.

I kicked myself for not deflecting him with more grace and ground my teeth at his predatory opportunism. The rhino stared at his back, then whirled like a quarter horse and trotted across the enclosure.

A burrito and soda with a good view of giraffes took care of lunch, but I was hot and depressed when it was time to go find the personnel office. If word got around about how my husband died, management would have questions that I didn't want to answer. Like why I still wanted to work with large carnivores, why I still wanted to work at a zoo at all, was I unstable. I wanted, needed, a job offer.

Maybe Greg wouldn't discuss it with the hiring manager. Maybe I was worrying for nothing.

I introduced myself to the middle-aged receptionist. She gave me an application form to fill out. That done, she ushered me into a cool, dim conference room.

Waiting to interview me, minus the sunglasses, was Greg.

Chapter Fourteen

The interview did not go well, but I stayed until Sunday evening anyway, through both of my days off. I needed the time. I called Jackie and made her change the tickets and tell Wallace that the crates wouldn't be back until late Sunday. Cindie put me up on her sofa. The extra days could be justified as research into moving to L.A.

My mother promised to pick up extra dog food and told me to have fun. Bessie could easily survive a couple days without food. My dad reminded me about the ad for Rick's truck, which I'd completely forgotten. The phone could collect any messages, and I'd deal with it later.

I spent Saturday roaming the Los Angeles Zoo, ignoring all the other blandishments of the big city. Cindie invited me to join her at a Halloween party, but I declined. Sunday I toured the La Brea Tar Pits.

Sun, traffic, thick air—so many people, so many *different* people. I'd just fallen off the turnip—no—log truck. I ate sushi and Thai pizza, bought mirror sunglasses and an L.A. Zoo ball cap. My nose and cheeks turned pink. I picked out a hummingbird tattoo to get someday and decided to have my hair highlighted soon.

Two days touristing in Southern California prevented conscious thinking and planning. Instead, new fears and suspicions settled in. Implications and connections formed in the fertile mud below the clear stream of conscious thinking. The outrage did not erode.

Cindie arranged a ride to the airport for the crates and me. I offered to return the hospitality if she ever got up to Portland.

On the flight back, I stared out the window at side-lit pink and gray clouds, regretting and editing my responses in the job interview. Greg had had the grace to look as embarrassed as I'd felt and had explained he was a last-minute substitute. He hadn't known he'd be interviewing me. In light of what he'd learned about me earlier, ordinary questions such as "why would you like to work here?" were complicated and slippery. I answered that one honestly, keeping to the surface: working there seemed like moving to fantasyland. Cool animals—black-footed cats, snow leopards, maned wolves—and excellent facilities. For the other questions, I ignored widowhood and brought up my experience with the clouded leopards and training the lions at every opportunity. The conversation was stilted from beginning to end.

I let go of regrets and leaned back in my seat. I'd done my best. Maybe it would be good enough.

If I got the job, it would be a fresh start, not running away. A step up professionally to a much bigger zoo. Tempting…leave all the ugliness behind. And maybe, someday, there would be another man. Thank Greg for that idea.

Interesting to hear him say that Dr. Dawson had a wife. Another thing to ask Jackie about.

Except that Jackie was coming up with these unsettling theories.

All the problems submerged for two days thrashed to the surface. The simple conviction that Rick was a blameless victim wavered. Nudged by Greg's prowling, infidelity crawled out from under a rock.

What woman did Jackie think Rick came to the zoo to see? Linda? Any of a number of zoo volunteers? Not Jackie herself. Rick didn't much like her, and she was ten years older.

Benita? He had been helping with her sick rattlesnake.

Benita and Hap. Hap's friends understood that Benita kept him on a short leash and that this was, all things considered, an excellent strategy. The story was that she gave him his name.

Biker friends called him Hazard, but Benita had scoffed that he was just haphazard, and it stuck.

Once when I'd inquired about his life before the zoo, Hap pulled up his Harley T-shirt to show me an appalling scar snaking across his belly. "This souvenir is why I don't get rowdy or hook up with women anymore. Hardly anymore," he'd told me. "Got into this fight at a rally and woke up with tubes in me in the hospital. All my friends came to visit 'cause I was there for weeks. Except not the one that was totaled by the same guy who got me, and not the one in jail, and not the one that was hiding out over in Malheur County. Benita sits down to talk to me and this time I can't walk off, and I hurt too bad to bullshit her. So I walk the damned line. Mostly. At least I don't get shit-faced and fight anymore. But if you ever need some help, Iris, you let me know. I can still take care of business when I have to."

Then there was the famous scene at Hap's annual party the year I started at the zoo. I'd come alone, hoping to nudge new work relationships toward friendship. Instead, I'd been holding up a dining room wall, nursing a beer and watching the crowd. Across the room, Hap was large and festive in a Hawaiian shirt, pink shorts, and plastic thongs, laughing with people I didn't know. A woman with hard miles on her, yellow straw hair, a leather vest and ripped jeans, punched him in the shoulder, ragging him about his muscles, feeling his chest. She was no one associated with the zoo, that I was sure of. Grinning, he'd thrown her an air punch. She grabbed the big fist and inspected tattoos on his hand, then his arm, rolling up his sleeve to see the length of the cobra. She moved her body against his and I heard her suggest they move to a bedroom so that he could show her the full set. Hap shook his head the way you might at a cute puppy that tinkled on the carpet.

Peroxide-woman was well fueled and had spoken too loudly. Benita wafted up to her, shimmering in a silky blue body suit, high neck, no skin exposed, but the tight fit telegraphing her thong and absence of bra. I'd wondered all evening whether she could get out of that thing to pee without assistance. Benita took the woman's hand, moving it off Hap, and put her other hand on top, a friendly, confiding gesture, a thousand-watt smile on her face. In four-inch heels, she tiptoed higher to reach the woman's ear, honey-and-chocolate hair loose on her back, breathy voice in a whisper too low to hear.

After a second's paralysis, the hard woman jerked her hand away, made fists, and stood with her jaw thrust out and color rising. Hap folded his arms across his chest, noncombative. She took a step toward Benita, wavered in the glare of that stainless smile, then wheeled around, grabbed a leather jacket and her soused boyfriend, and hauled them to the front door. At the open door, she hesitated long enough to drop her ratty pants and moon us—flat, pale ass—then shrieked some combination of "bitch slut dyke" as she slammed the door behind them.

Benita rotated her spotlight to Hap, who raised eyebrows and flared his fingers in a "not *my* fault" gesture. Benita's gleaming smile never reached her eyes, but she nodded, finally, and turned to rejoin her guests. A peculiar little grin twitched on Hap's lips and was gone.

I sagged against the wall. Benita had scared the nuggets out of me ever since.

Within two days, the zoo people had the story pieced together and the Legend of Benita never died. I'd been careful that the pleasant little buzz between Hap and me had stayed little.

Like Greg, Benita treated sexuality as an Olympic sport, one she'd medaled in. She'd asked for Rick's help with her snake. A scenario flowered: Rick and Benita meeting at the zoo to look at baby garter snakes or the python eggs. Benita deciding to give Hap some of his own back and making the moves on Rick, out of revenge or genuine attraction, or merely because she could. The two of them drinking together? Drunk and passionate. Hap suspicious, trailing Benita, walking in on them and going berserk.

Or was Jackie simply wrong? Who might actually know if Rick was having an affair? I made a list of people to ask, a short list. That kept me occupied for the rest of the flight.

Chapter Fifteen

The plane landed in late afternoon and I wrestled the two crates and my backpack onto the parking lot shuttle. The air felt moist and clean, kindly, after the eye-stinging atmosphere of Southern California. I'd never noticed how benign Northwest daylight was, all soft pastels, or the multiplicity of shades of green. Some muscle behind my eyeballs seemed to relax, no longer hard-clenched to withstand the exuberant Los Angeles sunshine. Could I adapt and live happily with reliable sun and a well-funded zoo? Or was I moss and mud to the core?

I drove to the folks' house and said hi to delighted dogs and to my mother, who was happy to have me haul them away. Winnie had tipped over all the wastebaskets looking for tidbits, and Range had trampled the fall cyclamens chasing squirrels. I promised a hard day's digging come spring to pay my debt. I kept quiet about the job interview and declined the offer of dinner.

My house was cold and dark, still tainted with stale smoke. I almost missed the tang of spilled beer. I had five phone messages, four from people interested in buying the truck and one from Marcie. She's the one I called back. After giving her the rundown on my weekend, I set up dinner for Monday night. The truck could wait.

Next was feeding Bessie Smith, who loathed me even when she was really hungry, then checking the mail. It included a surprise—the first installment on Rick's life insurance, $40,000, more money than I'd ever seen with my name on it. The usual amount of insurance was a year's salary, but Rick, ever susceptible to a sales promotion, had popped for double that. The insurance company had called a couple of times and I'd filled out forms, but the whole thing had seemed like a fairy tale.

I stared at the little piece of paper. What on earth should I do with it? What if the burglar returned? I folded it up and put it in my wallet next to about $8 in bills. I took it out again. I felt like Winnie with a fresh bone, carrying it around, inside, outside, what to do with it?

The house felt isolated and vulnerable.

I put the check under my pillow, locked all the locks, and fell into bed feeling like the sacrificial virgin on a cold stone altar. I was weary enough to sleep, but woke up on my feet when the dogs started barking at four in the morning. I locked the doggy door to keep them inside and cowered in the dark bedroom with the pipe wrench until we finally dozed again.

The next morning, the check was missing. I searched the bedroom, still half asleep, until a scary thought jerked me awake. I examined every door and window lock. No sign of intrusion. I stood still in the bedroom and pulled myself together. Coffee first, then think. After the first cup, I found the check where it had slipped behind the bed's headboard to the floor. I drank a second cup over a bowl of granola and stared at the little piece of paper. Getting paid for Rick's death was somewhere between peculiar and perverse. I stuffed it in my pocket with my wallet. I'd drop by the credit union after work and deposit it.

At the zoo, I hauled the crates back to the Commissary and checked the schedule. Three more days of training with Calvin, then Wednesday and Thursday off. I'd solo at Birds on Saturday and Sunday, Calvin's days off.

I chatted with Hap about L.A. for a bit, looking for guilt, regret, or self-righteousness and finding only his rough-edged friendship. An opportunity to ask him what he did after the party didn't materialize.

No way would Hap kill Rick. My imagination had run away with me.

I walked toward the Penguinarium with a gentle drizzle misting my sunburned face. Back in my own world, back at Finley, Rick's death seemed a lot more like an accident and the dangers to me more like…no, not like fantasies and coincidences. Uncertainty and ambiguity returned, but an icy core of conviction did not thaw.

Finley Memorial Zoo seemed smaller, older, and poorer than it had the week before. Much of it had been built in the sixties and seventies and the exhibits showed their age with rusting metal, worn paint, and outmoded design. Vancouver citizens had stepped up to the problem, I told myself. The bond measure they had passed would make a big difference, if the construction was ever finished. I wanted to be around to see that, to see a fine orangutan exhibit and classy housing for Asian cats, birds, and reptiles. Many of the new spaces would be filled by animals we already had, and all the staff were eager to see their circumstances upgraded. In a small zoo, I could make a difference. At Los Angeles Zoo, who knew whether that would be possible?

I took the long way to the bird kitchen, swinging by the future Asian Experience complex to see what progress had been made. Wallace and Dr. Dawson were in front of the construction site when I arrived. Dr. Dawson was carrying a long pole, the kind that holds a syringe full of some drug so you can poke it into an animal from eight feet away, if you're quick—and Dr. Dawson *was* quick. Wallace had a little curved hoof knife in his hand, so I guessed some antelope was in for a nap and manicure. They were both in parkas with the hoods down, indifferent to the rain in the best Northwest tradition. They looked companionable, two men with a chore they didn't mind doing together.

"Those penguins delivered?" Wallace inquired.

I stepped to one side of a puddle. "No problem. I left the crates at the Commissary."

"You talk to the people in L.A.?" He peered at me intently.

"You bet. I interviewed with a senior keeper. It went okay." No, wrong tone—safety required enthusiasm. "They loved my experience with servals and clouded leopards. What a great place." I needed to work on this—too stilted to convince people I really hoped to quit and move to L.A.

Wallace looked pleased. "I'll let you know if they call me for a reference."

"They've got fabulous animals in really cool exhibits," I added, warming up. "We don't have anything that comes close."

Dr. Dawson's chin went up a little. "It's a world-class zoo. You would be fortunate to have a job opportunity there."

Wallace turned toward him, annoyed. "Asian Experience is going to be as fine as anything at L.A. or anywhere else. The orang-utan piece will be state of the art. We've waited years for this."

"Of course. You're quite right," Dr. Dawson said in apologetic agreement.

I waved at the mud. The bulldozer was gone at last. "Yeah, it'll be great when it's finished, and I suppose this is how it has to be done, but it's hard to see our little woods torn up and scraped bare." I thought of clear-cuts visible from the plane, and it came to me for the first time that the whole zoo had been a forest long ago, thick with trees and ferns and wildflowers.

Wallace shifted impatiently. "No one's going to miss scrub second growth. They'll pour the foundations soon, and it'll start taking shape. In a year, we'll be up for design awards."

"And nobody will know or care what's gone," I mused aloud.

The alpha males gave me disapproving looks and departed toward their pedicure at the hoof stock barn. I walked on toward the Penguinarium, wondering about Dr. Dawson and his wife, or ex-wife. His aloofness now seemed to hold a hint of vulnerability, or perhaps my imagination was running away with me. I didn't know for sure that his wife had left him. Maybe he left her.

"How did those birds travel?" Calvin asked.

"They were fine. Their quarantine area is about as nice as our display area."

"They got the dough and we don't."

He was relieved to hear the penguins were in good hands and just nodded when I told him I was considering moving to L.A. He seemed more amiable than usual. I noted a few moments of

teamwork. I'd be on my own after a few more days of his tute-
lage.

I got in the groove and burbled to everyone I ran into about
the glories of the L.A. Zoo—the bongo breeding project, the
gerenuks, the botanical specimens. I felt disloyal to Finley, and
the other keepers' faces were careful and polite.

At day's end I trudged through the twilight rain to the
Administration building, wind ruffling my hair. Canada geese
circled overhead, wild voices invisible in the clouds.

My first goal was to resolve Jackie's speculations about Rick and
another woman while attracting the minimum possible attention.
It didn't feel safe to ask questions, L.A. job possibility or not, but
it had to be done. I had multiple strategies in mind.

The first was a failure. George, the security guard, was delighted
to chat with me from his tiny office. He'd seen and heard nothing
and nobody at the zoo the night Rick died. He might as well have
been in San Francisco or a coma for all the light he had to shed.
And, no, he'd never seen Rick at the zoo after hours. Benita either.
He'd seen the night keeper, of course, but was foggy about who
exactly had been on duty that night. Not Diego, he was pretty
sure. Sort of. He had, however, seen a possum on the grounds
recently and once, months ago, a house cat. I eased away before
he finished a story about a pet crow he'd had as a boy and trudged
to the Commissary and the time clock.

Denny was sitting on the counter by the bulletin board,
swinging his feet and talking steadily. He'd changed from his
uniform to brown cargo pants and a tattered gray sweater. He was
keeping Arnie from leaving by explaining the difference between
contrails and chemtrails and speculating that the government
was using airplane emissions to drug us all into docility.

"I always wondered about that," Arnie said vaguely and
ambled out to the parking lot.

I rummaged through the wastebasket for a scrap of paper and
found a ballpoint pen on the countertop behind Denny's rump. If
I were matter-of-fact about this, maybe Denny wouldn't notice.

"Thanks for waiting for me," I said as I wrote out my question and folded the note over Diego's time card. "I wanted to ask you about a few things in private."

Denny slid down to the ground. "Yeah, Ire. I've got a few questions for you, too. In my van. It's out of the rain." His jaw was set and his shoulders looked tense. My eyebrows rose.

I climbed onto the passenger seat of his battered Chevrolet panel truck. He sat rigid in the driver's seat, with the motor on. The wiper blades whapped back and forth while the defroster fought the windshield fog and lost. It felt like a distorted reflection of my last night with Rick.

Outside, the last of daylight was fading. Inside, fish smell rose from my clothes, mingling with a musty smell from Denny's snakes and lizards or maybe from the big pillows in back.

Get his issues out of the way first. "What's on your mind?"

"I hear you're getting serious coin from Rick's life insurance."

"That was fast. Who told you?"

"I got ways of finding stuff out." He sat with his wrists draped over the steering wheel, staring moodily past the wiper blades.

Jackie, most likely. "So…you asking for a loan?"

He kept on looking through the cloudy windshield, not at me. "You heading to L.A. got me thinking."

I stared at him, baffled.

"I'm trying to picture it. What, you got mad 'cause he was drinking and clocked him with a rock? You got the temper for it, God knows. Thought he was dead and wanted to hide the evidence? I tried to picture you doing it for the money, but I can't. Mad makes more sense. Is that what happened? Did you lose it after the party and do Rick, then drop him in the moat?"

My ears started to roar and I felt hot blood flushing my face. "Denny, you are *such* a jerk. I…I…" I stammered. I couldn't talk. I tried to open the door to get out and away, away from him and his vile notions, but parts are always falling off with that van and the door handle came off in my hand. I dug around on the floor for it so I could jam it back on to get the door opened and flee. I could hardly breathe from shock and rage and hurt.

Denny turned his head to look at me, chin shoved out, truculent. "I don't believe he just fell in any damned lion moat. Something by God happened that night and I want to know what the hell it was."

I had the handle back on the door and pried it open. "You are a flaming asshole," I enunciated clearly. "You are insane. And *how could you* even *think* that I would murder Rick?" Braining Denny with the door handle crossed my mind, but even in a rage, I could see that would tie in too well with his theory.

"I want to know what happened. You two were smokin' hot for each other, but you kicked him out like you kicked me out, then it looked like you were getting together again. Then he dies. So what *happened?*"

"So maybe *you* killed him? Did you ever think of *that?*" I snarled.

That caught him by surprise; he started to laugh, but went serious. "Now why would I do that?" he said, but his face showed he knew where I was going.

"You said it yourself. I kicked you out and married him. Maybe you were jealous and glad when we broke up. Maybe you lost it when we started working through it. Maybe you're the one who got mad and bashed him."

"Nah."

"Nah? What kind of declaration of innocence is that? I'm starting to think you *did* push him in the moat."

"He was my best friend. I was even down with the marriage thing. I know I got commitment issues, and it wasn't going to work out between you and me."

"Commitment issues? You been reading magazine articles at the dentist's office?" I sneered.

"Yeah, you weren't exactly clear why you dumped me. I've been thinking about it. Chicks always dump me sooner or later. Sometimes I'm just as glad, sometimes not. Anyway, I never held it against Rick. We were friends before and we stayed friends. Well, after a while."

"I didn't know you two were all that tight. He had all those people he met at bars and listened to music with. I never saw you there." Rain blew in through the open passenger door.

Denny shifted in his seat. "I didn't exactly feel welcome around you. But where did he go when you threw him out? He came to my place and I put him up."

"True." We sat in silence for a minute.

It was cold and wet with the door open, so I closed it. "I didn't throw him out. I left."

"Whatever." Denny was looking at me, frustrated, hands tight around the steering wheel.

"Where'd he get drunk that night?" I asked. "And who with?"

"I honest-to-god don't know. I thought you knew and weren't telling."

"Nope. Not a clue. I left him sober at about midnight." My head was clearing. I felt an odd pang of tenderness for Denny, that he was still being Rick's friend, in his unpredictable, quirky way—Rick's friend, but not mine. "You seem to have forgotten I'm the one who keeps asking what happened."

"Yeah. I figured maybe that was to smoke out who had suspicions or to mislead us."

I blew out a breath. Denny could incorporate contrary evidence into his theories with startling ease.

He turned toward me. "It was the money at first, then the L.A. job. I thought you'd found somebody else, but I don't see any sign of a new man."

"You are psycho, wrong, and plain mean. I am going home." I pried the door open again and got out. "I'd forgotten the money until it came," I said, slamming the door shut.

Denny started the van moving, but I had time to kick another dent in the side panel.

I was never going to get any useful information out of him.

Driving home to feed the dogs before dinner with Marcie, I thought about what Denny believed. Denny believed that the world was run by a black-hearted conspiracy of billionaire capitalists who would lose their fortunes if hemp were ever legalized, that marijuana brought him closer to the spiritual center of the cosmos, that spirulina algae would keep him healthy regardless of what else he ate or drank or smoked. He'd been wrong about computer viruses destroying civilization, wrong about women not caring how often a guy bathed, wrong about water boiling faster if you left the lid off the pot.

He agreed with me that something was fishy about Rick's death. That troubled me considerably.

Chapter Sixteen

Dinner with Marcie was a mess, both of us anxious and off balance. Thanks to the state I was in after talking to Denny, I'd forgotten to deposit the insurance check. I could almost feel it in my wallet, vibrating from unidentifiable emotions. The food at the Thai restaurant was good, as always, and the conversation went a little better after we'd eaten our ginger beef and green curry. Never again would I discuss anything important on an empty stomach.

When I suggested that Rick might have been murdered, Marcie didn't laugh or try to pack me off to a therapist. Instead, she went quiet.

"Marcie, there's something else."

"What?" Her hands were fists on the table.

"Denny has the same suspicions about Rick's death. Denny's theories are always cracked. Plus, his working hypothesis is that I did it. It's too confusing."

She relaxed a little. "I can assure you, his theories are not your biggest problem. Nobody takes them seriously, not even him. It's a hobby. It's the way he processes."

"He takes this one seriously. No one can tell me why Rick came up to the zoo. I need to talk to him—he's got to know something about Rick's last few days because Rick was staying at his place. He sincerely believes I might be a killer and I want to strangle him every time I see him. So I want you to be there." Marcie was the only candidate: Denny and I both knew and trusted her, she was calmer than either of us, and she was good at clarifying emotional situations.

Marcie picked at her food and seemed to be thinking it over. Finally she said, "I set you up. At the dog show. I talked you out of blaming Rick for all your problems. You started asking questions at the zoo and the bad stuff started happening. You better not get killed because I'll never forgive myself."

Her conclusion was that I had to quit the zoo immediately. Dodging with a vague promise to resign soon and take the L.A. job if it was offered, I got back to Denny. Would she mediate?

"Of course," she said. "I'll invite him to dinner and we can all talk."

That's when I realized I was probably putting her in harm's way, and the conversation deteriorated again into self-recrimination and ultimatums. We reluctantly agreed there was no point in going to the police without more information. Over fortune cookies that contained quips but neither valuable advice nor useful predictions, we decided to go ahead with inviting Denny to dinner. That settled, we limped our separate ways, exhausted. Still, it felt like progress.

I called the people who wanted to buy the truck and put them off until the next weekend. I had enough on my plate, and I didn't need the money anymore.

Tuesday morning, I deposited the check on my way to work. At the Commissary, I found the note I'd left for Diego folded over my time card, with the answer to my question added at the bottom in his careful printing, the name of the keeper who had the night shift the night Rick died. No surprise—I'd been told before, but had forgotten, as I'd failed to remember so much since Rick died.

I walked into the Penguinarium and forgot all about it again.

Calvin was in a near-tizzy. He was too deliberate to achieve a genuine tizzy, but he was as close as he was ever likely to be. "Gol-durned raccoon got in the aviary. Lousy cheap fencing. Killed one of the nene babies. It's still in there; can't find its way out. I'd like to shoot the son of a B," he ranted while ransacking the storage closet. So much for taciturn.

The three hatchlings weren't exactly babies anymore. They were full-sized, nice looking geese in gray and buff with black heads and bills.

"What are you looking for?" I asked.

"Where in Sam Hill is my catch pole?" He gazed around the kitchen, flushed and agitated. "I need to noose that forking varmint and haul him out before he kills every bird in there. Then I'd like to throw him in the river with a brick tied to him. Or kick his little behind out on the freeway at rush hour."

My, my.

I stood in front of Calvin to get his attention. "Do you have a catch pole? I can go get one at Felines if you want."

He focused on me briefly. "I used to have one, then Arnie or somebody borrowed it and never put it back. Maybe it's at Bears. I'm going to get a lock for that closet and never loan anything again as long as I live. Beans-and-rice-on-Friday. I got to fix that mesh or we'll have every raccoon in the state in there." He started toward the door, presumably to head for Bears.

I was still working on the beans and rice as I stepped in front of him again.

"Calvin, Felines has a catch pole. I'll go get it. You pretend you aren't swearing and meet me at the aviary."

He flinched.

I loped off to Felines and found Linda outside picking up the cougar yard. She didn't protest at my brief explanation, which I took as permission. The pole was in the kitchen, mixed in with the nets; I trotted back.

Calvin was standing inside World of Birds near one corner, glaring upwards. I looked up at the trunk of the artificial tree he indicated. A little masked face peered at us from about ten feet up, mostly hidden by the trunk and a branch. "It's a youngster," I told him.

"Get it out, or it's not getting a day older."

I'd never actually used a catch pole, aside from a brief practice session on a fat old possum during my early training. The possum hadn't minded, since he was quite tame and eating dinner at the time. The little raccoon was smaller but a lot more agile than Pa Possum and she was clearly contemplating climbing higher. If she made it all the way up the trunk, I'd never be able to reach her.

Superb starlings—that's their name—swooped down to perch near me, flashes of iridescent blue and chestnut. They had food on their mind and weren't worried about the intruder. The nene parents, on the other hand, rushed me, hissing with their heads held low in threat posture, pecking at my boots. "Hey, I'm the good guy," I told them. "Calvin, I need a ladder." The other birds were hidden in foliage or crammed into far corners, except for the little Hottentot teals, who paddled about in the stream unconcerned. They should have been worried; a raccoon that could handle a young nene could munch them right up.

Calvin went off obediently. I moved away from the perpetrator to take the pressure off, in hopes she wouldn't climb any higher. The nenes followed, hissing like teakettles. "Back off. I know what I'm doing," I lied.

Calvin brought a stepladder, still muttering, and we set it up. He seemed willing to let me handle the varmint side of bird keeping, so I shooed him out of the way, and climbed up. I was careful not to look at the raccoon, although I didn't fool her any. She knew I was after her. I teetered on the top step, the one labeled Do Not Stand Here, and adjusted the loop of lightweight cable at the business end of the pole. The cable ran through the pole and out the other end. I knew the theory—stick out the pole and loop the cable over the critter's head and one foreleg, then tighten by pulling on the cable at the far end. At my end of the pole, the cable had a loop with a plastic handle for me to pull on. The catch pole was supposed to allow controlling the animal without choking or injuring it.

I got my balance and took a quick pass at the raccoon. She scooted around the trunk, evading the loop, and climbed up another few feet. I climbed down, moved the ladder, and tried again. Same result. The culprit looked like she was planning a jump to the next tree over, which would put her into dense foliage.

"Calvin, you stand here," I ordered, placing him so that the raccoon couldn't move away from me without moving toward Calvin.

I climbed back up the little ladder and positioned myself, hoping that the third time was the charm. Calvin surprised us all by winding up and hurling half an orange from a food tray, beaning the kid between the ears. The raccoon nearly lost her grip and I swooped in and got the cable around her neck and one—no—two forelegs. The cable was around her middle, behind the front legs. It wasn't what I had in mind, but it didn't look dangerous for her. I snugged it tight, but not too tight, and hauled her down the trunk, her claws scrabbling frantically as I teetered on the ladder. She fell the last couple of feet and whipped around to bite anything nearby. I clambered down, knocking over the ladder and further inciting the parent geese. I towed the littlest outlaw out of the aviary as she screeched raccoon death threats at me.

"Get a box or something," I said. Calvin grabbed an empty garbage can and dumped it on its side. Together, we wrestled the kid inside and stood the can upright. Then I let some slack into the cable and eventually we got it disentangled from the raccoon. The youngster was hissing and growling savagely, but she didn't look any the worse for wear. Calvin rounded up a hand truck, clapped a lid on the can, and hauled it off, promising to release the raccoon in some scrub forest on his way home. I went back into the aviary and collected limp fragments of goose, blocking the hostile parents with a feed bucket.

Calvin came back and we set to work fixing the hole in the mesh fence, kneeling on damp ground in the drizzle. A vivid Mexican green jay supervised from a nearby branch. The other small birds weren't coming out of hiding, not yet. "Millions of dollars for the zoo and it all goes to new animals. Nobody gives a goldurn about the animals we already have," he muttered, pounding a metal stake viciously.

"You could bring it up at the next staff meeting," I suggested. "Put a little heat on Mr. Crandall."

"I have talked myself blue in the face. This happens every blessed year—we lose something to rats or raccoons or possums. They've got all kinds of holes under the perimeter fence. This aviary needs replacing, but we got to have fancy exhibits for brand new stuff like clouded leopards."

How could anyone be blind to the glory of having clouded leopards? I contemplated various responses, but they weren't going to mean a thing to a bird keeper.

He unrolled a scrap of heavy hardware cloth and I tugged on two corners to help straighten it out. "You'd think Wallace would care about the perimeter fence," I said. "He has to get the Children's Zoo yard resurfaced because of water damage from the vandals that got through a few weeks ago."

"He should care, but the truth is, Sam and I walked the fence the next day and couldn't find where those kids got in. Usually you can always tell. They cut a hole or smash down the bushes. We didn't find a hole big enough for a person, even a skinny kid." Calvin flattened the wire carefully and bent the edges back to eliminate sharp points. "I wonder who that was and what they thought they were doing messing around at the kids' zoo."

He started fastening the patch over the hole the raccoon presumably used. "A new perimeter fence is next on the schedule after the Asia exhibit is up, but I haven't heard boo about new bird construction. They better start planning, or I'm going to the city council about it."

I handed him pliers and baling wire as needed, a familiar role from working with my father on house projects. "Um, while we're planning better bird exhibits, can we ask for shift cages for the eagle and the other raptors?"

"You bet your Great-Aunt Fanny. I told Wallace to get us a way to manage that eagle properly or ship her to someplace that can." He spoke with heat and looked up to see how I reacted.

I nodded and had the sense to keep quiet.

Calvin finally straightened up, stretching his back to indicate we were done. "You did a nice job lassoing that thing."

I almost dropped the pliers.

"I expect you weren't a bad cat keeper," he added.

That left me flummoxed. Was he saying I was good with cats, but crappy with birds? I gathered up tools and scraps of wire and followed him back to the Penguinarium.

At lunchtime, I looked around the café. The person I wanted wasn't there. I walked through the steady rain to Felines. A few seconds standing and listening in the hallway told me that Linda was cleaning the small cats. I said hi to Raj and the leopards and sat down in the kitchen. Linda had made changes. The Gary Larson cartoons were gone. A framed poster hung from a nail, a still life of luscious yellow pears and droopy purple flowers. Two beautiful hand-built cups with an iridescent blue-green glaze sat by the sink.

Linda came in after a few minutes, sturdy and cheerful in her uniform. She'd cropped her chestnut hair even shorter and added a third earring to her right ear. "Hey, good to see you. Where's your lunch?" She pulled hers out of the fridge, a bowl of cottage cheese covered with chopped fruit. It looked like parrot food.

"I'll stop by the café later. Part of Rick's life insurance came. I can't figure out what to do with it and thought I'd ask you."

"Put it in the bank. Should I make coffee? Was it a lot of money?"

"Coffee would be good. The glaze on the cups is wonderful." I pulled out a chair and sat down. "It's only the first installment, but it's a lot. For me, anyway. It's in the credit union."

"I'm working on bowls to match the cups. Why don't you buy a house?" She activated the coffeemaker, another new feature— I'd always used a cone. She sat down opposite me.

I fiddled with the cup. "Don't know if I could afford that in L.A. Houses are for millionaires down there."

"The L.A. job is for real?"

"Not yet."

"I can see why you'd want a fresh start, but I would really miss you. You're the one person who helped me out when I was new. I haven't forgotten those first months."

"You don't need any help. You know what you're doing."
Still, it was good to hear.

Linda settled in to her lunch. "Wish *I* could afford a house.
With a nice garage or basement for a kiln."

So much for the amiable windup. Time for the curve ball.
"Linda, you worked the night shift the night Rick died, right?"
I watched her open face go cautious.

"Yeah. Diego asked for the night off. His daughter starred in
a musical at her high school, one of the brides for seven brothers.
He wanted to go on opening night. I didn't mind doing Diego
the favor and the money was nice, but night work half kills me.
Sorry, bad choice of words." She eyed me warily. "Everyone knows
all this. I told the police and Wallace and…everyone."

Linda got up and poured the coffee. She pulled crummy
low-fat milk out of the fridge.

I added milk and sipped. Not too bad. "I got sent home after
my interview and I wasn't paying much attention. I'm trying to
piece it together. So when were you here that night?"

"I punched in at 4:00 PM and out at 12:30. I got back at
7:30 AM for the day shift. I was supposed to work Primates; I
walked by the lions. You know the rest." She crossed her arms
over her chest. "You want to know if I saw anything that night.
The police asked me, and Wallace asked me, and Mr. Crandall
asked me, and Denny asked me, and I told them all no. You asked
me twice when you first came back. Remember? I didn't see a
damn thing, not until I saw the body first thing in the morning.
I don't think Rick showed up until after I'd left."

I nodded. "I wondered how the schedule had worked. Diego
said you were on that night, but I saw you in the morning. Pulling
your jacket over Rick." We were both silent for a minute.

Linda's eyes went unfocused. "The lions were wild for days.
They looked at me like they'd finally figured it out and we
couldn't fool them any longer. Creepy."

I thought about what the lions had figured out and shivered.
"You never mentioned that before."

"I shouldn't have now. They've calmed down. Spice's training is back on track."

"Linda, I have to ask you this. Did Rick come to the zoo to meet you that night?"

Linda's eyebrows went up and she stared straight at me, green eyes wide, a spoonful of chopped banana halfway to her mouth. "Meet me? Oh. As in 'show up for reasons of sweaty passion?' Oh, Iris. No, he didn't do any such thing. If he had, it sure wouldn't have been with me. You can let that one go."

"Why not you?" I asked stubbornly. "You liked each other. You're not in a relationship."

"Well, I didn't. He didn't, at least not with me. It didn't happen. For one thing, I was too busy and too beat." She looked at me with pity and dismay.

When I didn't nod acceptance, she jabbed at her cottage cheese uncomfortably. "Iris, hello? Have you ever known me to have a boyfriend? Look at me."

"How would I know about your private life? You never talk about it." She waited. I did look at her. "I never understood why you whacked off that fabulous red hair. Most women would kill for it. Guys love…" I wound down to silence.

I'd known Linda for over two years, trained her on Felines. She was my best zoo buddy, her and Hap. And I hadn't known… "Okay. You're telling me you're gay."

"Queer as a three dollar bill. Don't feel too left out—I didn't figure it out myself until a couple of months ago." She was still waiting, those green eyes steady on my face.

"What?" Lord, I could be dim. "Hey, I'm not going to demand my socks back and scream if you touch me. Relax."

She didn't, not quite. "You don't have to go announcing anything."

"Of course not. Look, I'm a little distracted. Not at my best, friend-wise."

"I'd want to know what happened to Rick if I were in your shoes. I want to know in *my* shoes. I can't believe that Rick was up here for romance, or sex, or whatever. He was probably checking

out something over at Reptiles. His death was traumatic—
anybody would be upset for a long time. He cared a lot for you,
that's why he had all that life insurance."

"Maybe so. Or maybe it was just a good salesman."

"You aren't being fair to Rick. And Iris, like I said before,
our health insurance plan probably covers grief counseling. You
ought to look into it. It should help you move on and not get
stuck in grief."

"I'll get unstuck when I know what happened. I can't live
with not knowing."

Another dead end. I couldn't let it go. "You were close to
him, pulling your jacket over him. Did he smell like whiskey or
beer?"

"That's a very weird question." Linda pushed the last of her
lunch away, looking ill.

"He was drunk and there was a whiskey bottle nearby. It's
puzzled me—he drank beer."

"He smelled like scotch. Iris, I don't think…"

I interrupted before she shut this down. "Did you see George
that night?"

"Yeah." This was easier for her. "He puttered over to the
Commissary in his cart and wanted to chat for hours instead of
keeping an eye on things."

"No one else? Wallace, Denny, Mr. Crandall?"

"No. I told you that. The place was deserted."

"So yours was the only car in the parking lot? Yours and
George's? What about Rick's truck?"

"George takes the bus. Rick's truck wasn't there. I'd have
noticed." Something flickered on her face and was gone.

"What?"

She looked hesitant, then trapped. "Nobody ever asked me
about the parking lot. I just remembered I saw a motorcycle. It
wasn't there when I came in, but when I left, I looked around
for a coyote that Diego said had been hanging around the lot. I
saw a motorcycle, over by the shrubbery on the edge."

"Scaly dragon eye painted on the tank?" I was clutching the cup.

"Well, yeah. Yeah, I did see that."

"Hap's, then. Was he around?" I tried for a relaxed voice, less steely.

"I never saw him at the Commissary or anywhere else. I don't think he was here until maybe just before I left. Or else I didn't notice it when I came in." She brightened. "Maybe the bike broke down and he left it there all night. Got someone to take him home."

"I'll ask him. What else?"

"Iris, I feel like I've been strip-mined. That's all I know." She looked tense and unhappy. "It really was an accident. Be careful about accusing people of things."

"Wouldn't dream of it," I said and got up to go. "Linda, thanks. Thanks for putting up with me."

"That's what friends are for." She sounded doubtful. "I really will miss you if you go to L.A." That sounded more sincere.

"I'd miss you, too." I meant it.

I found Hap still at the café, but so were other staff. Our chat about Rick's last night would have to wait. But I didn't plan to wait long.

Calvin and I met in the penguin kitchen at 3:30 to finish the day's reports. Generally I spent it cleaning and he spent it bent over the daily log with a pencil crushed in his grip, printing meticulous details of who had eaten what and how they had behaved today. Generally he ignored me.

This afternoon, the atmosphere was subtly altered. "Hey," he greeted me as he came in. After a few minutes writing, he added, "Take a look at the green band male. He look sluggish to you?"

I pulled my head out of the refrigerator I was wiping down and checked the exhibit. Mr. Green was cruising slowly around the doughnut-shaped pool.

"Looks okay to me. Why?"

"Didn't eat much today. We need to keep an eye on him."

I wiped counters, pleased that he'd asked my opinion, and gathered my nerve. After he'd finished most of the log but we still had ten minutes before day's end, I spent some of the credit I'd earned raccoon-wrestling. "You still think that heat lamp was set up by a kid fooling around? I've been wondering about it."

"I have no idea." He didn't look tense.

"Suppose it was set deliberately. Who at the zoo would know how to do that?"

"Lots of people, I suppose. Especially Maintenance guys. Why would anybody do such a thing?"

"I'm just asking. Wallace isn't the only one worrying about accidents—I could have been killed. Or you."

He put the pencil down and tidied up the papers. Looking at them, not me, he said, "Mishaps—accidents—happen. Tragedies happen. Lots of time you never do find out why. You have to go on." Another pause while he got up and put the pencil in a drawer and sat back down. "Southern California's a big change."

I dumped out and rinsed the strainer from the left sink. "True. Makes me nervous. But Wallace wants to get rid of me. He doesn't like the accidents."

"Wallace doesn't have ordinary sense. Man's a fool in a lot of ways."

"Uh, thanks. Do you think he has anything else against me?"

"I have no idea. He used to be a more agreeable person, I'll tell you that. Now he can barely say a civil word to anyone except the vet and Mr. Crandall, so don't think you're getting special treatment."

He had a point there. "How long have you worked with him?" I sprinkled cleanser in the sink and used a sponge to scrub it.

"I been here over twenty years when Wallace started, same year as Dr. Dawson, about maybe eight years ago. He got the foreman job maybe five, six years ago."

"What was he like when he started?" This was idle curiosity and a simple desire to keep Calvin's slow, heavy voice going.

"Wallace? We got a lot of good work done. My wife liked him. He never married, though I thought he would. That might have taught him some loyalty and manners." Calvin looked at his hands, quiet on the table before him, blunt and battered, with short chipped nails. He gave his square head a small shake. Throwing off old sorrows?

"A guy at the L.A. Zoo said Dr. Dawson was married." I tackled the second sink, which needed a swipe or two.

"He was."

"What happened with his wife?" I washed my hands and scrubbed under the nails to get the fish goo out.

"Up and left him. Surprised everyone, especially him."

I pushed it farther. "I can't see why anybody'd want to leave him. No bad habits that I can see."

Calvin studied me for a minute. "He's a good vet, but nobody's perfect," he said in his gravelly voice. "She was a pretty woman."

I wiped my hands dry on a paper towel and squirted lotion from the bottle on the counter. "Why'd you think she left him?"

Calvin stood, knees cracking, and stretched. He pulled his jacket on. "No idea. About time to head for the barn. I got some pictures from when we first got the penguins. I'll bring 'em in someday."

The clock ticked and he opened the door, walking slow and steady to punch out and drive home. I walked with him, but we were done talking. Had I learned anything new? Perhaps only that Calvin was now willing to talk to me. For a little while. On some topics. And that Dr. Dawson had been dumped. Maybe his tense, formal style was a consequence.

At the Commissary, Hap and Diego were reviewing the night's food deliveries. I punched out and lingered in the little room where dirty uniforms were left and clean uniforms were delivered. Diego left and most of the keepers had come through and departed by the time I came out.

I found him cleaning knives, getting ready to go home. "Hey, Hap. Got a minute?"

"Always got time for you, girl." He looked tired and only mildly interested.

I leaned a hip against the counter. "Hap, I'm trying to fill in some of the blanks for Rick's last night. I wasn't paying attention and I don't remember a lot of things people said. Like, I think you said you were up here late that night, right?"

Hap's face froze for an instant. "I was holding a party, remember? You were there."

"Yeah. But Rick came up here after the party and I thought you did, too."

"Where'd you get that idea?"

A beard and mustache make a face hard to read. I had never noticed that before. "I can't remember if it was something you said or if someone told me they'd seen your bike in the lot."

"Who told you that?" He wiped down his cleaver and hung it on a nail.

"Hap, I said I couldn't remember. I'm trying to sort it all out."

"Benita and I had to clean up after the party. Why the hell would I come up here anyway?" His voice was easy, perhaps a touch nettled.

"I don't know. I'm just asking."

"George or Diego tell you I was here?" Hap's voice was a little sharper.

"No. Diego was off that night. His daughter was in a play. George wouldn't notice a rock concert in the elephant yard."

Thick sandy eyebrows bunched together until the answer came to him. "Linda."

"Hap, I'm not trying to make trouble. I'm trying to find out what happened that night."

"I don't like people making up stories about me, especially not under the circumstances."

"Hap, was your bike in the parking lot that night? Did it break down or did you loan it to someone?"

"I don't loan my bike. Linda needs to explain why she's spreading bullshit. I'll get this unkinked tomorrow morning." He pulled on his scuffed leather jacket and took his helmet off a hook.

"Chill out, Hap. It's a misunderstanding. Don't start a war."

"Yeah. No problem."

It *was* a problem. Hap would confront Linda and she would regret she had told me what she'd noticed. "I'll see you tomorrow."

"Sure thing."

I walked to my truck replaying Hap's words. I'd finally learned something new about Rick's last night. Hap had been at the zoo. I'd bet on it.

It wasn't hard to imagine. Rick and Benita. Rick was strong and fit, not easy to push around, even drunk. But Hap was bigger and experienced in real fighting. Hap picking up Rick, tossing him over the rail. The lions surprised and fascinated, ready...

Hap had lied to me. My stomach roiled.

Not Hap, please not Hap.

Chapter Seventeen

Denny lounged in a corner of Marcie's white sofa, wearing pale jeans, a purple T-shirt from a band I'd never heard of, and a green kerchief tied around his head. He looked surly and piratical, if not criminal. The Princess was a cream and brown oval in his lap, purrs grading into snores. I was surprised to see him serving as heated cat furniture, but surprises were Denny's specialty. Six-Toes was hanging out hopefully in the kitchen watching Marcie cook and The Impossible Kitten was mauling a catnip mouse on the rug, adding a lighthearted note to a sullen ambience. The kitten's white paws looked stylish against a black pelt that at last had a healthy sheen.

Marcie's apartment ran to white, with a shiny brass and glass coffee table, prints by great masters on the walls. Shelves held pretty vases, books arranged by size, pictures of her mother and grandparents. Serene and quiet, clean and careful. I wondered if Marcie would ever put a jukebox in the dining room or paint a wall crimson.

I also wondered if I'd get through the evening without punching Denny. I declined Marcie's offer of wine, the better to keep the lid on. Rational, calm, persuasive—I could do it. I had to do it. Denny was the only source of information left.

He and I grunted at each other, exchanged the legal minimum of small talk, and drank our beer (him) and soda water (me) until Marcie called us to dinner. It seemed we'd taken a vow of silence until the opening bell, which apparently Marcie controlled. She chatted at us until we'd eaten our curried chicken, rice, baked squash, and apple cobbler. This menu seemed unlikely to accommodate his latest dietary obsessions, but Denny ate everything put in front of him.

After clearing the table, we had an awkward time deciding whether the dining room table or the living room was better for serious conversation. Denny and I ended up at opposite ends of the sofa, with Marcie on a chair across from us. Cats distributed themselves, shifting about.

Marcie smiled brightly at us. "Denny, Iris and I are hoping you will tell us everything you can remember about Rick's last couple of days. Iris is trying to piece together what happened."

Denny put his elbow on the sofa back and crossed one ankle over the other knee, aggressively relaxed, looking at Marcie. "That's what this is all about? I figured she was going to sue me for defamation of character. I was going to counter-sue for damages to my van." He wasn't making a joke. "I already told her everything about Rick." He glanced at me. "You think I'm holding back some big news?" The Princess returned to his lap, one tentative paw after another, and curled her old joints into a round cat pillow.

I suppressed an urge to hurl a glass at him. "If you could focus on the question, maybe you could tell me *again* about those last few days?"

Marcie said, "*I* don't know what happened. Tell me." Her hands were relaxed, folded in her lap.

Denny shifted toward her, surliness replaced by patience. The Princess' tail twitched. "He called me up, said he needed a place to stay. I said 'no problem.' It wasn't hard to guess why. He said, could he bring Ranger; I said we'd give it a try with Strongbad."

"The dog's name is Range, not Ranger," I said. "I've told you that a dozen times. And calling a big dog 'Strongbad' is asking for trouble."

"Be quiet," said Marcie.

Wasn't she supposed to be on my side?

Denny put both feet on the floor and straightened up, talking to Marcie. "Didn't work out with the dogs, too much shoving and growling and no good way to keep them separated. So he took Ranger back home. He left him there, picked up a few things and came back."

"Do you have his computer?" After my house was broken into and I couldn't find it, I'd forgotten to ask.

His eyes swept toward me briefly. "It's still at my place. Forgot about it."

"I want to take a look at it. Maybe it's got something to explain that last night," I said.

Denny ignored me.

"What did Rick do when he wasn't at work?" Marcie asked.

"Nothing special. Listened to music, watched TV. We went to a concert once. Did some Net surfing."

"What was he looking for on the Internet?" I asked.

"Didn't say." Denny slumped back on the sofa, tapping his foot. "He spent a lot of time getting my printer to work with his PC."

"Was he drinking while he stayed with you?" I asked.

"Not that I saw. Maybe a beer. I didn't really notice."

"Well, he sure got lit that last night. Was he drinking at the party after I left?"

"No. You two were gone a long time. Marcie and I talked."

Marcie nodded, all attention.

Denny hunched forward, coiling into tension. The Princess stuck out a paw and hooked a claw into his jeans at the thigh. "Rick came back to the party and took off. Just grabbed his jacket and left. Iris didn't even come back for hers." He unhooked the paw without looking down. "I went around to all the bars and liquor stores near the zoo with Rick's picture from the paper, that article they did on his death."

"And?" Marcie asked, still sitting with her back straight, hands in her lap, perfectly composed.

"Nobody remembered him. Nobody remembered selling him any beer or anything."

I was impressed at Denny's initiative—and still baffled. "I checked the Vultures' Roost. He hadn't been in for a few days before he died. Did he drink at your place?"

"I don't think so. I had some beer in the fridge and half a bottle of vodka. They're still there. I think he went straight to the zoo after the party. It wouldn't make sense to drive all the way to my place first."

Looking at Marcie while he talked to me or about me—it was getting annoying. Did he still think I'd hit Rick with a rock and dumped him in the moat?

"The paper said that Rick died between one and four in the morning. Before that, he got tanked *some*where," I insisted.

Denny dumped The Princess on the floor and stood up. She stalked stiffly to her bed, radiating elderly Siamese annoyance. Denny started pacing, engaged at last, filling the room with restless tension. "There's lots of places he could get a bottle. What I want to know is, what did Iris tell him?"

"Tell him?" I didn't get it. "We talked. About his drinking, whether to get divorced. We decided to give it another try."

"There's another possibility we could explore. I'm not saying it's true, just something I've been thinking about."

He had his back to me.

"What would that be?" Marcie asked.

"I'm thinking it's possible Iris drop-kicked him same as she did me and isn't coming clean about it. Maybe she tells him the two of them are through forever, says it was no good from Day One and it's his fault."

I could feel heat rising in my face. "Where do you get off, calling me a liar?"

Denny wasn't done. "Here's Rick, torn up good, because he was kicking himself for wrecking the home scene, trying to pull it back together, and she rips him a new one. He gets a bottle, goes to the zoo because he doesn't want to see me or anyone else. Iris convinced him he's a juicehead and a negative-energy loser, so what else is he to do? He really tanks up—codeine for the soul, you know?"

"Denny, this is psychotic raving. You are out of—"

Denny plowed on. "And then the lions start looking like a solution. She'd find him in the morning, and everyone would know it was her fault. Only no one thought that. Everyone was sorry for her instead, and before that wears off, she starts acting like she's trying to find out how he died."

I stood up, knees shaking, ears ringing. "Denny, get out. Get out of here. Now."

He looked at me at last, his jaw stubborn. "It's a possibility, that's all. I don't *want* it to be true, but it fits the facts. Prove I'm wrong. I'm listening."

"Prove what? That you are certifiable? That any friendship you had with Rick doesn't count if you have a conspiracy theory to ride? That blaming me is all that matters?"

"Iris, sit down. It's important to get this resolved." Marcie's calm was evaporating fast, her voice going breathy.

"I'm leaving," I said, my voice coming from some cold, tight place far away. "Do you want help getting rid of him?"

"No, no. It's all right." She was standing, too, fingers spread in agitation.

In my truck, I leaned my forehead against the steering wheel and turned the rage loose, snarling curses at him, close to sobbing. Denny was nobody I'd ever understood, a vicious paranoid. I was pathetic. Nothing I tried worked. I might as well buy a ticket to L.A. and give up now.

I started the truck and headed home. Rain slicing through the half-open driver's window cooled my face, but my hands were clenched on the steering wheel.

Reason crept back, ready to flee if the tidal wave of anger swept in again.

Denny was never going to help. He was locked into blaming me for Rick's death, still smarting from our abrupt breakup a year ago. When we had lived together, he'd seemed to be in a parallel dimension, impervious to anything I said or did. He'd looked more disconcerted and miffed than heart-broken when I told him to move out. I had not understood his vulnerability at all, or his bitterness. He would not be an ally. My sense of loss surprised me. I'd always thought we'd make it to friendship, if only he weren't so obnoxious. What a fool I was.

At home with the dogs, I remembered Rick's computer. What else did I have to work with? Nothing. I rounded up the scattered anger for fuel. I wasn't quitting because of Denny.

Marcie answered on the second ring.

"Marcie, don't say my name. Is Denny still there?"

"Yes. What's up?"

"Keep him there as long as you can. I'm going out to his place to get Rick's computer and take a look around for anything else Rick might have left."

"Let's talk about this later. I think we can come up with something better."

"Just do your best. I'll call you when I get back."

How to handle Strongbad? Denny's dog was big, young, and untrained. Unruliness didn't bother Denny. Strongbad would be set on defending hearth and home. I needed a distraction to get past him, and two possibilities wagged their tails at my knees. Winnie was a good choice—Strongbad was an intact male. Winnie was never going into heat, but he wouldn't know that and would be interested in making her acquaintance. I clipped on her leash, generating considerable enthusiasm for an excursion. Range waited for his leash, dancing with his front feet, and whuffling through his lips. He was a poor candidate; best to leave him behind. When he had stayed at Denny's with Rick, the two male dogs had never reached a truce. Brown eyes in an eager face won out over common sense and he came, too.

Denny lived thirty minutes east of my house, on a gravel road in a neighborhood of decaying wood-frame bungalows with corrugated metal storage sheds behind them. The house on the left looked deserted; the house on the right had a spotlight on the driveway, illuminating a drift boat on a trailer. Denny's house had a gravel pullout instead of a driveway, a sagging porch mostly concealed by runaway ivy, and no porch light.

Strongbad opened up full volume when I tried the front door, which was locked. I searched for a key on the ledge above the door and under the mat. No luck. Winnie and Range preceded me to the backyard, sniffing and pulling on their leashes, having a great time. No rain here, but the ground was soft and the air was damp. The back door was boarded shut. That left the windows, which required two hands. Strongbad lunged and bellowed at the window nearest to the drift boat. The neighbor hadn't come out to yell at me, and the light was better on that side. Maybe nobody was home next door.

I tied Range and Winnie to a rhododendron bush and tested the window. It gave a little. Strongbad reared his forefeet against it and barked his black and tan head off inches from me. I stood back and rethought. I'd met the dog once. He wasn't a nut case, just young and undisciplined. Hard to predict what he'd do if he got out.

I considered dropping this project and heading home. Not an option. A bite was something I'd have to risk.

It was hard to get any purchase against the double-hung window, but I shoved at it and got a little more movement. With a third leash in my hand, I clawed at the bottom of it and got it up an inch, increasing the Strongbad volume considerably. The plan was that I would calm him down before the window was open enough for him to take a chunk out of me, or he would focus on Range and Winnie, I would clip on the leash, and… Well, the rest would come to me.

I shoved the window up farther and a black muzzle was immediately crammed into the narrow space, the volume dropping to muffled yelps since he couldn't open his mouth. I pushed gently to open it barely enough to get my hand in, but Strongbad shoved hard with his nose and the window flew up a couple of feet. "Stay!" I said, reaching for his collar, but the big dog launched himself through space and I missed, fingertips clawing at slick hide. He landed chin first in the mud. Staggering to his feet, he lunged for Range. While grateful my face was still intact, I was alarmed for Range, who was twenty pounds smaller, not as aggressive, and tied up.

I could see only dark blurs, moving fast and sounding like six grizzly bears in a bar fight. Another spotlight came on next door, illuminating three dogs in a vociferous whirlpool of brown and black, with broken rhododendron twigs flying at the ends of two leashes. My dogs wouldn't be tethered victims, but the potential for serious wounds was high for all three.

Strongbad focused on Range and finally got a grip on the skin of his shoulder. He paused to savor the moment and Winnie nailed him on the flank, grabbing skin and muscle and shaking her head ferociously. Range pulled loose and clamped down on Strongbad's neck. I grabbed leash ends, leaves and all, and started pulling, yelling at my dogs to knock it off.

Range was willing to listen and Strongbad had learned caution, but Winnie was keen for blood. I tied Range to a much sturdier branch, not easy with Winnie roaring and lunging against the leash looped around my elbow. Strongbad growled and snarled, working himself up to another try at Range, when the neighbor walked over, spotlighting us with a huge flashlight. He was middle aged, in need of a haircut, in a black T-shirt and jeans. His tennis shoes were untied and he had one hand held behind his back.

"What's going on here?"

"A dog fight. Hold this one while I catch the other one." I thrust Winnie's leash at him. It took him a minute to decide to take the leash, then he had to bring the pistol from behind his back and shove it in his waistband to free a hand.

That was when I realized Denny had arrived. His white van sat in front of the house, driver's door ajar. He stood openmouthed, taking in the snarling dogs, neighbor, the pistol, and me.

"Get your dog," I ordered.

He nodded thoughtfully and started slowly toward Strongbad, who ignored him, full attention on Range.

"Be careful," I warned. "He's pretty excited."

Denny paid no attention and grabbed the big dog's collar. Strongbad shook his head, but didn't snap.

With the neighbor holding Winnie, I was free to hand Denny the spare leash. He clipped it on as Strongbad pulled toward Range, barking and growling with fresh enthusiasm, now that he had his own team.

"Thanks for your help," I told the neighbor, taking Winnie's leash. "Denny said I could stay here, but I couldn't find the key. He said his dog wouldn't be any problem. Boy, was he wrong about that!"

"That dog barks day and night."

Denny towed Strongbad closer to the house to inspect the open window. He seemed stunned. "You broke in. You came here and broke in."

So much for covering with the neighbor. "You wouldn't talk to me. All you do is blame me. You won't *help*."

He looked at the dogs, back at the window, and at me. *"Good freakin' grief,"* he muttered to himself. "Unbelievable."

I didn't recognize it, but it was the sound of a paradigm shift.

"You want me to call the police?" The neighbor sounded genuinely curious.

Denny noticed him for the first time. "What good would that do?"

"Is everyone all right?" It was Marcie, stepping carefully through the dark and gravel, eyes huge, arms folded protectively across her chest. Her little blue Saturn was tucked in behind Denny's van.

"What are *you* doing here?" Denny asked.

"You wouldn't stay so I followed you," Marcie said.

Winnie leaned on her leash toward Strongbad and opened up with a volley of frustrated barking, saving Marcie from a real explanation.

The neighbor looked at Marcie and then Denny. "Son, you got a lot of woman trouble, but at least they're pretty women. Don't let's have anymore ruckus tonight." He clicked off his flashlight and shuffled toward his house, shoelaces flapping. He opened his door and turned to look back at us. A voice from inside said, "Earl, what on earth was that all about?" The second spotlight went out and we heard the door close on his reply.

Marcie, Denny, and I looked at each other in the dim light.

"Iris, of all the impulsive, thoughtless things you've done, this has to take the prize," Marcie said. "I can't believe this. That man might have shot you. The dogs could all be injured. You could end up in *jail*."

No point in arguing with her. She was too rattled to listen and of course she was right. "Let's go inside where we can see and check the dogs," I said.

Denny unlocked the front door and turned on the lights. A mounted deer head on an end table gazed toward the ceiling with its antlers pointed threateningly at the couch. The room was a stoned garage sale of odd chairs; stacks of comic books; a TV on the floor connected by a long string to its remote control, also on the floor; a life-size cardboard cutout of Spiderman with a sweatshirt draped over it. Denny swept his battered couch clear of clothes and magazines so Marcie could sit on threadbare maroon fabric.

He towed his dog toward the kitchen, but stopped and stared at bright blood on his hand. I made Marcie hold my dogs while Denny and I checked out Strongbad. The hair on his back was up and he was anxious to resume the fray, but not hysterical. Blood was dripping steadily from a nick on one ear. He kept flipping his head, spraying red droplets everywhere. I felt his neck and flanks and found another cut where Winnie had grabbed him, but it was barely oozing. He didn't limp, but soreness was likely tomorrow. Denny got a bandage and we put it on the ear to stop the mess. Strongbad hated it and kept trying to scrape it off, still growling steadily at Range and Winnie.

"If you take him to a vet, I'll pay the bill," I said. "I'm sorry he got hurt." My mother's training reared its head. "And that your rhododendron got busted up," I added lamely.

"He's tough," Denny said.

I gave Range and Winnie a quick inspection. Both still had eyes, legs, a tail. No blood, no obvious limps.

Now what?

"Denny, I never would have done this if you hadn't…" I started.

"Sit down, both of you," Marcie said. "You both have some apologizing to do."

Denny obediently dragged a chair toward her, leaving Strongbad enough slack in his leash to stalk stiff-legged toward Range.

"Denny, hold him. I'll get my dogs out of here." I shut them in the truck with the windows rolled down a couple of inches and returned to face the music.

We sat facing each other once again in a living room.

Marcie crossed her arms over her chest again, but not in self-protection. Her soft face went stern. "Iris, apologize for breaking and entering and for risking the dogs. That was outrageous and irresponsible."

"Oh, I don't know," Denny said.

He let the silence sit for a moment before going on. "You never would have risked the dogs if you weren't being straight with me. I got carried away. You wouldn't maul Rick and he wouldn't crater himself. I couldn't think of anything better, and I was still kind of mad at you for dumping me so you could take up with Rick. Marcie's helping me get centered with it."

"Iris still has to apologize," Marcie said.

"Okay. I apologize. Now can you get Denny to talk to me?" I sagged back in my hard wood chair, very tired.

Marcie did not look appeased. She ran both hands through her hair and shook her head. "You two don't make anything easy."

Denny retreated to what I assumed was the bathroom. Strongbad got to his feet, already a little stiff, and followed him, shaking his head.

I looked around for Rick's computer and spotted it parked on a dusty treadle sewing machine in a corner. Marcie joined me. I got her a wooden chair and pulled up a metal stool. On top of a bookcase next to the sewing machine, a box tortoise scrabbled in an old aquarium.

Marcie sat down at the computer and reeled in the mouse dangling by its cord. The computer made a little noise and started to wake up. The dark screen gradually lightened, little icons emerging. "When did you shut Rick's computer off last?" she called.

"I never touched it. I thought it *was* off," Denny called back.

"Nope. Just asleep. Good. The browser's still open from the last time he used it." She moused around.

Denny returned with Strongbad still at his heels, but minus the bandage.

Marcie said she needed to get online. Denny disconnected the phone cord from his own computer, surrounded by towers of old comic books on a card table in a corner, and plugged it into Rick's. She opened a list of recently visited Web sites and clicked on some of them.

"Rick was studying Northwest Native Americans and the laws around ancient remains," I summarized. "And alcoholism." At last, promising new information. "That's why I found CDs of Native American music in his truck. He must have bought them while he was staying with you, Denny. The packages weren't open yet. When anything caught his interest, he looked for music related to it. Did he mention the CDs?"

Denny shook his head.

"How about Chinook Indians or alcoholism?"

Denny shrugged.

"Nothing at all? Didn't you guys ever talk?" I pressed.

Denny shrugged again. "We talked some about you."

Before I could follow up on this unsettling possibility, Marcie said, "Let's see if he has any email." She pointed and clicked. He had eleven new messages, aside from solicitations to purchase a counterfeit watch and increase the size of his penis. Denny pulled up a chair and we jammed in together, hunching over to catch the screen at the right angle. Two were postings about reptiles from a list group he subscribed to. Three had to do with animal training. Older emails were personal letters from friends at other zoos, asking or answering questions about animal-related matters.

Marcie took a look at his out mailbox. He'd sent two messages the day before he died. Both were to universities, asking whom he could call for information about prehistoric Native Americans of our area.

"That's all I can see to check," she said at last. "Anything else?"

Denny and I shook our heads. Marcie was way ahead of both of us.

We took a break from cybersnooping to search the house for anything Rick left behind. We found a T-shirt from a zoo-keeper conference and a pair of jeans. I folded them up neatly as dammed-up grief threatened to spill over. I pushed it down—not here, not now.

"Denny, you said he'd hooked up your printer. Where's that?" I asked.

It was on a card table in the corner, hidden under newspapers. The output tray was empty, but a paper grocery bag serving as a wastebasket was more productive. I found two crooked printouts from the archeology sites. Blurry ink offered details of the Native American Graves Protection and Repatriation Act. "The paper jammed, and he had to reprint these. When I saw him that last night, he had a manila envelope in the truck, full of papers. I bet it was stuff he'd printed from these sites. He didn't say anything about Indians when we talked in the truck. Did this have something to do with why he went to the zoo?"

Denny rocked his chair back on its hind legs. He had that intent look again and he started tapping his foot. "Why is he so interested in Native Americans all of a sudden, right before he dies? And why didn't he talk about it? He never said a word. Here's a theory."

"Oh, brother. Here we go," I muttered.

"You got a theory?" Denny inquired acidly. "Then you go first."

"Go ahead, please," said Marcie.

"It's the construction site. Rick found old artifacts, a village or grave. He read up on the Antiquities Act, like we saw on one of those sites. Everybody knows you can't mess with something like that, big federal penalties. State, too, maybe. So that would shit-can the new exhibit, right? So he keeps it a secret…no, why would he? Maybe he tells Wallace and Wallace asks him to keep quiet about it."

"Would he tell the director instead of the foreman?" Marcie asked.

Denny and I shook our heads. Mr. Crandall was either in his office with somebody important or else off to meetings.

Denny focused on the far distance and tapped his left index finger in time with his right foot. Marcie and I waited, energy ebbing out of me.

Denny got up and started to pace. Strongbad sat up, watching the action. "That's it. He tells Wallace, Wallace figures it will stop the construction. He gets Rick to shut up about it, then offs him when he gets the chance. Then he has to shut up Iris 'cause she's asking around. That would explain the accident in the aviary."

Of course he knew about that. Jackie would tell him if no one else did.

Denny nodded, pacing. "I bet," he mused in my direction, "Rick would have told you about whatever he found if you hadn't been fighting. All this might not have happened."

"Thanks for rubbing my face in it. Incidentally, your theory doesn't hold up. How could it possibly be worth it to Wallace to murder somebody because a zoo project gets delayed?"

"That would require a financial motive, a big one. Or he needed to cover up something else," Marcie said.

"I'll find out," Denny said, spinning on his heel and striding back.

The wisp of an idea dissipated into sleepiness. "Denny, shut up and hold still. I want to think." The construction site. A metal wheel leaned up on a gate. Mud. I shook myself. I was looping out into space like Denny.

"Iris, spit it out," Marcie demanded. "I can see the wheels turning."

Denny sat down next to her and threw a leg over the sofa arm.

"Somebody opened the water valve at the Children's Zoo a night or two after Rick died," I started slowly. "They removed that heavy wheel that shuts off the water and leaned it up against the gate, so that all the petting zoo animals could get out and away from the water shooting everywhere." I walked through the event in my head, trying to pull the fragments into a whole. "Diego is busy at the front end of the zoo. The security guard, too. Right—that same night, somebody dragged the elephant area's hose someplace where it got muddy, like over to the construction site."

Denny was up pacing again. "Sam bitched all day about his hoses. And that same day, the bulldozer gets stuck in the mud."

"Yes! Because somebody hosed the hell out of the construction area and it was a lot soggier than the driver thought it would be." Now I was up and pacing. "Destroying evidence or washing it out so it could be removed." At last, pieces fitting together. "Rick finds artifacts in the mud. The killer offs Rick, checks out the mud the next day. Maybe can't find anything, but worries about more construction activity turning up bones or whatever, comes back at night, creates a distraction, hoses it to reveal anything else, removes whatever he or she finds."

"Plausible, but couldn't anybody have done it?" Marcie asked. "Anybody could climb the fence."

"Calvin says vandals usually cut a hole in the fence to get in," I said. "He checked and couldn't find anything. A zoo insider would have keys to get in. And would know about the water wheel."

Denny nodded. "Definitely zoo staff."

Definitely? *Possibly* was as far as I would go, but I let it pass. "The animals were let out to delay Diego longer while he rounded them up, or maybe whoever it was didn't want them to get wet and chilled from the spray."

"Right," said Denny, "a killer who doesn't want the dear little goats and pony to catch a cold."

Made sense to me. Marcie nodded. Denny shrugged, conceding the point. Murder is one thing; neglecting an animal is another. More evidence for a zoo staffer.

"That gets the candidate pool down to—what?—fifty people?" Marcie calculated.

"It's Wallace." Denny was undeterred. "He suspects I've figured it out and that's why he's trying to get rid of me."

"Trying to get rid of you?" Marcie inquired.

"He won't. He's not going to bluff me into quitting."

I wondered what he meant. I hadn't heard any gossip about Wallace gunning for Denny's departure, but maybe the foreman was really cleaning house. Not just me?

"This would be more convincing if we actually knew what Rick found," I said. "Where is it? Did he have it with him when he went to the zoo? Did whoever killed him take it or did he hide it somewhere?"

"Yes," Marcie said. "Where's the potshards or tibias or arrowheads?"

"He probably went to the zoo to meet the killer and turn it over," Denny said. "We'll never find anything."

Oh. "Um, I have a possibility." I rubbed my face. It had been a long day and brain fade was returning. "Denny, you remember when I cleared out Rick's locker? The snake shed in the jar and the little tooth in the mud? I thought it was a deer incisor, but maybe not. Maybe he found a skull and stored it in his locker and the tooth fell off. It was small and hard to see."

"A skull," Denny said. He strode briskly from one side of the living room to the other like a pendulum. "Ancient gravesite. That's got to be it. We need to get that tooth to an anthropologist. Wow! This could be another duel in the courts like over Kennewick Man. Tribes versus scientists, rebury the remains or study them."

Marcie's head bobbed enthusiastically.

"Uh, that might not work out," I told them.

"Why not?" Marcie asked.

"I don't have it anymore." I gnawed on my lower lip. "Wallace said I had to turn it over to the Education volunteers. I didn't intend to, but he caught me on the way out of the zoo and took the jar."

We all stared at each other, wide-eyed. We had a real candidate as Rick's murderer.

"Forget ever seeing that tooth again," Denny finally said. "We'll have to do without it."

I needed time to think. Denny wanted time to find out whether Wallace had a financial connection to the construction. Marcie wanted to go to bed.

"Let's not get carried away," I said. "I'm beat. Let's talk tomorrow. Marcie, thanks for dinner. And everything. Do you want to follow me out, or can you find your way?"

She said she could find her way. I stood up and started for the door.

Denny said, "Night, Iris."

That was all, but "Iris" stopped me. Not "Ire." "Hey, Denny. Thanks for helping."

"Glad to oblige," he said.

"Sleep well," was all I could think to say, and left them.

The dogs were subdued on the ride home, but I felt a trickle of elation. Denny was on the team, his suspicions and energy no longer focused on my perfidy. That was a considerable relief. I had no stomach for mutual loathing.

And at last I had something to work with, some idea of what Rick might have been up to. The pieces might not fit together the way we'd outlined it, but at least there *were* pieces.

And, so far, none of them included Hap.

I carried the little bundle of Rick's clothing into the house. Range forgot his good manners and reared up, forefeet at my waist, to shove his nose into them. I checked—they did still smell of Rick, smelled like warm arms and good music and sex. My tears were only salty, lacking the old bitterness.

Chapter Eighteen

"What's up?" I'd clocked in a little late, but Calvin always got to the Penguinarium first. He should have been chatting with the penguins or laying out fish for their vitamin amendments. Instead he was standing at the low gate between the kitchen and the pool, hands clasped behind his back, watching the birds. They were hungry and braying at him, but Calvin just stood there.

The little silence gave me time to switch focus.

Ever since my bare feet had hit the rug next to my bed, I'd been sorting through the implications of Wallace murdering my husband. Over coffee and cereal, I'd concluded he was strong enough, especially if Rick was falling-down drunk. He could have let Raj out on me and he could have set the booby trap with the heat lamp. On the drive to work, I'd added Wallace pushing me to apply for a job elsewhere. Walking to the Penguinarium, I'd concluded that the scenario wasn't perfect. Keeping the construction project going didn't seem like a sufficient motive. Wallace breaking into my house made no sense, but perhaps it was truly unrelated and someone else entirely. There was still the problem of Rick drinking whiskey instead of beer.

Wallace was an unpleasant man, rough-tongued and ungenerous, but I felt no satisfaction in his possible guilt. At a fundamental level, I'd trusted him, as I did all my coworkers, trusted in his basic decency and his commitment to the zoo. Zookeeping had its dangers and we relied on each other. The thought of him picking up Rick and throwing him to the lions was nauseating. I'd been feeling that way often.

"Anything wrong?" I asked.

This time Calvin turned when I spoke and pointed with his chin toward a black plastic bag on the floor by the fridge. I squatted down and opened it. The black and white corpse, already stiff and dull-eyed, had a green band on the right wing.

"Ah, shit. Mr. Green," I said, running a finger gently down the smooth, dense little feathers on his back. The bare skin under the bird's eye was pale, not the healthy pink it had been. Yesterday Calvin had mentioned that the penguin was off his feed. He had looked fine to me, but Calvin had seen more. The birds were not interchangeable ornaments to him; each one was an individual with a personality and its own habits. Just as Raj was an old friend of mine, Mr. Green was an old friend of his.

I closed the bag and joined Calvin at the gate. "Mrs. Green okay?" She was at the far end of the island, away from the noisy crowd in front of us.

"She was standing by. Tried to keep me from taking him." He turned away from the gate. "I should have talked Dawson into putting him on antibiotics. We should have caught him up and made sure he was hydrated."

"Putting in a stomach tube is stressful. It might have done more harm than good. Maybe it was his time and nothing would help. Nobody's fault."

"He was one of the first we got here," Calvin said, "probably the oldest. I brought pictures today to show you. Wouldn't you know, on the day he dies."

"Let's do that this afternoon." Like a wake, I thought. Maybe that would help us feel less bummed out.

Calvin nodded and shook his shoulders loose, ready to get back to work after allotting a moment for grief. "I got to take him up to the hospital. Neal's last appointment with Dr. Dawson."

"Neal?"

"We named him after the vet, before we had the wing bands." He picked up the small bundle. I could see the head flop, the sharp beak threatening to poke through the plastic. Calvin carried him out.

The rest of the morning was feeding and cleaning, a familiar routine at last, the awkwardness and inefficiencies worked out. Pleasure in new competence, sorrow for the dead penguin, and anxious musings about Wallace eddied and churned.

Denny caught me on the way to lunch. "Ire, I want you to come talk to the foreman at the construction site."

"Now? I'm hungry." I was "Ire" again.

He was already striding off, assuming I'd follow. I trailed after him, wondering if feeling irked at Denny would ever change. It *was* an improvement on fury.

He led me to the future Asian Experience. A front loader sat idle off to the side. It looked clean and had different appendages from the machine that used to be half-sunk in the mud. Erosion control barriers, long sausages of straw-stuffed mesh, snaked across the mud. A slight dark-haired man in a white hard hat sat on the running board of a mammoth green crew-cab truck. He spooned up soup from a plastic bowl in his lap, intent on not spilling. A stainless steel thermos sat at his feet. Denny and I stopped and stood looking down at him.

"Mark, this is Iris," Denny said. "I want you to tell her what you told me."

"Pleased to meet you," Mark said, looking a little alarmed. He set his soup bowl on the running board and stood up to shake my hand. He was about five foot eight, slender, with neat, sharp features in an intelligent face. Maybe it didn't require brawn to manage a construction site.

Denny waited a heartbeat. "Tell her about Wallace."

Mark looked definitely wary.

I gave him my best nonthreatening smile. "I'm Iris Oakley. I work in Birds. You guys have made a lot of progress here. What happens next—pouring cement?" Give the guy a minute to think.

Denny answered for him. "If the weather holds, they'll pour next week. Nobody found any bones or artifacts, as far as Mark knows. Tell her about Wallace."

"You've met our fearless leader?" I asked, working the smile again. "I hope he's not interfering with your work. Wallace gives micromanagement a bad name."

Mark managed a faint smile of his own. He looked at Denny, then me, and seemed to make a decision to get this over with. "Denny asked me whether Kevin Wallace has any connections to the project. I mean, except for his job at the zoo. This is Huddleston Construction." His wave encompassed the mud and machines. "I told him that John Huddleston is married to Wallace's sister. That's all. It's not illegal or unethical."

Denny nodded several times. "Thanks, Mark. I owe you."

Mark looked as if he seriously wished he'd kept his mouth shut. His eyes shifted, relief on his face. "Hap, how's it going?"

I looked over my shoulder.

"Same old, same old," Hap said. To us, "Checking out the field of dreams?" He turned back to Mark. "That front loader running right?"

"Yeah. Thanks for the help. My guy is useless for electrical."

"He'll learn," Hap said. "I like getting my hands on big iron."

Denny and I watched on the sidelines. Hap was his usual relaxed self, not full of injured innocence. He looked twice the size of Mark. I wondered if he had accosted Linda yet.

"I'd love to see that 'Vette you guys dropped the engine into," Mark said, slurping soup where he stood.

"I'll see what I can do," Hap said. "Gotta go."

He swung around on his heel and left, broad shoulders moving with his steady stride.

Mark looked surprised, possibly wondering, as I was, why Hap walked a considerable distance out of his way to join a friendly conversation, only to depart almost immediately.

"C'mon, Ire," Denny said. "I've got to get back to work, but I want to talk first. See you around, Mark." He walked fast and spoke fast, intense and certain. "His sister's husband got the contract for the site preparation and a lot of the cement work on the new exhibit. Think 'kickback.' It's got to be a major conflict of interest. I really, really doubt the zoo board knows about the connection."

"Maybe the board does know and doesn't care," I said. "Maybe there isn't any kickback."

"No way. It's got to be against some policy or other. And it gives Wallace a financial motive to keep the construction going."

"I'd say it gives Huddleston a motive to keep the construction going. A legitimate motive."

"Maybe they're in this together."

Left to himself, Denny was certain to promote this to everyone who would listen. At the door to Reptiles, I said, "Denny, keep quiet about the connection. This might be important and it might not. We don't have any evidence. We need to work on this."

"Let's meet tonight."

Not my first choice, but I didn't see any way out of it. "Fine. Come to my place."

"Yeah, that should work better than last night. Marcie cleaned up the blood."

I winced. "Strongbad is okay?"

"He's fine."

"Seven o'clock, my place. And don't say anything."

"Just Marcie. I'll tell Marcie and she can meet us at your place," he said and disappeared into Reptiles.

I looked at the closed door, wondering. He hadn't asked me for her phone number. So maybe he already had it. Last night, I'd left them alone together twice, once at her place and once at his. Marcie and Denny? Unimaginable.

I left to sample the latest culinary biohazard from the café.

I was late and found only two visitors, middle-aged women with ice cream bars. I ordered the hamburger to go—no mayo, double tomato—and started back to Birds. I spotted Jackie leaning against the outside of the Administration building having her post-lunch smoke. She hailed me and I walked over, peeling the wrap off the burger and bracing for another emotional assault.

But she wanted to make peace.

"I'm sorry for what I said about Rick," she said. "I forgot you're kind of fragile right now. It's my allergy pills. Something comes over me when I take them three or four days running."

"Is that so?"

"You got all the bad news anybody can handle. Rick was crazy about you. We all knew that. If anybody would have played around, it would have been you, I suppose, not him."

"Jackie…" I started.

"Now I didn't mean a thing by that. Don't you take me so *seriously*. I'm trying to *apologize,* for Pete's sake."

My mother taught me it was petty to refuse an apology and that feuding ruined the complexion. "Whatever, Jackie. Let it go."

She inhaled with satisfaction. "Good." That out of the way, she launched into her current grievance. "What's the world coming to, anyway?" she said. "I am up to my eyeballs in monthly reports and Mr. Crandall wants me to stop everything and research this complaint from some moronic third-grade teacher about the presentation the Education volunteers did for her class. It was this thing about frogs, and they had the kids croak at each other and hop around."

She paused to take a drag and exhale. I shifted to the upwind side and stuffed maverick tomatoes back into the bun.

"The teacher wants to know if we understand what croaking really means—it's like, hey, baby, I wanna do you. And it's like we're pressuring these kids to have sex. Can you believe it? Frog sex. She thinks the kids will be doing frog sex in the gym showers."

"Uhhh," I said with my mouth full, trying to picture immature humans in amplexus in a shower stall. "I don't think elementary schools have gym showers."

"Whatever. It's as goofy as anything Denny's come up with. Hey, did you know Wallace put him on probation?" This seemed to take the sting out of frog research.

Denny had mentioned Wallace having it in for him. "What happened?"

"He mouthed off at visitors again." Jackie smiled. "You remember when he found those kids poking a peacock with a stick? Had it trapped in a corner with an overhang where it couldn't fly. Now that was an educational experience for those little criminals."

"And this time?"

"Yesterday morning. A mom and her four boys throwing marshmallows at the black bears, in front of the No Feeding sign." She paused to let me picture the scene.

"What'd he do?"

"He told her to quit it. She says the bears love marshmallows. He says, 'If I shoot your kids up with heroin, they'll love it too, same as bears with sugar.' They yelled at each other until Wallace showed up. Put him on probation. Arnie said he'd get Denny a six-pack as a thank-you."

"Denny will survive. He does his job."

"He won't survive if he pisses Wallace off any more. He's always late and he's always keeping things stirred up. That boy has the cutest butt and the squirreliest ideas of anybody here." She stubbed out her cigarette on the side of the building and tossed it into a trash can. "I gotta get back."

I tried the door of the Education Outreach office. Locked.

"No one around today," Jackie said. "That huge woman who giggles might be in about ten o'clock tomorrow. She's the volunteer who's been doing the schools. Can't you picture her hopping? Good grief."

Calvin brought out penguin pictures a half hour before quitting time. I realized, a little late, that he was a shy man and glad to have something to share. We sat at the kitchen table. He handed me a color photo of four people facing the camera in a line. Mr. Crandall had his arm around a smiling dark-haired woman, who in turn had her arm around another man. With a little imagination, he could be Wallace minus the belly, plus a full head of hair. A lean Dr. Dawson smiled to their left, not touching anyone. This amiable group was standing in front of an animal crate. I could see what might be a penguin peering through the wire front.

"That's when we got the first penguins," Calvin said.

"Mr. Crandall looked exactly the same," I observed.

"He don't change, except his hair's grayer. I s'pect he's immortal and he'll run this place forever." It wasn't a rousing endorsement.

"And the woman?"

Calvin took the picture back and peered at it. "That'd be Winona Dawson. That crate there's got the Africans we named after the Dawsons. The names was Wallace's idea, as I recall. Can't remember what zoo we got them from, somewhere's back East. They called them black foot penguins back then. Or jackass penguins. Same thing."

Winona Dawson. She seemed pleased and excited in the photo, looking directly at the camera with shining eyes. Thrilled to be part of the new exhibit? Happy to be hobnobbing with the director, her husband's boss? "What was she like?"

"Nice. A lot of fun."

That wasn't much use. I gave up.

"What's this picture?" I asked.

"That's the pair of them in the new exhibit. And our first chick." I admired pictures of penguins in a bright new exhibit, none of the chipped paint and wear that showed now. There were several adult birds in the picture.

"You must have ordered penguins from all over the country."

He nodded. "We got pairs from maybe three more zoos. I was going out to the airport a lot. Except for the last pair." He shook his head.

"And?"

"That was bad. They came up by truck from California; one of their maintenance staff drove them."

"Problems on the road?"

"No. Weather was fine. It was the crate. The guy who drove the truck was the idiot that knocked it together. Dr. Dawson helped me open it. Nails poking through the bottom, big

—splinters sticking out of the boards. Those birds had their feet all tore up, blood and guano all over them. I thought Dr. Dawson was going to hurt that man in a big way. My heavenly days, he was mad when he saw those birds. If I hadn't been with him, I don't know what would have happened." His shoulders moved. Remembering holding the vet back? "He worked on those birds for weeks, every antibiotic you could name. He saved one of them, the brown band male; the other two died."

"I can't imagine Dr. Dawson losing his temper. He's always been Mr. Self-Control."

"Imagine it," he said flatly. He took another look at the group shot. "I think Dr. Dawson never got over her." He stacked up the photos and slipped them back into their envelope.

He reached for his jacket. "Time to head for the barn."

I pulled out the group photo for a final look. If you didn't know him, young Wallace wasn't that bad looking.

<> <> <>

That evening, I sat in my minimally presentable living room with Marcie and Denny. Marcie was demure on the sofa; Denny was settled into the green recliner, foot twitching. I had dragged in a kitchen chair for myself. I had serious reservations about this Three Musketeers dynamic, but Marcie had brought a terrific chocolate cake with chocolate frosting. That helped considerably.

Marcie summed it up: "We have no evidence. The financial motive is weak. Anybody could have done it."

Denny hung tough on the motive. "The kickbacks are enough. And I'll get more information, now that I know what to look for."

"We have nothing," I said. "You want it to be Wallace because he's threatening your job."

"Because he's worried that I'm on to him."

"No, because you fight with visitors."

"Will you two stop?" Marcie snapped.

The silence gave me a moment to note that I had my own reasons for wanting it to be Wallace—I didn't want it to be Hap.

"Listen, I haven't told you that Hap was at the zoo the night Rick died." I recapped what Linda had told me and Hap had denied.

Denny nodded, not surprised. "Arnie says Diego told him that Hap had been hanging around the zoo late at night."

"Well, that's a reliable chain of hearsay."

Marcie gave me the look.

"It's all blind alleys," I said. "Our only hope is some sort of trap. But we have no bait."

A trap. Now that I'd said it, it sounded like a decent idea. As Marcie had once pointed out, I often learned what I thought by listening to what I said.

Chocolate is a powerful stimulant. A couple more bites and my creativity spiked. "Look, we can lie. We tell Wallace—no, *I* tell Wallace that Rick left a package at Denny's addressed to a university or agency. I took it home and opened it. There's a letter Rick wrote—which is almost true—and some bones and arrowheads that he got from the construction site. Then I ask Wallace what I should do with them."

"He'll tell you to bring them to him," Marcie said.

I scraped up traces of frosting and licked the fork. "I'll do it as a voice message. I say I'm going out of town Friday. I can't deal with it until I get back, but I want to know if I should mail the package to the university or not."

"And then you hide and watch," Denny said.

"Right. I do the preparation tomorrow, get my dogs out of the house. Then we see if Wallace takes the bait. He knows where I live—it's on my personnel records. He comes to lift the stuff and we know we're guessing right. Or he doesn't and we know that's not it."

"Or he brings a gun and shoots you dead," Marcie contributed.

Denny gave that a thought. "If he killed Rick, he'll kill you," he agreed.

"Maybe I take his picture ransacking the house. Maybe I disable his car and call the cops. I don't know; I'll figure it out."

"Better let me handle it. I can borrow a video camera and tape him," Denny said. "I can call tonight—I'm off tomorrow. I'll tell him Rick left the stuff at my place."

"Yes, let Denny do it at his house," Marcie said.

"If Wallace spots him, is he more bullet-proof than I am?" I asked.

"I've got a .22 rifle, but if there's serious ordnance around, I'm gone and he'll never catch me," Denny said.

"The shoot-out at the Comic Corral." I sucked a chocolate molecule off my fork and could see it: Wallace blazing away with a pistol, Denny dodging behind a doorjamb, peeking out to snap off a shot with his little rifle, stacks of collectable comics riddled with bullets, falling over in a cloud of dust.

"No," I told them. "Rick was *my* husband. It's my risk to take. Denny is not one bit more qualified than I am. I'd like to borrow that video camera, but I'll go buy one if I have to." I set my empty plate decisively on the coffee table.

"I think it's time we gave it a rest and went home to bed." Marcie's voice was calm, but her hands were knots in her lap. "We can think it over in the morning."

It was a safe bet she would call tomorrow and try to talk me out of it.

"Right." I gave Denny a hard look. "I'll call Wallace tomorrow after work, like I just found the package. Don't go shooting your mouth off or charging around wrecking everything."

"I forget. Who was it that died and made you Captain Picard of the Starship Enterprise?"

"My husband is the one who was murdered, remember?"

"My job is the one in free fall, remember?"

"Puh-leeze!" Marcie said.

"Relax," I told her. "This is what passes for conversation with us."

When she left, she took the cake leftovers with her.

Chapter Nineteen

After I'd slept on it, the plan to trap Wallace looked shaky. Either it wouldn't work and I'd look like a fool, or it would work and I'd be dead. I couldn't decide which was more probable.

No alternatives surfaced. Maybe if I had more of that cake… One thing that did occur was that if the plan failed and Wallace didn't show up, I could try it with Hap. I'd test everyone at the zoo until someone fell for it. No, that was wishful thinking.

Thursday, work was uneventful except for a little kid who fell in the waterfowl pond and was fished out by one of the gardeners. I arrived on the run, summoned by a hysterical teenage girl, as the mom was telling everyone that her little boy did that all the time. She and her sopping child wandered off to finish their zoo visit, leaving the rest of us worried about hypothermia and hoping for swimming lessons soon.

I was flying solo the coming weekend, but Calvin seemed unconcerned that I might kill off his charges through clumsiness or stupidity. He told me what to do if I had extra time after the basic routine, and that was about it.

"I'm off tomorrow. If anything comes up, you'll leave me a note?" I asked.

He shrugged. "Nothing will."

No lists of reminders, no home phone number. I recalled all the instructions and suggestions I gave Linda when I left Felines to her, most of which were unnecessary, all of which were probably annoying.

At home that night, I fed the dogs and iguana, then sat down and wrote a little script for my call to Wallace. I'd have only one shot, and I wanted to get it right and get it over. Marcie called before I finished, full of the same worries about The Plan that had been troubling me. I spent a long time describing all the safeguards I'd thought of, starting with pepper spray. She added another—borrowing her new cell phone. Nothing I said seemed to reassure her, and nothing she said persuaded me not to go ahead.

We signed off in mutual frustration. I finished the script, rehearsed it twice to two polite but uninterested dogs, and picked up the phone to make the call. The receiver beep-beeped in my ear. Denny had called while I was talking to Marcie. He wanted me to call back as soon as possible. Being Denny, he didn't say where he was. I called his house.

"Come on over. I've got someone you need to meet." He sounded twitchy.

"Why? Who is it?"

"It's better if you just come."

"I haven't had dinner yet. Can it wait an hour?"

"No. I've got some TV dinners. Now is good. Later is not good."

He hung up, probably figuring curiosity was more powerful than any reason he could come up with. He was right. I reluctantly got into my truck, leaving sad dogs behind. I could leave the message for Wallace later. That wouldn't be a problem.

I pulled up in front of Denny's at maybe 7:30 PM, full dark. His van wasn't there, but the lights were on in the house. No warning roar from Strongbad. That made me nervous enough to start the truck again and drive another two blocks to park.

I walked back in the dark, dodging potholes full of water on the gravel road, imagining all the dire possibilities that might be lurking. Native Americans used to tie a rag to a pole and let it flutter while they lay in hiding, ready to shoot arrows into pronghorn antelope that had more curiosity than good sense. I must have been a pronghorn in a previous life.

I circled the house, squishing through mud, to get to the living room side window, on the same side of the house as the bedroom window I'd jimmied two nights before. Maybe if anything really bad happened, the neighbor with the pistol would save me.

Moving rhododendron branches aside, I could see Denny sitting in a chair with his back to me. A woman was sitting on his couch. I didn't recognize her. Denny had a rifle leaning next to him. It looked as if they were drinking one of Denny's dreadful herb teas. He had a bloody bandage on his hand and a camcorder at his feet. I noticed several apples lying here and there and an orange or two on the floor. The room looked even more disheveled than usual. The situation was definitely peculiar, but was it dangerous? Denny looked calm and confident, chatting away cheerfully.

I considered my options. Leave and wait until later to find out what Denny wanted? Go get my dad or the neighbor as backup? Buy a handgun? I decided to hell with it, I was hungry and wanted to get this done. They both jumped a foot when I rapped on the window. I came around to the front door and Denny let me in. I looked inquiringly at the woman.

"Ah, Iris, this is Suzanne." He pronounced it "Sue-zayne."

Suzanne was short and, as my dad would say, built for comfort, by which he meant amply endowed. She was generously proportioned in the chest and hips and reasonably narrow in the waist, given that she was at least as old as my mother. My mother, however, did not favor black low-cut jerseys with black stirrup pants and black high heels. She sat on Denny's tacky sofa with her legs crossed, looking completely at home. A black knit cap was draped over one knee. Her hair was an expensive blond swirl, slightly mashed from the cap. Stray wisps fell over her eyes. A big emerald flashed on her left hand. It looked like her coral lipstick matched her nail polish, but it was hard to be sure.

She smiled winsomely. "I'm so glad to meet you, Iris. Freddie's talked about you."

Freddie?

"Mr. Crandall. She's, ah, an old friend of his." Denny gestured vaguely with his bandaged hand.

I followed his wave, which led me to glance at the ceiling and discover a large hole, clearly the source of the plaster bits distributed liberally around the room.

"Have a seat, Iris. Denny, could you get another chair for Iris?"

I took a stack of comics off a wooden chair and pulled it up. "So…what's going on? Denny asked me to come right over."

"Um, do you want tea?" Denny asked.

"No, I want dinner. I want to go home and get me some sleep. So tell."

Instead, Denny lurched toward the kitchen muttering about a frozen dinner, changed his mind, and hesitated. I scowled at him—no help—until he wisely decided to feed me first and tell all later. He headed toward the refrigerator.

Suzanne smiled warmly. "I tried to help a friend, but I made a fool of myself instead." She looked at the rug and swung her foot a little. She didn't really look contrite, but I supposed that was the intended effect. Microwave noises came from the kitchen. Denny came back and sat down.

It took a little doing, but eventually Denny got his half of the story out. He and Marcie had a chat after we parted the night before. They agreed it was far too dangerous for me to set the trap for Wallace. Instead Marcie would try to talk me out of it, and Denny would give it a try. Yesterday evening, he had come home from my place and left a message for Wallace, saying that he had found some Indian remains and artifacts in Rick's stuff. With them, he claimed, was a letter Rick had written to the university explaining that he found these at the new Asian Experience construction site. Denny had asked for advice, saying he would be out of town on his days off, but would deal with the package when he got back.

"Plans you make with me don't count for much, I take it," I said.

Denny was unrepentant. "Marcie was in."

He had parked Strongbad with Hap, who was not at all pleased to have a rowdy dog terrifying his parrots. "Did you tell Hap everything?" I asked.

"Sure, why not?" Denny said.

So much for trying the trap on other zoo staff.

Denny left his van on the next street over from his house and hid in the attic with a camcorder poking through a hole punched in the ceiling. The access was by a trap door in the kitchen ceiling, with a chair parked under it. The apples and oranges were provisions; the rifle was just in case. He had a water bottle and a big coffee can to pee in. He settled in with a pile of comic books and a flashlight.

Denny said he'd come down once to get a pillow and a sleeping bag and was about to climb down again to find some fresh batteries for the flashlight when he saw a light moving around below. "Man, was she quiet! I didn't hear her open the window or anything."

Suzanne said demurely, "I've always wanted to be a cat burglar."

Most of the rest was self-evident. He'd shut off his flashlight and tried to turn on the camcorder in the dark, knocking it through the hole instead. He tried to catch it and stepped off the floored part of the attic onto the plaster, which could not hold him. He landed on the living room floor with the camcorder, apples and oranges crashing down around him. Not to mention the rifle.

"And the can of pee?" I asked.

He ignored me. "I cut my hand on the way down. Suzanne used to be a nurse. She washed it and wrapped it up for me."

"Your turn," I said to Suzanne, who didn't look like any nurse I'd ever met. "Let's start with what the hell you are doing in Denny's house."

She was unflustered. "I was trying to help Freddie." This time I got the connection—she must be the girlfriend Jackie had mentioned.

"What's Mr. Crandall got to do with it?"

"Kevin Wallace told him about Denny's call and asked what he wanted to do about it. Kevin wanted Freddie to handle it. He didn't know what to tell Denny, whether he should bring the things in or turn it over to the state or what. He wasn't concerned, but of course Freddie was. He was so upset today that Asian Experience might be canceled or delayed or get a lot of bad publicity. After all his hard work, now this. He didn't know what to do. I told him not to worry, that it would all work out. I always tell him that and usually it's true, but this time I thought I could make sure. You have no idea how distraught he was. So I came on over and climbed in the window."

She shrugged and smiled. "I thought I would take some little thing to make it look like a robbery, then find whatever pots or arrowheads and throw them away. Then they would be gone and Freddie wouldn't worry himself into an angina attack. But Denny came crashing down on me and *I* almost had a heart attack!" She gave a throaty laugh.

"Wallace talked to Mr. Crandall and told him about the artifacts?" I asked.

"Oh yes. He thinks it's Freddie's job, not his. Kevin does animals and personnel and Freddie decides everything sensitive."

"And Freddie—I mean, Mr. Crandall—was worried?" I asked.

"Asian Experience is the jewel of his career. He's waited such a long time to do a major new exhibit. Well, you can't imagine how keyed up he is over every little thing. It's already three months behind schedule and over budget. You'd think the money was coming out of his own pocket." She sniffed.

"What about kickbacks? Is Wallace getting kickbacks on the construction?" Denny asked.

I heard beeping noises from the microwave in the kitchen, but curiosity won over hunger. Again.

"I have no idea. I doubt it's much money if he is." Suzanne was unconcerned.

"Does the zoo board know his brother-in-law got the contract for the bulldozer work?" Denny pressed.

"I'm sure they must. They review the big decisions and Kevin's made no secret of the relationship. At least not to me." She glanced down with a little smile that hinted of a lot of things not secret to her. She reminded me of Jackie, only far more upscale.

I looked at Denny. "Our theory is shot to hell. The microwave is done."

He left and came back with a TV dinner and a fork. Chiles rellenos, refried beans, rice with bits of something red, and cut corn. "It's organic," he told me. It sounded like an apology.

The edges were bubbly and the center was icy. I scarfed it. My primitive animal brain was suffused with gratitude toward Denny for feeding me, until my cortex kicked in again.

"Did you really find any ancient artifacts?" Suzanne asked me, perched like a quail on the sofa.

Denny and I looked at each other and didn't answer.

"Ah, then." She cocked her head to one side and smiled at Denny. "Perhaps you could tell me what you hoped to accomplish?"

"Denny," I said, "do you think you need stitches in that hand?"

He shook his head and opened his mouth to speak.

"You'd better start picking up this place," I said. "It looks like a bar fight."

Denny looked put out, but he shut his mouth.

Suzanne stretched, which nicely emphasized her chest. "I see." Blue eyes focused on me.

I said nothing, and Denny kept quiet.

At last she said, "The tea was wonderful, but it's starting to wear off and I need my beauty sleep." She tucked her chin a little and glanced at Denny sidelong through her eyelashes. "Oh, are those old Spiderman comics? My husband, bless him, collected comics. He's been gone many years. I haven't had the heart to throw them out." She said "gone" in a way that meant "dead." "I have boxes of Spirit and Pogo comic books, kept so nice in plastic sleeves. I don't know what I should do with them."

Denny's poker face slid into place with almost an audible clang. "Originals or reprints?" he asked indifferently.

"Oh, they must be originals. He got some from an uncle. Some he bought at those collectors' meetings. You collect them also. Isn't that interesting? You two are so different." She made it a compliment.

"So do you plan to sell them someday?" Denny's voice was steady but his fingers were tapping softly on his thigh.

"Oh, they aren't worth enough to bother. I was thinking of them more as a gift for someone, if I ever found anyone who would cherish them." She smiled and shook her head sadly. "He loved them so, I want them to be appreciated."

I looked at Denny in alarm. Surely he wouldn't fall for this? He would—I could practically see the hook through his lip.

"Appreciated by someone who wouldn't mention to the police or Mr. Crandall that you committed breaking and entering?" I suggested.

"Oh, Iris!" she chirped, looking at Denny. "No, I really am looking for someone to enjoy them."

Well, it hadn't been *my* window she climbed through.

"Why don't you stop in tomorrow or the next day? You could take a look and see if they are anything special. Suzanne Skutch. I'm in the phone book." She spelled out her last name, took her flashlight, and tap-tapped out the door in three-inch heels, leaving a trace of perfume behind.

"Wow! What a woman! I have to rethink Freddie from the top," Denny said grinning as the door closed.

"Chubby little thing," I said, charmed in spite of myself.

"Meow," said Denny.

"I'm going home," I told him wearily. "Wallace didn't murder anybody over Indian bones and neither did Mr. Crandall."

"Why not Mr. Crandall? I'd say Mr. Crandall is now a prime suspect, if you stop to think about it."

"I did stop to think about it. He couldn't wrestle Rick over the guardrail. He wouldn't know how to turn on the geyser at the Children's Zoo. And he wouldn't kill someone. Incidentally,

I am never going to work with you again on anything as long as I live." I looked around. "What a mess." I'm not sure whether I meant Rick's death or Denny's living room. Both qualified.

I slogged back to my truck in the dark and drove home, wondering how much worse Denny had made the situation.

I found out at eight the next morning. Jackie called, waking me up on my day off.

"Mr. Wallace wants you in his office in an hour," she said.

"It's my day off. Do I have to?" A pre-coffee crisis finds me at my most vulnerable, whiny and slow-witted.

"You do. Wear your best Kevlar," she said. "He had me call Calvin and Denny, too," and she hung up.

Denny arrived at the Administration building at the same time I did. We exchanged desperate glances and marched into Wallace's office together to meet our fates, a puzzled Calvin following.

"What the hell are you two trying to do?" the foreman greeted us from behind his desk. "I got Crandall climbing my tree, saying you two invented some prank to block Asian Experience. That is all I need." He turned on Calvin. "Did you put them up to this? Is this your big idea of how to get the aviary replaced?"

Calvin looked at me.

"No, he didn't know anything about whatever it is you're talking about," I said. "I mean, he didn't put us up to anything."

"What exactly *are* we talking about?" Denny asked.

Wallace shoved his chair back and stood up, his face red. "Don't act like morons. I mean that phone call to me about Indian artifacts. You didn't find any pots or whatever. All you're doing is trying to interfere with the construction and get even for the disciplinary action." He turned to me. "You've been nothing but trouble since…for weeks. I'm trying to work with your situation, but I got only so much slack for mental problems. For this, I gotta put a disciplinary warning in your file. Get your head straight, or you're gonna be out of here."

He turned back to Denny. "I'm starting the process to terminate you. You'll get the paperwork today." He glowered at Calvin and sat back down. "Out, all of you."

"What on earth was that all about?" Calvin asked as soon as we were safely out of the Administration building.

"Suzanne talked to Freddie," Denny said to me, ignoring him.

"No shit," I said.

Chapter Twenty

I sat in my pickup in the employee portion of the parking lot trying to grasp the full scope of the disaster. Denny was to blame for the misfire, but in truth, this would still be a catastrophe if I'd been the one to spring the trap.

Denny would appeal his firing, which might delay it long enough for Wallace to calm down, although that did not seem likely. I was in only moderately hot water—a warning in my personnel file was the least of my worries.

The big deal was this: if all the surmises and logical leaps were correct, Rick's murderer was wise to the trap, or would be soon, and, moreover, knew what Denny and I thought had happened the night Rick died. If we were getting close to the truth, and I thought we were, the killer needed to get rid of both of us, pronto.

Now Denny was at risk, too. What about Marcie? After consideration, I concluded she probably wasn't. Denny had mentioned her name to Suzanne, but it would take some work to find out who she was and where she lived. She was likely safe for now.

If Wallace was exonerated…I got out of the truck and walked back to the Administration building.

A peek through the window showed that the door to Wallace's office was closed. Jackie was sitting at her desk, on the phone and turned away. I nipped around the building to the side door. This time the Education Outreach office was unlocked. A large woman in a large dress printed with large sunflowers was pulling paper handouts, colored pens, and what, on a closer look, resolved into bat masks, off crowded shelves and piling them into a plastic crate. Materials for a classroom presentation.

"Good morning to *you*," she warbled, and beamed at me. "What can I do for you on this bountiful day?"

"I think I left a jar here. A jar with a little snake skin?"

"We have guinea pig skulls, ostrich eggs, porcupine quills, and a peacock foot. We have snakeskins in all sizes. Or can I interest you in parrot feathers or a turtle carapace or a freeze-dried hawk moth?" She giggled.

I edged around her and scanned the shelves. On the second pass, I spotted it, nestled into a mink pelt.

One small snake shed, two hatched-out turtle eggs, and—hard to spot—one small tooth.

"This is it. Thanks."

"Any time. This is your full-service nature's magic shop! Showing children *and* adults the spell of the wild!"

I fled with the jar.

Her voice followed me. "Have a *beautiful* day! Each one comes only once!"

Wallace's door was still closed. I stuck my head into the office.

"Jackie, come talk to me outside," I hissed. I didn't want Jackie spreading news about the failed trap. It was barely possible that the killer might not learn about it for a day or two if she kept quiet. I needed that slim advantage for a trap of my own. Of course, if Hap were the killer, which I could not believe, Denny had already alerted him to what we were on to.

Jackie didn't waste any time.

"What did you and Denny *do*?" she asked, as we huddled in her smoking refuge under the eaves. "I thought Mr. Crandall was having a heart attack."

I stuck close to the shrubbery. If Wallace came out, I'd vanish into the bushes like a hunted doe.

"Jackie, listen. You have to keep absolutely quiet about this."

"About *what*?"

"Everything. Look, I can't tell you. It's important. Keep quiet until…until next Wednesday. Then I'll tell you what's up. Honest. You owe me one, remember?"

Jackie sputtered, "How can I keep quiet if I don't know what *it* is?"

"Denny getting fired and me in trouble and the reason why."

"I never talk about that stuff. It's unprofessional. What *happened?*"

"I can't tell you. Just don't talk about it at all. You really, really have to do this. Or we won't be friends." Because I'd quite possibly be dead.

Jackie stared at me. "You are seriously flipping out. You need to get away from this place and calm down."

"No, I'm not crazy, but I've got to go. Wednesday you get the scoop." I checked that the coast was clear and started toward the parking lot. I stopped in two steps and turned back to Jackie, who was still looking at me as if I'd lost my mind. "Jackie, I got the L.A. job. Tell anyone you want. Tell everyone."

I sat in the truck again and planned my next step. Jackie would probably find out what Denny and I were in trouble for. She might or might not keep quiet about it. She certainly would share with the world that I had the L.A. job. That was the best I could do.

Now for the tooth.

Wallace *did* want it in the hands of the Education Outreach department. Wallace really *was* innocent, if the burial site part of the scenario was correct. And perhaps now I knew why my house had been broken into and set on fire. Someone other than Wallace knew about the tooth and wanted it out of circulation.

I drove to Portland to catch my dentist, Dr. Chen. I made it to her office in southeast Portland, not far from my parents' house, by 11:45 AM. The receptionist was new, with spiky frosted hair and a blue tattoo around her wrist. I said I needed to talk to Dr. Chen. She said I needed to make an appointment. I said I needed to see the dentist immediately. We went on like that for a bit, but I was prepared to spend all the time it took, and she wanted to go to lunch.

Finally she agreed to see whether Dr. Chen would talk to me, and what was it I wanted to speak with her about? The concept of a talk with the dentist that didn't involve actual dentistry on my actual mouth was difficult. I used the words "consultation" and "urgent" and "long-time patient." My patience was used up, and I said these words several times with escalating decibels.

She went off disapprovingly to the back of the office and came back to grant me "a very few" minutes with Dr. Chen when she finished with her procedure. I sat down, the only customer in the waiting room, to stare at the framed Chinese calligraphy on the wall.

In spite of the new receptionist, Dr. Chen was possibly the world's most perfect dentist. She was calm and had a motherly air, enhanced by her four-year-old who sometimes played in the reception area. You knew she wouldn't ever hurt you unless she really, really had to for your own oral good. She also had little fingers, a positive attitude, and a cool machine that showed live videos of your gums. I never exactly looked forward to visiting her, but I liked her enough to pay her bills instead of finding a dentist who would accept the zoo's dental insurance.

She was puzzled about the urgency of my mission, which I skipped explaining. "I need to know what you can tell me about this tooth," was as far as I went.

She wasn't entranced with the tooth, but she gave it careful consideration. "An incisor." She turned it over in her hand. "I'll go with upper right incisor, Number Seven. Where'd you get it?"

"Human?"

"What else could it be?" She sounded startled. "You work at the zoo, right? I have no idea what else it could be from. I'm not familiar with monkey teeth or anything like that. It *looks* like a human tooth. That's really all I can tell you." She walked to the sink and rinsed it and scrubbed it with her fingers and a little toothpaste. "See here? It's got a filling. This pale spot. I suppose that makes it more likely to be human, although a zoo animal might need a filling. I never get called for animals. Too bad. It would be a great change from the office."

"Could the tooth be really old, like a hundred years?" Maybe there were dentists a hundred years ago. I had no idea.

"It's a composite filling. I'd say the work was done no more than twenty-five or thirty years ago, probably much more recently."

Not from any ancient gravesite. I thanked her, took the tooth back. The receptionist stopped me, checked on the fee with Dr. Chen, and grudgingly let me go for free.

I sat in the truck and gathered myself, shaken. Rick really had found a skull; that guess was dead-on. But it wasn't ancient. It had nothing to do with Native Americans.

I spelled it out. A man or woman had died, probably a few years ago, and been buried on the zoo grounds. The source of the tooth in my hand had been murdered. Why else hide the grave in the woods at the zoo? The secret had been safe until construction had started. Now the rest of the remains were long gone, unearthed by hosing, then taken away and destroyed.

My break-in and house fire. He, or she, had come for the tooth. And was desperate to conceal the murder again, at the price of a new death. Mine.

I had a plan, but it seemed ridiculous, a piece of twine to hold back a charging Cape buffalo. Did I dare risk it? What else *could* I do?

If I went to the police now, I'd look like a hysterical widow afflicted with conspiracy theories. All I had was one tooth and a story. But not going to the police seemed stupid. I started the truck, pondering.

When I got home, I didn't call Marcie or Denny. I would handle this myself.

I called Linda at Felines to change my clouded leopard watch, and then I went shopping.

Chapter Twenty-one

Saturday was my first solo at Birds. I stayed alert, thanks to a restful night at my parents' house, and kept pepper spray in my pocket. I'd told the folks that I suspected the prowler had been back. As predicted, they insisted I stay with them and didn't make a squeak about the dogs coming too. I'd fed Bessie Smith and told her she was on her own for a day or two. She had bobbed her head at me, looking cranky.

Once the zoo opened, I stayed in sight of visitors almost continuously. Weekends brought out the visitors, even on a dull, cool day, and for once, I was glad to see them.

The penguins condescended to eat from my hand, after some initial consternation that I was neither Calvin nor Arnie, who was the customary weekend relief. Nothing dropped dead or bled or crippled itself or even looked ill. Nothing fell on me or zapped me or otherwise threatened my life. I worked steadily and got everything done without incident.

Jackie didn't work weekends. Neither did Wallace. The only keepers I talked to were Sam and Arnie.

I picked up the empty food pans in The World of Birds in late afternoon and sat in the Penguinarium filling out reports, tired and hungry, but cautiously optimistic about living through the day. After tidying up the insect shelves, which was on Calvin's "do if you have time" list, I was feeling modestly successful as a bird keeper.

Tonight I would take the offensive. I quivered at the thought. The plan was simple. I was signed up to watch the clouded leopards on TV monitors in the Feline kitchen. They were newly together and under continuous watch to protect Losa, the female, in case Yuri took a dislike to his roommate and decided to attack her. I'd be there, alone at night, me and the monitors. Waiting for the next attempt on my life. Only this time, I'd be ready.

My jacket was on and I was almost out the door when I noticed the blinking message light on the phone. It was Denny. The long message said he'd caught the same off-note I had when we had talked to his friend Mark of Huddleston Construction Company and Hap had joined us, then abruptly left. Mark finally admitted that Hap and his buddies used the zoo's Maintenance shop to work on their cars at night since it had an engine hoist and a grease pit. Wallace wouldn't approve, so Hap kept it secret. That was why he'd left the conversation when the topic shifted to cars. He hadn't wanted Mark to spill the beans to me or Denny.

Hap had been at the zoo the night Rick died, but it had nothing to do with Rick's death. I put a hand flat on the counter. Relief made my knees weak.

The rest of Denny's message said that Wallace was forced to reinstate him until a hearing on firing him, and he would be on nights until then. After a long moment's thought, I called Denny at his house. I needed backup, and he was, oddly, the one person at the zoo I could trust. I trusted him not to try to kill me and hoped I could, for once, trust him to do what I asked. I said I'd be on clouded leopard watch and to drop by every hour if he could.

"Scared, huh? Yeah, I'll come by when I can."

I would tell him about the tooth later, when I had time for an explosion of consternation and theories. I stepped out the Penguinarium door and was nearly run over by George, the night watchman. He leaned out of the window in the electric cart.

"I got a call some crazy visitor was trying to cut open a fence."

"Nobody here. I haven't heard or seen a thing."

"Caller said it was over by the aviary. He was real excited." George was distressed. He hated emergencies.

I got in and we tooled around the area and found a trash can tipped over, but no one engaged in vandalism.

"Some dumb crank call," George finally diagnosed as he watched me clean up the litter.

I was half an hour late clocking out, and there was a note from Hap asking me to find him before I left. I was not terribly surprised that he was working on a Saturday. He might need to take a day off later in the week. If he wanted to come clean about midnight mechanics, that would clear the air between us. More likely, he had a problem with the fish delivery for tomorrow. Everyone else had left, and I figured I'd missed him, but took a quick look anyway. I needed to eat dinner and show up at Felines for the clouded leopard watch.

The roll door at the front of the Commissary was open. I walked out and checked the loading dock. It was stacked with boxes of lettuce, carrots, and miscellaneous produce set out for Diego, the night keeper, to deliver to the animal areas. No sign of Hap. Back inside, I looked around the central space crammed with shelves full of supplies and glanced through the window of the big refrigerated room to the left. This building was possibly the only part of the original zoo that wasn't cramped and undersized. Toward the back was a walk-in freezer half the size of my house. The freezer door was open, and I heard Hap talking inside. The door was designed to swing shut to keep in the cold. It was held open by a claw hammer lying on the floor.

"Hap?" I called, walking toward his voice. Fluorescent lights overhead threw white splashes of light contrasting with dark shadows. The familiar space felt spooky and alien.

I stopped and put one hand in my pocket, reassuring myself with my new pepper spray. I took a good look at the maze of shelves full of vitamins, marmoset diet, canned peaches, and a thousand other items. Nearby, ceiling-high metal shelving held paper products, bags of monkey chow, and duck food. I didn't see anybody lurking, but this was a great place to skulk unseen. My shoulder blades started to prickle.

I stood rooted, about to flee, when Hap laughed, still talking with someone from inside the freezer, probably Diego, the night keeper.

"*Hap?*" I bellowed.

I heard Hap laugh again, relaxed and ordinary. It was possible they couldn't hear me. I was about a dozen feet from the open freezer door, and I was not going one inch closer. If Hap or Diego didn't stick his head out in two seconds, I was out of there. I pulled out the pepper spray and checked that I had it oriented so that I wouldn't spray myself.

The blow landed squarely between my shoulders and slammed me flat on my face and chest. The pepper spray went flying. A foot shoved my butt, skidding me across smooth cement into the freezer. The lights went out and the door pushed against the bottoms of my feet as it closed.

I scrambled to my feet, staggering back to hands and knees as I lost my balance, ruled by the primitive imperative to face my attacker on my feet. I fumbled for the light switch and lurched against the door as soon as they came on. The door held, the outside latch in place. The big concrete door was designed with a safety release. I grabbed the bar that ran through the door and pushed hard. Instead of engaging and disconnecting the latch, it moved forward without resistance, as if the latch weren't in place. I shoved the door again. It didn't open.

The door wasn't latched, it was jammed shut.

I hurled my shoulder against it, took a running start and did it again. And again. I panted from fear and exertion, but the door was not budging. I took hold of the safety release again and pulled instead of pushing, alternating pulling on it and shoving on the door with my aching shoulder. The door gave a tiny bit and moved a little more with each push or pull. Whatever held it shut was working loose. I was sweating from exertion and panic, yanking and slamming my shoulder.

The door stopped moving that little bit forward and back. I pulled and pushed harder, not believing it. After a dozen more attempts, I figured it out. Whoever had trapped me was still there. Whatever was jamming the door had been adjusted. This wasn't going to work.

Hap laughed, inside the freezer with me.

I looked around. I was alone with my pounding heart and fear-sweat, but Hap talked on. The voice was coming from fish boxes, herring in two stacks six feet high. A cordless speaker was perched on top. A recording. Even as I finally noticed the tinny sound of the voice, the freezer fell silent. The killer had shut off the tape player outside the freezer. Hap? Would Hap do this to me? My doubts flooded back.

It was bitter cold, probably close to the zero degrees Fahrenheit it was supposed to be.

Panic shuts down the brain. I tried two deep, chilly breaths, then spotted a hand truck with three fish boxes ready for Diego to wheel out. I threw the boxes off and tried to push the hand truck platform under the door to use as a pry. The door fit far too tightly. Quality construction.

My hands were cold and shaking. I tried the release bar a dozen more times, a dozen variations. This was my second lesson that a cell phone was more important to my health than medical insurance. I paused and tried the deep breathing again, taking a moment to thank the paranoid electrician who had put the light switch on the inside instead of the outside. Being trapped in the dark would be a thousand times worse. Better to die with a good view of boxes of ground meat, packaged in plastic tubes; donated berries; clear bags of white lab rats; boxed Popsicles for the monkeys. Six or seven whole salmon stared frostily at me from a work counter. Everything was rock-hard, hostile.

The lights brightened briefly and another jolt of panic went through me. If my assailant disabled the lights, I would become sincerely hysterical. But it was just the cooling apparatus kicking off. The open door had let warm air in and the equipment had brought the temperature back to its set point and shut itself off.

What among all this would keep me alive? Lots of cardboard boxes. I could start a fire. With what match? And the fire would use up all the oxygen and I'd suffocate. Breathing deliberately, I looked around the room really carefully. Nope, no other doors I'd failed to notice. I found the pepper spray and put it back in my pocket.

The lights flickered and dimmed as the motor hummed on again. A breeze I hadn't noticed before kicked up. I headed to the back of the freezer and started tossing boxes out of the way, examining each for a polar bear hide or a space heater, until I got down to the machinery. I found the power switch and slapped it off. It quit humming. The breeze died and the lights brightened. Not that this would do me any good. The room would probably stay below freezing for a good two weeks with the door closed, even with the cooler off.

I could stack up boxes and climb to the ceiling, but there wasn't any exit up there either. I tried waving my arms and jumping up and down to warm up. It was soon clear that I was only going to freeze tired.

I was out of ideas, desperate and despairing. Composing myself as an attractive corpse-sicle seemed like my last option. I wasn't shivering anymore—I was shuddering violently. I remembered reading that freezing to death was a pleasant way to go—you simply fell asleep. I had to disagree, based on experience so far. Being cold is loathsome. The cold saturated my jacket and pants, claiming arms and thighs. Numb fingers, icy feet.

Inactivity was still impossible. I staggered over to the freezer unit and began flipping the switch on and off. The lights dimmed each time it went on, then brightened again. Cold air pulsed briefly each time. Dully I thought that maybe the lights would flicker throughout the zoo. Maybe George or the night keeper would notice. Fat chance. I flicked the switch and tried to remember how Morse code for SOS went. Three shorts, three longs, three shorts? Or was it three longs, three shorts, three longs? Did it matter?

This was a great opportunity to reflect on how stupid I'd been, once again thoroughly outfoxed. Despair and frustration and cold put me in tears. "I figured out *why*, Rick," I said aloud, "and I tried to find out *who* did it to you, but I can't pull it off. Your killer is going to get away with it." And I was going to die alone. "I wish I could believe you told me the truth and just love you and miss you." The lie about quitting drinking ached—Billie Holiday's voice was breathy in my mind's ear.

Or was I asking the wrong question? Maybe all along I should have been asking how it could be that he told the truth and still died with a belly full of liquor.

Cold was congealing my brain. The lions knew *who*; no one else ever would. I flicked the switch faithfully, but I was drowsy and discouraged. On, off, on, off. The lights dimmed and brightened, dimmed and brightened. My hands weren't working well. I'd finally figured something out and forgotten it again, too tired and sleepy. Trusting Rick's word had something to do with the sick penguin getting dehydrated. Spice going down to the bottom of the moat—when and why did she do that?

I'd nap a little while, then maybe it would make sense. Nothing but sleep mattered very much anymore.

Chapter Twenty-two

After some indefinable time, a voice assaulted me, close by and too loud—disturbing. Slowly meaning penetrated: "Hey, you're going to wreck that unit!"

The voice emerged from George, the security guard, standing at the open freezer door. His broad, open face was baffled and concerned, blue uniform tight across his belly, belt lost under its slope. "What the heck are you doing? The lights keep blinking; you gotta stop that. Hap doesn't like anybody messing around in here."

I mumbled something and staggered from a hunched crouch to my feet. My legs weren't working right. George held my arm, protesting mildly and steadily, as I weaved to the laundry room. I found the thermostat and turned it up. The big heater hanging from the ceiling kicked on, and I stood shaking, facing the blast of warm air, inhaling it deep into my lungs. He shoved a chair under my rear and I sat back.

"Why'd you stay in there if you were so cold? I gotta put this in my report, you know."

"Do what you need to do." Muzzy intuition kept me from telling him the truth.

George dithered uneasily while my strength slowly returned. After several minutes, I was able to walk back to the freezer door, now closed—blank, inoffensive, normal. A door I saw and ignored every workday.

I found where a thin, tapered object might be inserted between the door and its frame to jam it. Hap's heavy wooden-handled cleaver sat on the stainless steel work counter ten feet from the door.

At the sound of George's electric cart, someone had pulled the cleaver out and vanished. George had saved my life simply by showing up. "George, did you see anybody when you came in here?" I looked around at the shadowy aisles.

"No. I didn't see nobody. I went to get my Popsicle. Hap says I can have one a night. What were you doing in there, anyway?" His voice was querulous. George was best at dealing with the ordinary.

If I told him the truth, tomorrow Wallace would boot me out of the zoo, one accident too many, with Marcie's and my parents' full support. My plan was to resolve this situation later tonight, but I might need more time. And keeping this secret was the unexpected thing to do—I'd reported the previous accidents. Maybe it would give me some advantage over my opponent. "I lost something. I was looking for it. Thanks for…Nice to see you, George." I turned the thermostat back down and started to walk, still shivering, out of the building. Craven and exhausted, I turned back. "George, will you run me to the parking lot?"

He was pleased to be helpful. "Sure. I guess I got time."

I climbed in and we rode through the twilight to the employee parking lot. We saw no one.

The truck heater roaring, I drove around Vancouver in circles until I was sure no one was following me. I felt terrible, in many dimensions. Shoulders, breasts, arms, and butt all ached from physical abuse. A headache was drumming its way to life. My bones were immune to warmth, permafrost below the surface. I was so tired I could hardly drive. Panic crouched icy and intractable at my core. Only basic survival instincts were functioning. They said that refueling was mandatory.

At the back booth of a little café I'd never noticed before, I sat facing the door, adrenaline spiking each time it opened. The waitress brought a charred steak glazed with grease, a damp baked potato wrapped in aluminum foil with a glob of sour cream and another of butter, and overcooked green beans. I ate it all, plus the stale dinner roll, and asked for more coffee. The waitress failed on chocolate cake, but delivered an acceptable blackberry cobbler.

Now what?

I had Rick's life insurance, a sizeable stake. My parents would help me pack the truck. I'd call the landlord and leave a check for the last month. Forget the cleaning deposit. What about Bessie Smith? Denny. She could go to Denny. I'd spend the night at the folks', leave town tomorrow. Tell them I wanted to see some of the country. No permanent address for a while. Give it a couple of months, then settle down in some little town far away. Maybe find a job in landscape work or at an animal shelter.

I couldn't bring Rick back, and there was no point in getting killed trying. I could still be sleeping in the freezer, beyond fear or obligation or responsibility.

The waitress orbited by with more coffee. I ordered the peach pie. Skip the à la mode. She removed the berry cobbler remnants—a fragment of crust and a smear of juice. The headache was gone and I seemed to be approaching 98.6 degrees throughout.

I could be safe again. No more looking over my shoulder, wondering what deadfall I was about to trigger. Just me and the dogs. I'd talk to Marcie and my parents by phone every week. Maybe Linda too. I could change my name, no law against it if I wasn't defrauding anyone.

I yearned for this like a seedling straining toward a sunny window.

The peach pie vanished. Not in the same league as my mother's, but not bad. Apple pie didn't sound good. I sipped the last of the coffee and sighed. My waistband was tight, a comfy feel.

Turkey vultures circled over my new Eden, drawn by the smell of decay at the foundation. This new plan offered tenuous safety based on hiding, hiding from myself as well as any pursuer. Living with failure; betraying Rick's love. A rotting base for a new life.

The problem was, I knew who had killed Rick and had come so close to killing me. I'd reconstructed my insights from the freezer. As soon as I asked the right question and believed what Spice showed me, the answer emerged again, like a trick image resolving out of a chaotic background. Once I knew who, then I knew where the tooth came from and why Rick died.

If I fled instead of sticking with my original plan for the evening, the killer was going to get away with two murders.

Chapter Twenty-three

The cougars were up and about. Their pale shapes rose and fell in the cool, moist night as they romped. They chirped like birds, one of their many un-catlike sounds, and thumped solidly as they landed. My stomach was still tight against my jeans, but now it felt stuffed and heavy. I'd rested for a few minutes in the parking lot and weary muscles had stiffened up. Fear crouched in its den, waiting. I stood in front of the exhibit and watched longer than I should have.

I wasn't going to get any smarter or stronger standing in the dark. A dull, iron resolve finally pulled me away from the cougars and around the building toward the staff door. Bagheera, the black leopard, stalked me from behind the wire as I walked. He was invisible but for dim light glinting off his satin coat, a deeper black sliding in and out of shadow.

I unlocked the service door and walked inside the Feline building, shutting it quietly behind me. Ahead of me was the kitchen door. The familiar hallway stretched to my right and left. I could see the lions' night cage on the right, but the cats were lying out of my line of sight. A cool breeze touched my cheek, probably from the cat door to the cougars' night enclosure on the left. I'd need to close it later, when they were willing to come inside.

No more skittish uncertainty. This time I knew full well I was walking into a trap. Baiting the trap. I was the goat staked to the tree, waiting for the tiger.

In the kitchen, one new monitor showed an empty outdoor enclosure and the other an empty indoor holding area. Both screens floated from overhead brackets at head-height. Linda sat at the metal table with a clipboard in front of her, watching the monitors. It was a little after eight.

"Where's the cats?" I asked, pulling up the second chair.

"Yuri's in that shadow. You can see his tail. He's been sleeping for the last hour." She was still in uniform and looked tired.

"Where's Losa?"

"She's in the den box inside. You can't see her."

"Fascinating."

"Huh. You want fascinating or you want peaceful? Boring is good. What's with the duffle bag?"

"Food. A blanket."

"You'd better not fall asleep."

"No worries."

She pulled out the instruction sheet and walked me through the standardized data collection. Every fifteen minutes I was to check off what each cat was doing. "Sleeping" had a long row of check marks. I flipped through checklists from the previous night, the first the clouded leopards had ever spent together. The cats had slept until about midnight, then started moving around. Linda's notes included "M. and F. sniff noses," "F. flee," "M. footscrub." M was male and F was female.

"Use the checklist first. Then you can add a note if anything interesting is happening." She reviewed the definitions of foot scrubbing (urinate, then use hind feet to rub it into the ground, a territorial signal), sniff noses, snarl, attack, and the favorite, sleep. "Mostly they're pretending the other one isn't there."

I didn't remind her that I'd developed the checklist myself.

"Can you stay awake until one?" Linda asked again. "You look kind of wrecked."

"I am kind of wrecked. But I won't fall asleep."

"What happened to your chin?"

I got up and checked the little mirror over the sink. "Fell down and bumped it."

Linda cocked her head at me. "It was dumb to ask you to be here in Felines. I wasn't thinking. I can stay with you."

"I'm fine. Go get some sleep."

Linda shrugged. "Board meeting tonight. People might drop by. Call me if anything comes up. You know what to do if they fight—the hose is set up."

Marcie's cell phone bulged in my jeans pocket next to the pepper spray. I'd driven to her apartment, told her I would feel safer with the cell, and dodged her questions. I'd taken other steps as well, everything I could think of to ensure my survival. As soon as Linda got herself gone, I had a few more steps to take. She took a final look at the monitors, gave me a doubtful look, and left.

Alone in the kitchen, I finished my preparations. The bait wanted to both entrap and survive. All I had to do was wait for the man I expected, confirm he had murdered my husband, and survive until Denny and/or the police showed up. I had the cell phone, pepper spray, and my dad's big pipe wrench. In case I couldn't call 911 myself, Marcie expected to hear from me every hour and would phone the police herself if I didn't check in.

Done, I settled in at the table. Lions grumbled from their side of the building; a cougar yelped from the other direction. The building creaked as it cooled; something dripped. On the motionless monitors, all color faded into gray concrete, dark shadows, black corners. The clouded leopards slept on. The metal table was cold under my wrist. I marked the checklist.

I made a cup of coffee, drank it from one of Linda's gleaming cups, and marked the checklist. It came to me that I had failed to advertise my presence. I'd called Linda only the day before to change to this shift. Would the killer even know I was here alone? I shrugged. My enemy had been ahead of me every step so far. I had bigger worries.

I wandered around the kitchen and shut off the faucets hard. They dripped anyway. Meat for the next day hadn't yet been delivered. The stainless steel counters that ran along two walls were spotless and mostly bare. Small bottles of cheap perfume and jars of spices lined the back counter, interesting scents to spot around the outside yards for olfactory excitement. Gear for catching small cats was stashed in a corner by the door, including various size nets on long poles.

I marked the checklist and countered ragged nerves by fantasizing about Losa and Yuri. They'd get used to each other and, maybe in spring, she would go into heat. Passionate cat love would ensue. We'd separate Yuri for safety's sake and tap our fingers, waiting for the birth. Darling clouded leopard cubs would frolic at their mother's feet.

I had used up that sweet scenario and was about to head down the hall to visit Rajah when the outer door banged shut. I flinched. It was Wallace blowing in with a blast of wet night air. He looked surprised to see me and not pleased. I guessed he had come from the board meeting.

"Any action?"

"Both sleeping."

"Good." He walked behind me to see the monitors and stared at them. Touchy topics floated through the air. I made marks on the checklist. Losa got up and wandered around the inside enclosure, barely visible. She stepped outside through the little door and settled herself in bark chips sheltered by an overhanging ledge, head up, forepaws in front of her. Across the yard, Yuri slept on.

Wallace stood behind me and watched. It made the back of my neck itch. "Uh, it's looking good," I said, getting to my feet and turning toward him. I stretched my arms and back theatrically. He wasn't my first choice for killer, but he wasn't completely out of the running either.

He stepped back a little. "Why wouldn't it look good? We've done everything by the numbers. She'll go into heat soon, he'll breed her, we separate them for safety, and then it all depends on whether she's going to be a decent mother or not."

I tried a small test. "You don't think he'll beat her up?"

"No. It's going fine. People think they're so smart, predicting the worst. These two aren't that old. They can learn to get along."

Neither of us found anything else to say until he finally took his leave, with a gruff "don't fall asleep."

I called Marcie from the phone on the counter rather than use up her cell phone minutes. She was watching a Jane Austen movie with cats in her lap. I put my jacket on, shifted around on the hard chair, and marked the checklist.

Dr. Dawson was next in, also startled to see me. He scanned the monitors and riffled briefly through the checklists.

"Nice and peaceful. Looks very promising," I said, never taking my eyes off him.

His brows drew down. "He may be fine for months, then he could decide he doesn't want to share his territory, and he'll attack her. It's the way clouded leopards are wired. We'll hope for the best." He would never trust Yuri. He stayed only a moment, the door shutting silently behind him.

I watched another forty-five minutes, my anxiety level escalating. I called Marcie, who sounded sleepy. Unable to sit still, I picked up the pipe wrench and headed down the hallway to see Rajah. The old boy was lying flat in the inside den. I watched his ribs rise and fall, nostrils fluttering. Without any voice in the matter, the cats had traded hunger, parasites, and maybe a broken jaw from a frantic hoof for steady meals and good medical care. In exchange for accepting a tiny territory and few choices, the zoo provided a life with little risk. Their own kind was the major source of danger, just as it was for me.

In the dim hall light, I looked at the cat door and the bar attached to the cable that would pull it open. I pulled on the cable a little. The door opened six inches, squeaking softly. Raj raised his head, looking puzzled. I let the door close gently.

The day Raj jumped me, I'd heard that sound. What I hadn't heard was the main service door banging shut, the way it did when most people used it. If I had it right, whoever had let him out on me had known the service door slammed and had closed it carefully and silently.

I turned around to check the common leopards on the opposite side of the hall. The inside quarters were empty. Their little door to the outside was open, letting in brief cold gusts. My face was near the mesh as I tried to spot them outside, looking across the night den and through the cat door. No sensible keeper puts face or other body parts directly against mesh or bars, vulnerable to a quick claw or beak. I could see only a black square of darkness and neither the black male nor the yellow female. I half-turned to leave and, with only a flicker of movement and a tiny thud, a black leopard hung inches from my face, white teeth in a gaping crimson maw, black claws hooked on the mesh. I jerked back involuntarily, lost my balance, and banged hard into the bars behind me. Bagheera dropped agilely to the floor.

He'd timed it perfectly, lurking in the darkness until my attention shifted. Invisible against the black night, he'd vaulted through the little door and up on the fencing. I scrabbled to my feet, heart pounding. He leaped easily up to the sleeping platform and settled in, licking an inky foreleg with a long pink tongue, ignoring me. I told him he was a jerk and limped off, leaving him to savor his feline joke.

Frayed nerves still vibrating, I checked the monitors. Losa was up, wandering around. Yuri was still in the shadows, still not moving. I marked the checklist. Losa lay down again in the bark chips.

The door banged and I jumped as Denny slipped in. He was in uniform with a big flashlight clipped to his belt on one side and a cluster of keys on the other side. "All good?"

"Yeah. Quiet. When's your termination hearing?"

"In a couple of weeks. Arnie's doing Reptiles, but at night I can fix whatever he screws up. Suzanne says she'll get my job back. Listen, I've got a couple of new ideas about Rick."

"We need to talk, but not tonight. I've got to focus on the cats. Just come by every hour. Please."

He stared at the monitors, another person enraptured by shadows. He tore himself away. "Will do."

"Denny, watch yourself. We've stirred up the hornets."

He waved that off, invulnerable.

Alone once more, I watched the monitors and watched the clock in a strange state of suspension, drifting between sleepiness and stomach-clenching anticipation. What else could I do? What would I regret not thinking of?

One of the lions coughed twice. I walked back and stared at them, slack tan bodies resting. Three sets of golden eyes stared back, mouths a little open, outlined by black gums. Spice stood up, turned around completely, and lay down again with a little grunt. I saw her climbing down into the moat, checking out something *interesting*—Rick, stunned and helpless. "I thought I could accept that you killed Rick because you had the chance to do what lions do," I said aloud. "I thought it shouldn't matter to the keeper part of me, but it does. It does matter."

I went back to the kitchen, marked the checklist, and thought about anger and relationships. I got up, stiff and chilled, and paced around the kitchen. I looked at the observation schedule, taped to the wall by the sink. An unfamiliar name, probably a volunteer from the Children's Zoo or the Education department, was scheduled for one to five in the morning. Denny hadn't come back. I heated leftover coffee in the microwave and stood staring into space. I'd almost used up my full store of resolve.

The clock had crept almost to midnight, and it was time to call Marcie. I used her cell phone to test it. It didn't work. I was redialing when Dr. Dawson walked in again. He'd come through the outside service door silently and had opened the kitchen door as quietly, but I'd been facing that way and saw him immediately.

"I completed a lab test on the male penguin that died," he said. "I'm heading home, but I remembered you were here and thought you might be interested in the results." The hood of his parka was down, and he had water spots on his glasses. He stood at the closed kitchen door and fussed with the glasses, struggling to get a handkerchief out of his pocket to dry them, half turning away from me. That done, he moved a few steps into the room, toward me.

"The door didn't bang," I said.

"What?" His chin came up, alert.

"Most people let the door slam shut." I stood at the far end of the table with the cell phone in one hand and the other resting on the wrench. He didn't get it, and I didn't explain.

From about ten feet away he said, "Most cell phones don't work in this building. I imagine it's all the concrete and metal. Here, try mine." He pulled out his phone and tossed it to me in a quick, smooth motion. I automatically grabbed for the sleek silver object and, still in the same motion, he flowed forward and captured the pipe wrench off the table. He was astoundingly fast.

I jumped back, both phones clattering to the concrete floor, and pulled a chair in front of me like a circus lion tamer. But *I* was the animal, one more for him to outmaneuver and far from the quickest. But he didn't come for me. Instead, he examined the heavy wrench and tossed it into the bin with the nets. It clanked on the bottom, well out of reach, and he withdrew back to the door. I looked at him and thought of Rick, gone from me forever; my beautiful lions used to kill him. "You murdered Winona and buried her in the forest like a road-killed possum, and when Rick found her bones, you fed him to the lions." My voice was shaky, ragged with loathing and adrenaline.

His chin jerked up. "You have no idea what you are talking about." He scanned the room carefully, then stepped aside and glanced toward the hallway, looking through the window in the door. I took a step toward him with the chair raised, when he turned back to me. I froze, indecisive.

Whatever he'd seen, or not seen, was reassuring, and I was no threat. He relaxed. I'd heard him tell keepers, "Stay calm and take your time. Work with the animal, don't rush, and you can accomplish almost anything without trauma." Now he said quietly, "You think you have it all figured out, but you don't. I loved Winona. We had a good life—a nice house, enough income. I was never unfaithful or unkind to her."

"You *murdered* her," I said.

"I did no such thing."

"She dumped you and you killed her." I would goad him, keep him talking, as I had planned, and it would be okay. He would talk and I would listen, and he wouldn't have time to kill me with the syringe sticking out of his pocket.

He was patient with me. "My wife was attractive to men, and she liked that. I couldn't always keep her away from them. Yes, it's true, one night she said she was leaving me. But if anyone *murdered* her, it was Kevin Wallace." He waited for that to sink in.

If he moved toward me, I'd keep the table between us and swing the chair at him. My heart thudded unevenly. "Liar. Wallace didn't kill her. You did. You murdered your wife." Where was Denny? Marcie should have called the police by now.

Still patient, he said, "You're not listening. He seduced her when I was out of town for a conference. She didn't want to tell me, but when I demanded the truth, she let it slip. She was leaving me for *Wallace* of all people. I'm sure you understand my shock."

"And that made you hit her. *You,* not Wallace."

His voice lost the soothing overtones. "Not murder. An accident. I came to my senses and she was on the floor by the fireplace with a broken neck. She fell back against the edge of the mantel and fractured a cervical vertebra. I would never hurt her. I miss her terribly."

"Normal people call 911. Murderers bury people in the woods."

"What better place to bury her than in the forest nearby? I planted ferns on her grave, and I stayed to watch over her when I could have moved on as we planned, on to a bigger zoo, maybe San Diego. She wanted to move to California. I would have done anything for her." His composure was back in place. He had long ago thought this through. "Nothing would bring her back. If I went to jail, all my education, all my skills, would go to waste. What good would that do? Finley Zoo would never find anyone else with my credentials at the salary they pay. What would happen to animal care?"

That stopped me for a second. I was jeopardizing the animals by trying to stay alive? I blurted, "You stayed because you were afraid. Your worst fear happened—the construction turned up her skull and Rick found it."

Twin spots on his pale cheeks reddened. The syringe was in his hand now. I knew well enough what it held. A drug to leave me unconscious—at best—while he disposed of my carcass at his leisure. I was one more big primate to immobilize. I'd set up my security measures so carefully, but nothing was working. "You were lucky Rick didn't tell anyone else, just you. How did you lure him up here?" Had Marcie called the police? I couldn't call them myself, not and hold the chair and watch him and try to evade him.

He edged toward my right, and I circled away from him. His voice was quiet. "I told him we needed to discuss the matter privately and that I would be in my office late running lab tests. He couldn't come until after midnight. But I was patient, and he showed up eventually."

"And you hit him on the head and poured scotch in him using a stomach tube stuck down his throat. You're the only one who could tube a mammal. Birds are easy, but mammals are hard." I leaned toward him to hear better, to hear him confirm what mattered so much.

He nodded acceptance and spoke in confidential tones, almost a whisper, circling slowly, the syringe held low. "He refused the scotch, even beer, to my surprise. But he was not suspicious. It was easy enough to distract him and cosh him with a wrench. Like your wrench." He smiled ruefully. "It was simple to insert the tube before he woke up. A shame it had to be that way. I liked him."

A brief weird joy flickered. I'd finally gotten it right. Rick *hadn't* lied to me.

A subtle shift betrayed his intention, and suddenly aware of my own gullibility, I straightened and stepped back. His murmuring voice had lured me closer, but not close enough to trigger an attack.

"Normal people don't use lions to kill other people." I spoke loudly, abruptly. We kept edging around the room with the table between us, an ominous dance. I kept an eye on the monitors, but only to avoid banging my head. Denny had forgotten me. Marcie was asleep.

"Don't keep saying I'm not normal!" he snapped back, abandoning whispers. "What choice did I have? It was his life or mine. It was a gamble—he might have survived. It's not as if I murdered him. You can't predict what wild animals will do in a new situation."

The thoroughness of his denial was stunning, infuriating. "Bullshit! It went exactly as you planned. I turned Winona's tooth over to the police this evening. You burned my house and pawed through my stuff for nothing—it was never there." I threw the words like poisoned darts. "They'll reopen Rick's death as a murder investigation and you'll fry."

He stopped moving to set me straight, narrow lips in a little smile. "No, they won't. They blew Rick's postmortem, after all. They didn't notice that one head contusion was earlier than the other. With Rick cremated, that evidence is gone, and a tooth doesn't prove a thing. No one will give his death another thought."

"Denny's coming by and the next volunteer is due any minute and my friend has already called the police. You might as well go home and call a lawyer."

"Denny's unavailable, on ice, so to speak. The next observer won't show up for half an hour. We'll be done by then. Relax. It won't hurt. I'm very good at this, and you haven't a chance."

"If I die, you think nobody will notice?"

"It's surprisingly simple to manipulate these situations. No one ever thought Winona was dead, until you and Rick made a mess of it. I even arranged for Wallace to fire his new girlfriend when she stole gate receipts, or so it seemed. He'll always be a bachelor instead of having my wife. I did that! Now everyone thinks you walked into the exhibit with the tiger because you were distracted by grief. See? It's easily done."

Why was he bragging? He stood easily, waiting. For what? I felt the day's physical insults weighting me down. Exhaustion was slipping in through the panic. He knew that. He was giving it time to work.

"You won't be dead," he said. "It will be like Winona. You'll leave town and never come back. I called Los Angeles. They've gone with an internal candidate. But I appreciate that you announced that you got the job. Everyone will assume you followed your dream."

I knew that dream. He had me there.

I opened my mouth to shout that he was wrong, doomed, when he struck like the black leopard, in swift, silent steps. His right arm shot out, syringe in hand, reaching over the table. I leaped away, the needle scoring my arm through my jacket, banging my head on the monitor. I yelped, not sure whether he had injected the drug or not. He kept coming as I dropped the chair, dodged around the table, twisting the handle. But he'd turned the latch while he was fussing with his glasses, and the lock stuck. I fumbled the pepper spray out of my pocket, tried to turn the sprayer toward him, and instead dropped it as he came at me again. Trapped in the kitchen, I bolted away, throwing a chair in front of him. That slowed him enough for me to get the metal table between us again. I glimpsed the pepper spray deep under the counter.

My head ached. He'd jumped me when I was positioned to hit the monitor. We circled faster, each looking for an opening. He'd abandoned subtlety and would simply overpower me. He was bigger and so confident, so fast with that syringe. He leaned forward again, and I fell back into the counter. I grabbed one of Linda's beautiful cups and threw it at him, but it missed and crashed on the floor. The second one hit him in the shoulder, but didn't slow him. He glided on his feet wolflike, hair-trigger aware, syringe held low.

He surprised me again, hurling himself at the table, brute strength. With a shattering screech of metal against cement, it slammed into my belly, my spine crushed against the wall, shoving the breath out. He flowed around the table, quick and intent.

I shoved the table back a few inches and twisted down underneath it. I could feel his body heat as he lunged above me, feel the needle catch on the back of my jacket. I scrabbled on hands and knees out from under the table, cutting my palm on broken pottery. I shoved the table up with my back as I stood, felt it collide with his body. He hurled the table away, knocking it over with a metal clang. I lurched upright and away.

Panting, I edged toward the door, the fallen table between us. He paused, looking at the underside of the table. "I suspected a tape recorder. That's the first place I would have looked." He kicked it twice, striking with leather hiking boots. I heard the plastic crunch as the table slid toward me. He looked at the syringe in his hand and, astonishingly, unscrewed the bent needle and tossed it on the floor. He took a fresh needle from his pocket and attached it. His movements were quick and automatic, doing what he'd done many times before.

I stood flat-footed, missing my opportunity. He was so much quicker than I was, with a longer reach. My panic strength was almost gone. The cut palm throbbed and my legs were shaky. I slipped a hand into my jacket pocket and gripped the only hope left, Winnie's chain leash, left from our last walk. It was cool against my fingers.

One of the lions let loose with a roar that shook the building. We both startled with ancestral fear. A roar or maybe a scream tore my own throat as I charged him, crouched low to avoid the monitor. I slashed his face with the chain and connected across his cheek. His glasses smashed to the floor. He yelled with surprise. I slashed at his face again, wanted to keep beating him with the chain. Anger, my old nemesis, my folly, was an ally at last, flooding me with power when true strength was used up. I dropped the leash and spun the overturned table toward his legs. It caught him on the shins, but he scrambled over it, coming at me half-blind and furious. I raced to the door, but knew I would never get the latch open in time. Instead, I grabbed the six-foot catch pole leaning in the corner in a tangle of nets.

I kept moving, carrying the pole low and horizontal. He turned to get between me and the door and his foot slipped on the leash. He fell to one knee. As he staggered to his feet, I slipped the snare over his head and around his neck like implacable justice. I yanked on the loop at the end of the pole—slippery with blood from my hand—pulling it taut, tighter.

His momentum shoved me back, but the pole kept him from closing in on me.

His yell clogged in his throat as he clawed at his neck. My jaw clenched, lips peeled back. I snarled as I pulled. The wire bit in; flesh and skin bulged above and below the snare. He couldn't get his fingers under it. I liked that. He dropped the syringe and clawed at me, reaching for my eyes, but the pole was too long, longer than his arms.

He grabbed the pole with both hands and yanked, throwing me off balance. I braced myself and shoved back, slamming him against the counter edge. Eyes panicky, he pulled the pole right and left, up and down, jamming me into the wall. I hung on with my last reserves as he battered me about the room.

My end of the pole punched me in the belly and I nearly threw up. I tried to keep the end off to one side, but that meant my right hand was battered into the wall. He backed me into a corner, alternately jerking and shoving on the pole while I flopped around. I was getting weaker, feeling my vision start to dim, when he went down to his knees.

He was faking. I kept the wire taut with all my strength, waiting for him to get up and fling me around again. But he didn't get up. His face was swelling; his eyes rolled back. He went limp and fell over. His weight on the pole pulled my arms straight.

After some indefinable pause, I realized I had to slacken the cable or…not.

I relaxed my bleeding hand, let the cable loosen, ready to tighten it as soon as he leaped up. He didn't move. His tongue was protruding. He looked old and stringy and repellant. Had I killed him? *Should* I kill him?

I let go of the pole and it clattered to the concrete floor. He didn't move. After a stunned moment, I fumbled in the cupboards for a tangle of yellow nylon rope from some forgotten project. Forcing myself to touch him, I wrestled his hands behind his back—no resistance—tied them with the stiff, uncooperative cord, tied his feet together as well. A breath rasped in his throat, then another.

I stood back, wild-eyed and bloody.

Denny. He'd said Denny was on ice.

I glanced back at the limp body as I fumbled with the latch, and lurched out the kitchen door, then the service door into the cold night air. I recalled that I loathed cold. He'd left the electric cart outside, waiting to haul my body away, to his car and then some remote grave. My right hand didn't work. My left hand turned the key clumsily. I could run faster than the cart would go, except that I couldn't run. I could barely sit upright and steer.

Outside the Commissary, overhead lights created a mosaic of light and dark, leaving deep shadows along the building. I staggered inside, leaving the cart and its illusion of safety. I hit the inside light switch. Stacked boxes were brightly lit, the aisles behind them dark and full of secrets.

The freezer door was closed. I released the latch and yanked on the handle. Stuck. I dragged a box of carrots over to the door with my good hand and stood on it. Hap's cleaver was jammed into the crack between the door and its frame, up near the top. I wiggled it out. It clanged and skittered on the floor. I kicked the box aside and pulled open the heavy door.

Denny was curled up on the floor just inside. He mumbled incoherently as I stuck my hands under his armpits and dragged him out. Relief steadied my legs. I left him in a heap and ran to the phone. The 911 operator wanted details, but I demanded police and an ambulance at the zoo immediately and hung up. I turned up the heat in the uniform room and got Denny sitting up on the floor. I unzipped my jacket and sat behind him with my arms and jacket around him, sharing my body heat. The paramedics, the police, and Wallace arrived more or less simultaneously and found us huddled together, shuddering.

While the medicos tended Denny, I blurted out the evening's events and the story of Rick's death in disorganized bursts to Wallace and the policewoman. She was apparently responding to Marcie's call and the paramedics to mine. It wasn't clear who had called Wallace so that he could get them into the zoo. The policewoman had the paramedics bandage my hand before she'd let me in the patrol car, and then called in a report before she would drive me across the zoo.

I was frantic to get back to Felines, and not only to turn Dr. Dawson over to the police. I'd had time to remember the clouded leopards. They were surely disturbed by the noise of the fight. Losa was at terrible risk and no one was there to help her if she needed it. It seemed hours since I'd fled.

At last I turned the key in the Feline door with my good hand and walked in with Wallace and the policewoman behind me, not sure whether I wanted to find Dr. Dawson dead or wanted him alive.

He was definitely alive. His hands were still tied behind his back, but he had been working hard and his legs were free. He was standing at the counter sawing awkwardly at the tough nylon rope with a paring knife. He was a mess—blotchy face and rumpled hair and clothes. He pulled himself together and croaked, "Thank God you've come. She tried to kill me. She thinks I murdered her husband. Keep her away from me." He looked truly frightened.

A young man in a University of Washington sweatshirt followed us in, looking alarmed. The policewoman looked startled also, hand at the pistol on her hip.

"Are you the late shift volunteer?" I asked.

"Uh-huh. What's up?"

"Don't worry about it. Just keep an eye out for the female. I, uh, got distracted and I don't know if she's okay. The male might have attacked her."

He sat down at the table and watched the monitors, with furtive glances toward us.

The policewoman untied Dawson's hands. Wallace looked at Dawson, then at me, his face unreadable. The vet rubbed his wrists with shaky fingers and rasped, "She's insane. I dropped in to check on the clouded leopards, and she starting ranting at me about murdering Rick. She got the catch pole over my head. She almost killed me. Has she got a weapon?"

While the policewoman patted me down, a list of the people who would believe his story, believe that I was nuts, scrolled by. Wallace. Jackie. Linda. Mr. Crandall. Maybe Hap and Calvin. I had to hand it to Dr. Dawson. Poor Iris, deranged by grief, had lost it at last, and he was the victim.

When the policewoman was satisfied I wasn't packing, I stepped on the empty chair and up to the tabletop. Wallace asked what the hell I was doing, and the policewoman stepped back and moved her hand to her gun again. Reaching up, I dislodged one of the acoustical panels in the ceiling, shoved it aside, and felt a rush like really good sex.

I had beaten the son of a bitch. *Again.*

The police officer received the little tape recorder like she might a nice package of nitroglycerin.

"It's all in here," I said. "And in case it's not..." I climbed down and looked behind the fridge. He hadn't found that one, either.

"How many tape recorders did you hide?" the volunteer asked, incredulous.

"Five." I unearthed the other two and handed them over. "Three different models, all voice activated. At least one should have worked. You get back to those damned monitors. We *have* to find out if Losa is all right."

I tested one. Wallace's voice first, fast-forward to Dr. Dawson again—"...came to my senses and she was on the floor by the fireplace with a broken neck." Poor audio quality, but understandable.

Wallace looked stunned. The policewoman looked skeptical, but I wasn't worried. Even if the tapes weren't enough to convict the bastard, they would activate a serious search for Winona's dental records.

"We'll sort this out," she said, a promise or a threat.

"Losa," said the volunteer.

And there she was, safe and sound, walking around the outside enclosure. I sagged into a chair.

Chapter Twenty-four

"This is not kicky and sexy. This is a lunatic science experiment."

"Shut up. I'm following the directions exactly." Marcie did vigorous things to my scalp. She was wearing "old" clothes: a decent pair of dark blue sweats with an apron to shield them from the dye.

"Are you sure this isn't toxic? I don't want toxic."

"Iris, women have put henna in their hair for centuries. Probably millennia. Hold still."

"I am holding still. How long is a millennia?"

"Millennium." She pulled a shower cap over the whole wet mess. "There. It has to soak for thirty minutes. You'll look great in the trial coverage. Seven o'clock news, People magazine, who knows."

We wandered out of my bathroom into the living room. It was Sunday evening, two days since I'd battled Dr. Dawson. Linda had arrived during my beautification. She was curled up on the sofa, dogs at her feet, reading a huge bird encyclopedia Calvin had loaned me.

I started to sit next to her, realized what henna leaks would do to the sofa and took a seat in the kitchen. Marcie removed the lid from a casserole dish on the table, unveiling an experimental chocolate bread pudding.

Chocolate pheromones drew Linda in. Marcie set out plates and forks. Linda distributed napkins and sat down. "Can we talk about this thing? Everyone at work is obsessing, and I'm supposed to report back. Did you really figure out it was Dawson or just wait to see who walked in and tried to kill you?"

"Figured it out. I finally tried believing Rick when he said he'd quit drinking. Then it had to be Dr. Dawson. No one else had the skills to tube a mammal, to get the whiskey into him by stomach tube. Calvin showed me with birds—it's pretty easy—but it's hard with mammals. You're likely to drown them if you don't know what you're doing."

Linda nodded thoughtful agreement. Marcie carved out three servings and shoveled them onto plates.

"And I tried trusting Spice," I added.

Marcie swiped at a drip on my neck with a paper towel. "You said something about that before. It didn't make sense then and it doesn't make sense now."

The dessert was swell, crunchy bread chunks on top and custardy ones below, chocolate chunks interspersed. "No, it's true," I said. "Linda, think back. For days after Rick died, every time Dr. Dawson showed up, Spice would climb down into the moat. I thought she was trying to get away from him because he's the vet, but I think she was hoping for a repeat."

"I remember seeing her do that," Linda said. "She moved like she was stalking. I thought she was wacko from the whole episode and didn't connect it to Dr. Dawson."

Marcie looked puzzled, then she got it. "Iris, that is truly gross."

"Yeah. It is." I hesitated, put bad images away and went for another bite. Range and Winnie pushed out through the doggy door on squirrel patrol. The backyard was a sea of mud. Rick's grave would be muddy, too. "It's touch and go with the case against him. The tapes and the tooth are about it for evidence. The rest of her bones have disappeared. His fireplace had ashes that looked like Rick's printouts, but that doesn't prove much."

I'd called Greg at the Los Angeles Zoo and told him the story. He said he still had some of her poems. Learning that she wrote poetry made her death more than bones in the mud and bad luck for Rick. A real woman had been cheated of her life.

"He'll be gone from the zoo, one way or another," Linda said.

I scratched absently at my soggy head.

"Leave your hair alone. You're going to mess it up." Marcie rearranged the shower cap.

"Rick didn't lie to me, that's the important thing," I told my friends, the familiar ache in my throat again. "He really did mean to change. He never got the chance. He might have told me about the skull, I might have gone with him to see Dawson after the party, if we hadn't still been feeling our way back together. It could all have been different."

Marcie's voice was gentle. "Maybe he didn't think an old grave was important, not as important as getting back with you."

"Did you have your talk with Wallace and Calvin yet?" Linda asked.

"I did. Yesterday. I didn't expect them to cry and hug exactly, but I thought it would mean something to Calvin to know who set up his daughter and that it wasn't Wallace. But Calvin acted like it didn't matter—he thinks Wallace should have stuck by her regardless. Wallace didn't say much."

I didn't mention the private conversation I'd had earlier with Wallace. That he had normal emotions was not something he would want others to know. The police had confiscated the tapes before anyone could hear them, and he had called me into his office to ask about the confrontation with Dawson. I'd told him the whole story. Winona's murder hit him hard. He said he'd gotten an email from her after she vanished telling him she'd left to find herself and didn't love him anymore. Dawson had covered his tracks and exacted revenge at the same time. Wallace had honestly believed that Dr. Dawson was his friend. The murder of a woman he loved and the levels of betrayal left him blank-eyed and silent. He hadn't seemed to notice when I'd left.

Marcie distributed seconds on dessert as the dogs bounded in happily, squirrel patrol accomplished. Both shook vigorously before I could grab a towel and wipe them down.

Marcie took a light hit on her sweats. "You're going to ruin that towel, getting mud all over it like that. You'd better pre-soak it."

The dogs flopped down and began improving on my rub-down, licking their legs and sides. I tossed the towel on a chair and sat back down.

"About Denny…" Marcie crossed her arms.

"What about him?" I asked.

"He was right about a lot of things. He deserves some credit."

"He was also wrong about a lot of things. He needs to get that dog neutered, for example. And to clean up his house. And quit picking fights with visitors."

"Iris, you are extremely critical and judgmental about Denny. How he leads his life is not really your problem."

"It is if he's sleeping with my friend."

Linda tried to look invisible.

"Some surprising couples work out fine," Marcie said, possibly a little smug. "Your clouded leopards haven't killed each other."

Linda's face said she had a good point there.

"That's another reason I thought it was Dawson," I said. "He was so sure it wouldn't work out with the clouded leopards. I think he was projecting from his own experience. Of course, with Denny, I'm projecting from *my* own experience."

Marcie narrowed her eyes. "Denny can change, like anyone else. Even me. And you. Time's up."

I followed her docilely to the bathroom. After I was rinsed and dried and fluffed like a red-brown poodle, Marcie eyed me critically. "I think it works for you. Just a touch of highlights, adds life and energy to your hair."

Linda was pulling her jacket on and Marcie gathered her coat and purse to go.

"Wait a minute, guys, I need to tell you something."

They paused, mentally already elsewhere, patient.

"Calvin told me this story, about Laysan ducks, I think it was."

"You need to tell us about ducks?" Marcie queried, eyebrows raised.

"Shush. Anyway, this was like the most endangered species ever. It finally got down to one pair and she had a clutch of eggs, but some predator killed the male, then chased her off the nest so those eggs died." I paused dramatically.

"And then the very last duck died and that was that." Marcie shifted impatiently.

"No, then she laid another clutch, fertilized from the last time the male tread her, trod her, whatever you call sex for ducks. That clutch hatched and that is where all the Laysan ducks today come from."

"And the point of this is…" Linda inquired.

"Rick was the last of his family. Both his parents are dead and his sister probably is too; anyway, she doesn't exist as far as I can find out."

I had their full attention. Linda frowned, puzzled.

Marcie erupted, hands flying up. "Iris! I cannot believe you are using this, this *bird* story to tell me that you are…are…"

"Pregnant."

Linda looked skeptical. "Are you sure?"

"Uh-huh. Got the test today." I smiled at a bittersweet memory. "The night of the party. It's not easy in a pickup truck, but it can be done, and, um, done well. We'd always been careful, but not that night. Maybe we were both hoping for this, to glue us together. Which is stupid, sure. But that's what happened. You'll make terrific aunts. Your first assignment is to help me shop for a house that smells decent. I've got insurance money to spend."

Marcie balked. "Iris, are you sure this is a good idea? Being a single parent is not a great way to raise kids. I happen to know that for a fact." Her father had walked out on the family when she was six. He'd made his support payments, but she rarely saw him.

"I've had too much death. If the situation were different, I might not handle it this way. I can't apologize to Rick for not trusting him, but I can take care of our baby."

After finally insisting that the next day was a workday and I had to get some sleep, I stood with the dogs at the open door and watched my friends walk through the dark to their cars in the driveway, Marcie still perturbed. The night was clear and cold. Star-jewels stretched across the broad black sky.

I rubbed my belly, my peaceful belly.

No, no they can't take that away from me.

A final note from the author…

The natural world is everywhere in distress because of human activities. If you enjoyed the animal characters in *Night Kill*, consider supporting organizations that work for survival of the real animals in their natural habitats. Here are two good possibilities:

- Save the Tiger Fund: http://www.savethetigerfund.org

- The Penguin Project http://mesh.biology.washington.edu/penguinProject/

My own website, http://annlittlewood.com, lists other organizations as well.

Or contact your local conservation organizations and ask how you can help protect your native landscapes and wildlife.

To receive a free catalog of Poisoned Pen Press titles, please contact us in one of the following ways:

Phone: 1-800-421-3976
Facsimile: 1-480-949-1707
Email: info@poisonedpenpress.com
Website: www.poisonedpenpress.com

Poisoned Pen Press
6962 E. First Ave. Ste. 103
Scottsdale, AZ 85251

LaVergne, TN USA
28 July 2010
191250LV00004B/1/P